W9-CDE-766

Scrambled Eggs

Scrambled Eggs

Boris Riskin

Five Star Press • Waterville, Maine

First Edition
First Printing: May 2005

Published in 2005 in conjunction with Tekno Books
and Ed Gorman.

Set in 11 pt. Plantin by Liana M. Walker.

Printed in the United States on permanent paper.

Library of Congress Cataloging-in-Publication Data

Riskin, Boris.
    Scrambled eggs / by Boris Riskin.—1st ed.
        p. cm.
    ISBN 1-59414-291-2 (hc : alk. paper)
    1. English teachers—Fiction. 2. Runaway wives—Fiction.
3. Organized crime—Fiction. 4. Fabergé eggs—Fiction.
5. Art thefts—Fiction. I. Title.
PS3618.I73S38 2005
    813'.6—dc22   2005000927

Dedication

This novel is dedicated to Kiki,
my beautiful, talented, inspirational wife.
You have made my life whole.
I could not have done this without you.

Acknowledgements

This book could not have been written without the constructive criticism, patience, humor, devotion and encouragement of the Ashawagh Hall Writers Group, along with its intrepid and inspiring leader, Marijane Meaker. Many thanks.

I also want to thank Faith, my daughter, and Hal and Caren, my son and daughter-in-law, as well as the rest of my family and friends, who shared the process with me.

Chapter 1

"No way!" Even though Morty was my best friend, I told him I wasn't going to his annual shindig.

Sherri and Dr. Morty Adler threw one of the best parties of the Hamptons' season. The booze was Chivas, Kettle One, and Bombay, and the food was supplied by a caterer called *Bringing in the Sheaves*, who produced pots of beluga, bushels of plump oysters, and a dessert so drenched in chocolate sauce and strawberries that people waited in line for it, like the British queuing for a bus.

"No way am I going," I said.

"Asshole," Morty said. "You can't hide from her. You might as well come and have a good time. It's better than moping around the way you've been doing the last couple of weeks."

The "asshole" Morty referred to was, of course, me. The "her" Morty referred to was Rosalind, my wife of twenty-five years, who had walked out on me those same few weeks ago.

I'd only let a best friend talk to me like that, especially since I thought he might be right. I had to admit, I felt like an asshole because I hadn't had a clue that Rosalind was going to do what she did. Worse, I felt pain. Real, gut-wrenching pain.

Morty had been my best friend since about halfway

through second grade. He'd been just another kid who walked home from school in the same direction I did, when one afternoon he stopped at my house and we began horsing around in the front yard. He picked up a stone and said, "Watch how far I can throw this." His aim wasn't as good as his arm and the stone sailed through a neighbor's window. The neighbor was the kind of person who seemed to have nothing better to do than to yell at any kid who came near her property.

The glass shattered and we froze. Then I said, "Come on." We ran as fast as scared kids could into my house, where I hid Morty in a closet. In a short while, there were loud knocks on the door.

I knew I had to do something. Luckily, I was blessed with a mother whose love for me had no limits. I blurted out the story, then added, "It was an accident, Mom. We didn't mean to do it."

"I know." My mother smiled her beautiful smile at me. "Don't worry. I'll take care of it."

And she did. While I hid behind her, she defused the neighbor's anger by offering to pay for the repair of the window. I waited until the door closed, then let Morty out of the closet and introduced him. My mother gave us milk and cookies, and from that day on Morty and I were buddies.

Two years later, it was discovered my mother had breast cancer and nothing could be done to save her.

I followed Morty's advice. I put on my Ralph Lauren blazer, forty-four regular, and checked myself in the mirror. Even though I did my share of ingesting calories both liquid and solid, my weight was okay because I worked out at the gym, played tennis, and did a lot of biking. I still had all my hair, although it was obvious the gray was doing a blitzkrieg into the brown. Rosalind used to say I was handsome, but I never thought so. I went closer to the mirror and looked at my eyes. There were plenty of red streaks. I was sure a lot of that was due to my fast approaching sixty. Sixty. Hard to believe, since most of the time I still thought of myself as twenty-five. Not then. Not with the devastating amount of hurt I felt deep inside me.

"Never mind," I said to the guy in the mirror. "You're going to that party and you're going to have a good time."

I didn't.

Mostly, I hung around the bar and drank a lot of Kettle One. I also couldn't help being on the lookout for Rosalind. I thought she might be there with the friend she'd gone to stay with when she left me. This friend was the rather famous Toby Welch, the one with the TV show who instructed an audience of millions how to decorate a house with walnut shells and a few dabs of Elmer's Glue, or how to turn five dollars' worth of dinner napkins into slipcovers for a sofa. In the past few years, Rosie had put in a lot of time doing charity work. It seemed Toby did quite a bit of the same thing herself. The two of them had hit it off and become good friends.

I called there a dozen times. At first I tried to get Rosie to come back, but she wouldn't consider it. Then I tried to get her to tell me why she'd left. *Because I honestly don't know*, I said. *Then you'd better give it a lot of thought*, she said.

On my way back to the bar for about the fifth or sixth time, I bumped into Morty's wife, Sherri. Sherri was a beautiful woman but it was a hard beauty, as if she'd been sprayed with *Glo-Coat*. She gave me one of her looks. Sherri had a variety of looks that she directed at people. Depending on where you stood on the social (read monetary) scale, her looks could go from simple disdain to disapproval to contempt, or all the way in the other direction to admiration, or even, if she were regarding someone famous such as Toby Welch, adoration.

11

In my case, when Morty began going out with her and first introduced us, he was already on his way to being a successful surgeon and I was just a high school English teacher. So the first look I got from her was disdain. When she learned we were best friends, her look turned to disapproval. I was pretty sure she thought Rosalind had done a wise thing in leaving me.

"Hi there, Madame Hostess," I said. "Have you seen my wife, by any chance?"

"No," Sherri said, giving me her disapproval-contempt look. "And if you're lucky, she won't see *you*."

I continued on to the bar vaguely wondering what she meant by that remark when a knockout of a dish, dressed in white and adorned with gold jewelry, took hold of my arm.

"Are you Jake Wanderman?" she asked.

"I am, unless you're from the IRS."

"Could I talk to you?"

"Sure."

She pulled me into a corner. "Morty Adler said you would help me."

"To do what?"

"He didn't tell you?"

"No."

"Oh," she said. She had blonde hair and eyes the color of dollar bills. She sucked in her carmine lips. "He said he would explain everything."

"I guess he didn't have a chance," I said. "So why don't *you* tell me?"

She looked around as if someone might be listening. "Not here. Come to my house. We can talk there."

"Now?"

"It's vital."

I tried to grasp the concept of what she meant by "vital,"

but couldn't. Abruptly, my brain signaled that it wasn't working too well because I'd had a tankful of vodka. It also told me I had just about enough energy to get home and crawl into bed. "Why don't we make it tomorrow? I'm sure whatever it is can wait a day."

She shot me a green-eyed look that was like a jolt of electricity. She took hold of my hand, and in a minute we were outside. The night air was fresh and sweet. I gulped it in. "My car's just over here," she said, tugging at me. I stumbled after her. We came to a Jaguar. She got behind the wheel. "Hop in," she said.

I hopped as well as I could.

She went down Ocean Road, where she made a series of turns. I didn't know the names of the streets, but I knew we were in the neighborhood where tall, elegant women holding iced martinis smiled down upon their short, rich husbands.

We drove up to an iron gate. She pushed a button on the remote clipped to the sun visor and the gate swung open. A string of security lights lit up the curving driveway. We went about a hundred yards before we came to the imposing double-door entrance of what looked like Frankenstein's castle.

I expected to see Frau Blucher and hear a horse whinny, but instead, the door was opened by a small woman in a maid's uniform.

"Everything all right?" my driver asked.

The maid nodded.

"Good. You can go to bed now."

The foyer was the size of my living room. It was filled with plants as tall as trees. Hell, maybe they were trees.

"Follow me," the blonde said, and began climbing the marble staircase that led from the back of the foyer to the second floor. I followed, enjoying the interesting motion of her tush beneath the clinging dress, and wondering if she lived here alone or if there was husband or lover, and if so, where was he or she?

We went along a hallway and into a huge, brightly lit room. A king-size four-poster bed was placed against one wall. There were dolls propped up against the pillows on the bed, lots of them: big and little, long and short, wearing uniforms, dresses, gowns. Their eyes were open, staring, asking me what I was doing there. A secretary desk stood open, with a pile of papers scattered across the top. A crystal chandelier hung from the ceiling. The room was done in varying shades of pink: the walls, the trim, the furniture. There were enormous amounts of lace and ruffles. I had trouble breathing. I felt as if I'd been shoved into a rose.

"My husband had an office in another part of the house," she said. "I brought most of the stuff in here. I'm trying to figure out the checkbook: paying bills, that kind of stuff. Boris always took care of that, but I'm having a lot of trouble."

"Boris is your husband? Where is he?"

"Dead."

"Gee, I'm sorry. How long has he been . . . gone?"

"Since a week ago, yesterday."

She took a key out of her handbag and unlocked the bottom drawer of the secretary. "I want to show you something." She removed an attaché case, took it over to the bed, and sat down with it on her lap. She smiled at me and patted the bed with one hand. Her attitude seemed to underline the idea that she was not going to allow her status as a widow to be a hindrance to her social life.

Cautiously, I sat next to her, wondering what was going to happen next. What was in that case? Handcuffs? A whip? Curiosities made of black leather?

She clicked the locks and opened the case.

I leaned over to get a better look. Her perfume went up my nose. Heat came off her body as if she were a radiator.

The case was filled with white cotton. She took one section of cotton out of the case and unwrapped it, revealing an egg-shaped object. She gave it to me.

I held it in my hand and felt my fingers tingle. "Is this what I think it is?" I was ten years old when I first saw a Fabergé egg. My father was usually out hustling a buck, but after my mother died he tried to spend some time with me. One of those times, he took me to the Forbes Gallery on Fifth Avenue to see the collection old man Forbes had put together. It had been astounding to see those fantastic jewels. They were so exotic, so foreign. They seized my imagination and sent it soaring. I saw Tsars and Tsarinas draped in furs and jewels, icy landscapes with wolves howling in the background. It might have been then that I first began to dream of traveling to far-off places, meeting strange and glorious people, having great adventures. "What do you think, Jakey?" my father asked. "How would you like to have one of those for yourself?"

Now I was actually holding one. It had a background of royal blue and over it were concentric circles of gold leaves. In the midst of the leaves and encircling the egg was a diamond-studded snake with emerald eyes. I didn't know how much it was worth, but I knew it was a lot.

"There are six of them," she whispered. "All different. One is more beautiful than the next."

"Wow," I said. I handed it back to her, feeling a lot more sober than when I'd come in. "I'm impressed. But I have the feeling that beauty is only one part of the equation."

"Dr. Adler said you were smart."

"He's biased."

"I suppose you want to know where I got them from."

I didn't answer. Actually, what I was thinking was more along the lines of, *what do you want from me?*

"Well," she went on, "the whole thing was a big surprise because I found them by accident."

"Excuse me?"

She pointed to a painting on the wall that looked like Gainsborough's *Blue Boy*, only this boy was dressed in pink. "There's a secret closet back there. Boris had it made especially. I thought I ought to check it out after he died."

"Good thing you did."

"And how. There were also a few gold bars and some cash."

"I'd call that a nice closet."

"I thought so, too. Then I got a phone call. A man said he was a business partner of Boris's. He said Boris had something that belonged to him and did I know anything about it. I guessed he was referring to what I just showed you. I thought the best thing to do was play dumb. I told him I had no idea what he was talking about."

"You didn't know this guy who said he was your husband's partner?"

"I may have heard the name. But Boris never told me he had a partner. For that matter, he never told me anything about his business. That's why I needed you to come here tonight. Morty said you were very smart. You would know what to do."

"He did, huh?"

She put the flat of her hand on my chest directly over a nipple. I could feel the texture of the hand through the shirt I was wearing, the heat from it working its way through the epidermis, beyond the subcutaneous layers, and into the blood cells.

"I'm all alone," she said. "I don't know who to turn to. Will you help me?"

I did not have a clue as to what kind of help I could give her, but a feeling came over me. I felt a glow—maybe it was still the vodka—as if I were being bathed in a bright light from above. Suddenly, I was King Henry, he of the sceptered isle, raising my fist to my army, declaring victory for God and country. At the same time, I was aware of a hint of doubt in the far back recesses of my brain, but I didn't let it hold me back. "Of course I'll help you," I said.

"Promise?"

"I promise," I said, enjoying the idea of being reckless and bold.

"Thank you." She surprised me by kissing me, pressing her lips hard against mine.

"Does anyone else know about this closet?" I asked, after taking a deep breath.

"Not as far as I know."

"What about the people who built it?"

"It was built by one man, an old friend of my husband's, from Russia. He died only a short time after he finished the job. Boris gave the eulogy at his funeral."

Convenient. The only guy who could tell anyone about the closet just happens to drop dead.

"Okay," I said. "I think the first thing to do is put the case back in there and pretend you never saw it. Forget there's a closet altogether."

"All right." She re-wrapped the egg and put it back in the case. I followed her over to the pink *Blue Boy*. She did something at the bottom of the painting and the wall suddenly slid open, smoothly and silently. A light switched on, revealing a space just large enough to walk into, with shelves on the left side and a safe in the wall opposite. She placed the attaché

17

case on the middle shelf, stepped back, pressed something again, and the wall closed up.

"Would you like a drink?" she said. "We could have one downstairs, or I could bring it up here."

Something in my stomach rebelled. "Thanks, but no thanks. As a matter of fact, I think I'd better be getting home."

"Are you sure?"

"I'm sure."

"Okay. I'll drive you."

On the way back to Morty's house, I asked, "When did you say you first heard from your husband's so-called partner—what was his name?"

"Solofsky. He called me the day after the funeral. Couldn't wait, could he?"

"And he hasn't called you since?"

"Sure he has. But I haven't spoken to him. I told my housekeeper to say I wasn't taking any calls. But I'm frightened."

"The police . . . ?" I began, and stopped. We both knew that was out of the question. It didn't take much of a brain to know the eggs were not kosher. "What about Morty Adler? He know about this?"

She shook her head. "I didn't tell him anything. You're the only one who knows."

"Good. Let's keep it that way for now."

We were back at Morty's. I began to get out of the car when she leaned over and planted her mouth on mine again. "That's just my way of saying thank you. I really appreciate what you're doing for me."

"Fine," I said. "Fine. But if you're going to keep kissing me, I think I ought to know your name."

"It's Cynthia. Cynthia Organ."

Chapter 2

The party was still hot. The house was packed with the people you see photographed at charity balls in the Hamptons: mouthfuls of teeth, semi-exposed breasts, and, despite the warnings from the skin doctors, well-developed tans.

I was still a little confused about what had just happened. I was also pissed at my old buddy Morty for pushing me in the merry widow's direction. I wandered around looking for him. There were a lot of places to look. It was a large house with expensive art on the walls and sculpture on the lawns. Morty once told me the insurance alone cost ten grand a year.

"How come?" I asked. "I never knew you had such a great interest in art."

"It's not me. It's Sherri. She has an orgasm every time she gets one of these things."

"Nice you can afford it."

"I can't. But she's got a rich uncle. He gives her this stuff for presents."

I found Morty near the bar, surrounded by a bunch of people listening to him tell a joke.

"You want to know the difference between sexy and kinky?" he asked. "Sexy is when you take a feather from a chicken and glide it lightly over your lover's skin. Kinky is when you use the whole chicken."

After the laugh, I got him to one side. "I just met your blonde friend," I said. "She said that you said I would help her. It's funny you never told me. What's the idea?"

"Help, shmelp," he said. "She asked me if I knew somebody very smart. You were a teacher. Doesn't that mean you're smart?"

"Very decent of you, volunteering my services."

"You should be glad. Since you retired, you've got nothing to do. Wouldn't you like to help out a fellow citizen? Especially one with a lot of money and a body that won't quit?"

"I'm still married, remember?"

"Technically, yes. But I wouldn't give odds on how long. Face the facts, baby. It looks like you're going to join the crowd at the Friday night singles' bar."

"Thanks for your support. I really appreciate it. But could we get back to the widow? What's her story?"

"There's no story. She's a widow, that's all. Probably needs help with her checkbook, bills, credit cards, things like that. Most women do when their husbands kick off."

"That's it? You sure?" I was thinking about that secret closet and what was in it, but since Morty knew nothing about it, I didn't think now was the time to tell him.

"Sure I'm sure." He put his arm around my shoulders. "Listen to me. This will give you a chance to help someone and be a hero at the same time. And who knows where it might lead?"

He gave me a gentle shove. I let the momentum carry me back to the bar, where I ordered a large cognac. I thought about the beautiful Cynthia Organ and her soft lips on mine. More of that might not be so bad. I thought about how Rosalind had left me and how that empty space beside me made the bed very cold at night. I drained the glass in one swallow.

Then a voice in back of me said, "Don't you always get a headache when you drink brandy?"

I turned to look at my wife. After more than twenty-five years of being together, I still saw the young girl I'd fallen in love with at first sight: creamy skin, a Modigliani oval face, dense brows, and eyes that made me weak. Rosalind Mandel. Shakespeare's Rosalind:

> *From the east to western Ind*
> *No jewel is like Rosalind.*

"I already had the headache," I said. "But now that I've seen you, it went away."

"Sweet. How are you doing?"

"Not well. I'm lonely."

"Who isn't?"

"Ouch." I plucked an imaginary arrow out of my heart. "You don't have to be. You could come back."

"We've already talked about that."

"Not to my satisfaction." I wanted to reach out and take her in my arms. "At least explain it to me."

"No. I think you ought to be able to figure it out all by yourself."

"I've tried. But I can't. Why won't you talk to me about it?"

"Because I don't want to."

"I'm sorry to hear that. But I want you to know something."

"What?"

"I miss you."

21

"Better get used to it."

"You're cruel."

"Cruel?" She laughed her tinkling little laugh. "You know what? I think you've had more than enough to drink. If I were you, I'd go home and sleep it off."

"Nice talking to you, too," I said.

Chapter 3

The next morning I swallowed aspirin and stretched out on the deck. The sun was warm, the air cool. I closed my eyes. After a while I thought I heard the familiar and pleasant sound of Rosie's clogs, the scrape of the metal chair as she sat down next to me. I sighed, knowing it was only my imagination.

What wasn't my imagination was how many times I'd been woken up in the middle of the night from a sound sleep. Barely awake, I could feel Rosie's hand lying lightly on my chest. I knew what that meant. Slowly, slowly, as I knew it would, her hand crept downward. I didn't come awake immediately, but as her hand advanced I became more and more attentive. It's not as if I didn't know where her hand was going, I just liked the waiting for it, the way it finally eased itself under the elastic of my pants. By the time her fingers finally reached their objective, I was fully alert. And I was ready. I got out of my bottoms while she did the same, and not very long after, I'd be on top or she would. Rosie was not like other women I'd known. They were always telling me to slow down. Not Rosie. She was in a hurry. It took me a while to understand why. Then I realized it was because she was the one who started it. I don't mean she was always the initiator, I had my share, but four a.m. belonged to her, not me. Once I was up, and I mean up, I'd go in quickly. But just to show her I had something to say about it, I wouldn't move. "Hold still," I'd say. "Don't do a thing. I'll get there." She wouldn't answer, but she obeyed. And then, after what seemed like a long time but was probably not more than thirty seconds, with me fully aware of myself in that warm and heavenly place, I'd begin. Then she'd say, "Okay. I waited. I did my part. Now that you started, don't stop." And she'd thrust herself at me. What happened after that didn't take long, but the result was the same every time: the pleasure that comes from unexpected and soul-satisfying sex. And it was unexpected, even though it happened time and again, because neither of us ever knew when we went to sleep what might come to pass in the middle of the night.

From that lovely thought I segued to the last time Rosalind had been in the house. Was it only two weeks ago? We were having oatmeal for breakfast. She made it exactly the way I liked, smooth and creamy, perfect consistency. The night before had unfortunately not been interrupted by anything except a visit to the bathroom. She cleared the table, rinsed off the dishes, and put them in the dishwasher.

"I have something to tell you," she said.

"Oh?" I was looking at the front page of the *Times*, not thinking about anything but what I was reading. I read the *Times* first thing every morning. By way of not getting lazy and fat, I didn't have it delivered. I biked over and got it.

"I'm leaving," she said.

"When are you going to be home?"

"I'm not coming home." Her voice had an unnatural metallic sound, as if it were being amplified. "I'm leaving for good."

I went numb. My body froze but my brain immediately did

what it tended to do in moments of excitement or pressure, think of a line or two by Shakespeare, the genius who had known more about the human condition than any other man on earth. Back in the days when I wore a beard, and recited my poetry in smelly clubs in the East Village, I thought I was good. I thought what I had to say was important. But when I read William Shakespeare, I knew I was only a pretender to the throne. We, the other scriveners and I, were rutting about in the weeds while Shakespeare sat high among the clouds on the peak of the mountain.

I tried to speak, but before I could say anything, Rosie said, "And please, whatever you might say, do not quote Shakespeare at me. It used to be enjoyable, but now it drives me up the wall."

"All right, I won't quote anybody. Just tell me why."

"I've tried to tell you for a long time now," she said. "But you weren't listening."

She went swiftly out of the kitchen, leaving me holding onto the newspaper and, in spite of myself, thinking of the closing lines of Romeo and Juliet. After a while, she returned with a small piece of luggage. "I'll be back for more of my things later, when I've found a place for myself."

She was really doing it. "I'm listening now," I said. "Talk to me."

Her eyes had become the color of mushrooms. "I'll tell you this much: ever since you quit teaching, you're not the same person." She turned to go.

"Wait a minute. That's not enough."

"If I go into detail, we're going to have a fight. I don't want to have a fight. We've been doing quite a lot of that lately, or hadn't you noticed?"

She was right about that. I wasn't sure how long it had been going on, but we seemed to be picking on each other about everything, from my commenting about her lipstick on the bathroom glass as well as her lack of shopping expertise in the supermarket, to her saying I never seemed to have anything better to do than sit around and read a newspaper or play games with other not-doing-anything-of-interest persons.

"In the meantime, I'll be at Toby's," she said. "You can reach me there, if you have to."

"Toby Welch?"

Her smile was ice. "She's a good friend of mine. You know that."

"Sure I do." Toby was married to a guy named Herbert, but it was rumored she liked women. Rosalind had told me she had been introduced to quite a few of her women friends in the relatively short time she had known Toby but never saw any likely lesbians.

"I don't like the way you said that," she said.

"I don't think I said it in any particular way."

"You know what I mean."

"Believe me. I don't know what you're getting at. All I said was, I know who Toby Welch is."

"You weren't suggesting, by any chance, that I'm leaving you for another woman? In particular, the same Toby Welch?"

"Of course not. God forbid."

"Good. You may as well know, the rumors about her are not true."

"I don't care about the rumors. I don't care if she swings up, down, sideways, or around the world."

"Nice that you're still a liberal."

"I'm a liberal up to a point, the point being that I'm asking you not to leave."

"It's too late. I've made up my mind."

Rosie's making up her mind was like the slamming of a door. Before I could get my mouth in position to form another word, the door actually did slam behind her departing back, her VW convertible started up, and that was that.

Never was a story of more woe
Than this of Juliet and her Romeo.

Chapter 4

The phone rang inside the house, bringing me back to the present. I was out on the deck without the cordless. With considerable effort, I got off the lounge and went into the kitchen.

"Who is this?" an accented male voice asked.

"Suppose you tell me who you are; then I might tell you who I am."

"Excuse me. I am so impolite. Of course, you do not know who is calling you. My name is Solofsky."

It took only a second for the name to register. This was the guy who had called Cynthia, the one who claimed to be her husband's partner. "And just who are you looking for?" I said carefully.

"A person by the name of Jake Wanderman."

"You are speaking to him. What can I do for you?"

"I understand that you have been in touch with Mrs. Organ."

"Mrs. Organ?" I said. "I don't know anybody by that name."

"Mr. Wanderman, I ask that you are careful what you are saying. I think you do not know what you have connected yourself to here."

"I don't know what you mean. I'm not connected to any-thing."

"Let me repeat the question. Do you know Cynthia Organ?"

"I'll repeat my answer. No."

"Never mind. I shall be in touch."

The phone clicked. I wondered how this guy knew I had been in contact with Cynthia.

Chapter 5

Later that day, I threw on some sweat clothes, got my helmet, and bicycled the five miles to the health club. I found exercising at the club the best way to forget about the world and any problems I might have with it. I did some stretching and then worked out with the punching bag. I liked hitting the bag. It gave me a feeling of satisfaction each time I gave it a jolt. After about twenty minutes, I had managed to cover myself with a decent amount of sweat. After that, I walked around a bit trying to decide between leg lifts or working on my abs. I saw some familiar faces, then one I knew well. To say I was surprised to see Cormac Blather at a gym would be an understatement. Cormac was usually found in his antique shop wearing his customary white three-piece suit, a la Tom Wolfe. Unlike Mr. Wolfe, whose physique might be compared to a tree branch, Cormac's was more like the silhouette of Alfred Hitchcock. Yet there he was, outfitted in gym clothes and sweating mightily on a treadmill.

Cormac's shop was on Newtown Lane in East Hampton. His specialty was glass: Lalique, Tiffany, Venetian, that kind of stuff. Seeing him brought me back to the world I'd escaped for a few minutes. I couldn't help thinking he might well know something about Fabergé eggs.

I gave it the casual approach. "How's it going, Blather?"

He pinched his lips together in distaste as he walked on the treadmill. "Wretched. Murder and mayhem. Don't you read the papers?"

"I'm not talking about that kind of thing. How's business?"

"Excellent. The more expensive the piece, the better they like it."

"Listen, you're an expert on antique glass and jewelry, aren't you? Do you mind if I ask you a question?" Subtlety was not my strength.

"Of course I mind, but I am quite sure that won't hinder you."

"I was in the library the other day and picked up a book about Fabergé eggs. Do you know anything about them?"

Cormac's face could have been a St. Bernard's, all flaccid jowls and soft brown eyes. At the mention of Fabergé, he stared at me a moment. Was there a gleam in those droopy eyes? "I know a little. Why do you ask?"

"Just curious about what those things are worth today."

He carefully stepped off the machine. "It depends."

"On what?"

"On which kind of egg you're referring to. There are two kinds, you see. There are those called Imperial. One was sold at auction not long ago for about five and a half million. The non-Imperial are valued considerably less, perhaps between one and two million. But it's rare when either kind is for sale."

A rapid calculation informed me that the case in Cynthia's closet was worth between eight and thirty million, give or take a few. I almost said, "Wow," but held myself in check. "When I was a kid, my father took me to see some of them. I was awestruck."

"Indeed," he said. "It might interest you to know that giving eggs was an old Russian tradition. At Easter, they gave an egg, three kisses, and said, 'Christ is risen.' Then they started decorating the eggs. The Czar had the idea of going it one better. In 1884 he commissioned Fabergé to design a jeweled Easter egg. It took a whole team more than a year to make one egg. In all, The House of Fabergé made fifty-six eggs for the royal family, hence 'Imperial.' They made about forty-four for the commoners, the 'non-Imperial.' Not many, you see. That's one of the reasons they're valued so highly." He peered at me. "You know, there has been quite a bit of talk the last few years about Fabergé eggs. The biggest collection in the world was in the Armory Museum in the Kremlin. It was abruptly closed to the public some time ago. The gossip was that a considerable number of eggs had been stolen . . . directly out of the Kremlin itself. This has never been acknowledged. You can imagine the embarrassment to the Russians if that story were to be true."

I suddenly felt the need to get out of there, away from Cormac Blather. He seemed to be peeking into my brain, as if he suspected I wasn't sharing my real reason for asking all those questions. "Very interesting, Blather. You are certainly well informed. Thanks for the information."

I biked home. There was a black Lincoln Town Car in the driveway. I never locked my doors, so whoever it was had to be in the house. Wrong. There was nobody in the house, but through the patio doors I could see someone on the deck. I went outside to find a little guy regarding me with the air of a man used to being in charge. Even though it was the beginning of summer, he wore a black suit that shone like a mirror. Standing behind him, leaning against the railing, was a very short but wide guy, also in a shiny black suit. I didn't like the look of either of them.

The little man came toward me and extended his hand. "Ah, Mr. Wanderman, is it not? We are waiting for you."

I thought I recognized the voice as the same one I had heard earlier on the telephone. "Mr. Solofsky, I presume?"

"Jascha Solofsky. Sit down. Let us talk."

He pointed to the man against the railing. "That is Pyotr," Solofsky said. "He is my driver."

Solofsky's sidekick had a round face with stubble all over it, a small bulb of a nose, and eyes like pebbles. It struck me that he was the living incarnation of Shakespeare's pooch, Crab, the most sour-natured dog that ever lived. Shakespeare had given that dog a name. No other in all of his work had ever achieved such a distinction.

The man with the dog's face scowled at me.

"Relax, Pyotr," Solofsky said. "Mr. Wanderman is not going to give us any trouble." He smiled. "Are you, Mr. Wanderman?"

I did my best to smile back and appear to be cool. "What do you say we start even? You don't give me any and I won't give you any." I sat down.

Solofsky's chin was decorated with a pointy beard. He folded his hands under it. "I will get right to the point, Mr. Wanderman. Boris Organ was my partner. All of a sudden he is dead. His death is a shock to all of us who know him. Some people—I will be honest—do not care, one way or another. But me, I care. We are friends for many years. We do much business together back in the old country. We are *shabasniki*."

"What does this have to do with me?" I said.

"Allow me to go on," Solofsky said. "Simply put, *shabasniki* means we are capitalists in a communist country.

We buy and we sell. We make some money. Then we come to this country."

"I still don't get it," I said.

He sighed. "Allow me to finish. Boris likes the ladies. He decides to get married. He marries a lovely young woman. Her name is Cynthia. You remember we speak of her? Too young, I think, but it is not my business. But she is extraordinary handsome woman, is she not?"

"Gorgeous," I said, then realized he had suckered me.

He smiled just enough to show his teeth. "So it seems you are not honest with me on the phone. You say you do not know her, but you do know her." He didn't wait for me to say anything. "Never mind. I explain why I am here. I will be frank. Cynthia does not like me. Perhaps she suspects I am opposed to the marriage. I do not know. All I know is that I cannot get to speak to her. When I call, I am told she is not in. But I need her help. How do I get that help, I ask myself. Are you following me, Mr. Wanderman?"

"At a far distance. Why don't you get to that point you mentioned before?"

"It is arriving," he said. "When Boris dies, it is very inconvenient because we are in the middle of important negotiations. We are partners, you understand. He is in possession of certain things that belong not only to him but to me. Somewhere in his house is something quite valuable. I need to have it."

"So where do I come in?"

"You are a friend of the widow."

"I barely know her."

"You go to parties with her. You go to her house late at night. You stay a long time."

"How would you know that?"

He smiled. "It is of no importance. What is important is

that you explain to the young widow that I do not intend to steal what is rightfully hers. She shall have her share."

"Why would she listen to me?"

"More than money is involved. There are other very powerful forces. At the moment, I am able to hold them off. But I have only so much time. If what is in the widow's possession is not delivered, there will be serious consequences to her and, I might add, perhaps also to me. We will all be, including you—how do you Americans say it so charmingly?—in the soup. I do not wish for that to happen. I will do everything I have to do, to make sure that does not happen. Do you get my meaning?"

"You got the wrong guy. I'm not going to be able to get her to do anything. I just met her last night."

Solofsky ignored my protests. "Speak to her soon. I suggest, today. I am also suggesting that if you are thinking to go to the police or the FBI, you are making a fatal mistake." He looked over at his bodyguard—who forevermore I would think of as Crab, the dog—then looked at me.

Crab came off the rail and over to where I was. Before I could guess what he was doing, his fist smashed against my ear. I felt a stinging pain and a siren go off inside my head. I blinked a couple of times to get my bearings. My vision was blurred but I could see the son of a bitch was smirking. In spite of the pain I wanted to punch that smirk, but then he hit me again, this time in the stomach. The air went out of me and I doubled over, trying to get my lungs to work.

"Nothing personal, Mr. Wanderman. This is merely to show you that I am quite serious about this undertaking."

With an effort, I was able to straighten up and breathe again. I wanted to tell him to seriously fuck himself, but his bodyguard was standing over me eagerly waiting for the opportunity to hit me again. I barely managed to get the words out. "That's a helluva way to make a point."

"I am trusting then you have it, Mr. Wanderman. The point. I am getting in touch very soon with regard to your progress. *Dosvedanye.*" He waved, and they both were gone.

Chapter 6

I got a bunch of ice cubes from the freezer, wrapped them in a towel, and held it to my ear. It helped the burning ear but did nothing for where he'd socked me in the stomach. It also didn't do much for my peace of mind.

The excitement and the sense of adventure I'd felt about getting together with Cynthia Organ and her Fabergé eggs had changed considerably. What I'd thought might be a bit of a challenge, along with, I admit, an enjoyable hint of sexuality, was now something else altogether. The pain in my head and gut told me that. This guy, Solofsky, and his man, Pyotr, were real and dangerous. It didn't take a brain to figure out that my meeting Cynthia Organ had been a step into deep shit. And I knew I had to decide in a big hurry what I was going to do about it.

My first thought was that I'd like to kill my friend Morty for setting me up with her. But I then had to admit that wasn't fair. He wasn't the wretch soaked in vodka who had promised to help her. What was I thinking when I made that promise?

I remembered what I was thinking . . . that I was Henry V. I also remembered inhaling her perfume while her lips were pressed against mine. Being in love with your wife is one thing . . . lust is another.

Yet I knew it wasn't really lust that had made my blood sizzle. It was those hot eggs. I could still feel the tingle in my fingers when I held that jeweled ornament in my hand. I was a boy again, dreaming of romance, exotic faraway places. Ivan the Terrible. Catherine the Great. Rasputin, the Mad Monk. And I remembered how I felt growing up, surrounded by white middle class *ordinary* people. I wanted to be different, to do things that were different. That was why I trained in karate. I tried judo, yoga, even meditation. I got a kick out of all of them, although I was a failure at meditation.

I'd never been the violent type, but knowing martial arts had given me the confidence to deal with violence. In my single days I prowled the city a lot at night, and one very late night I was approached by a mugger with a knife in his hand.

"Give me your wallet, bitch," he said, moving the knife around as if he knew what to do with it.

"Sure," I said, "no problem." I handed him my wallet with my left hand and, when he reached for it, chopped his arm so that the knife fell. I then kicked him in the balls. He let out a yell I think could've been heard in the Bronx. I left him writhing on the ground and feeling pretty good about myself.

I also discovered hiking. I'd head out to the Adirondacks with only a backpack for company. Alone on the mountain, I'd get the feeling I could conquer the world. I'd tramp around, hoping to run into a mountain lion or a bear. Luckily, I never did. I'd write yards of poetry that seemed great at the time. The fact that later I would recognize it as not so great didn't change my love of being out there alone in the wilderness with the sense of unspoiled nature all around me.

But I was nineteen then, and the world was an endless vista.

By the time I met Rosie, I'd given up that part of my life.

I'd become a teacher, teaching English to a bunch of acned high school kids who had about as much interest in literature as I had in nipple rings.

Meanwhile, I had to think about what I could do about the current situation. One simple option, of course, was to back out. Renege on my promise. Even if I wanted to, I knew I couldn't do that. For one thing, Solofsky wouldn't believe me. Involving the cops was no good, either. What could I tell them, that some guy had assaulted me? I'd have to press charges and identify him. I knew just what would happen if I did that. They wouldn't even lock him up. My word against his. They'd set a court date . . . maybe. And all that would happen next would be another visit from the two Russians, and it wouldn't be social.

So what was I to do? I thought of the fantastic treasure I'd actually held in my hand, and Aladdin's cave where it had resided, and the glamorous, helpless widow who had the power to say, "Open Sesame." But even more powerful than those thoughts and the feelings they provoked was my desire to have Rosalind back. Wouldn't doing this help change her mind about me? Wouldn't this make her realize I was not really a dull clod who had nothing on his mind but games and the ability to quote Shakespeare?

It was about seven p.m. but it felt like midnight. I cracked a couple of eggs, added milk, salt and pepper, and a sprinkle of fresh parsley, crumbled in some moistened matzos, and fried it in half a stick of butter. While I ate, I switched on the TV, and watched part of a John Wayne World War II movie. Now there was a hero. I put the dishes in the sink and went to bed.

In the morning my stomach ached less but my ear was still tender. I rolled over on it a few times during the night and the pain woke me, but once I was up for good I forgot about it.

I needed to talk to someone. The only one I wanted to talk to was Rosalind. We'd spent our lives talking things over, often even after we'd had a fight. Aside from making love, yakking was the one thing we did together that suited us perfectly. The only question was, at this particular time, would she even want to see me?

There was only one way to find out. I called her at Toby Welch's and said I had to talk to her. It was very important.

"You're not going to start all over again, are you?" she said. "I thought we got that squared away the other night at the party."

"It's not about us. It's something else."

"Okay. I'm listening."

"I can't talk about it on the phone."

"Why not?"

"Just take my word for it, okay?"

"You're not stringing me along, are you? Because if you are, you'll regret it."

"I'm telling the truth, goddammit. Cross my heart and hope to die. I'll even spit if you want."

"Where do you want to meet?"

"How about Gibson Beach? We can walk along the ocean while we talk."

She agreed to meet me in an hour. I showered and changed, and drove straight to Gibson, even though I knew I'd be early. I was excited just knowing I'd be alone with her. At the same time I told myself not to act like an idiot and stick to the script.

It was still morning, so there were plenty of parking spaces on the narrow road. The Hamptons had miles of contiguous ocean beaches, but each area had a different name and a different feel. There was a beach in Amagansett called Asparagus, because of the singles who stood around like stalks of asparagus looking for pick-ups. There were others: Nude, Flying Point, Sagg Main, Bitch. Each had its following. My favorite was Gibson because it was small and usually uncrowded.

I took off my moccasins and walked barefoot on the sand. The breeze coming off the water was cool and smelled of salt. I took deep breaths of sea air and immediately felt calmer. The waves were not big, but were high enough to make a roaring sound as they broke against the shore. I walked to the edge of the water and let the remnant of a wave wash up over my feet.

I thought I heard a shout and turned around. Rosie stood at the entrance to the beach waving at me. I was continually surprised at how from a distance she appeared to be tall, yet was only a couple of inches over five feet. She walked toward me, sandals dangling from one hand. She was wearing denim shorts and a matching cutoff tank top that bared a narrow band of skin and a dollop of a navel, declaring that at forty-nine, although ten years younger than I was, she looked a whole lot better. I remembered what a different image she used to project in her role as a vice-president of Allied Stores. Then she wore tailored pinstripe suits and carried an attaché case, very much the businesswoman, but still damned attractive.

"You look great," I said.

"So do you. You're getting to look more like Paul Newman every day. It must be the blue eyes."

"The young Paul or the old one?"

"The middle-aged one."

I took her arm and we walked along the edge of the ocean, where I told her the first part of the Cynthia story: about Morty setting me up, her dead husband, her secret closet and what was in it. I left out the kissing.

41

"I'm guessing she wants you to sell them for her."

"She never said, but that's what I'm assuming. Contact the right people. Act as a middleman." I stopped. "But that's not the whole story." I told her about Solofsky, his bodyguard, and the threat. I mentioned the ear, figuring to get the sympathy vote.

"He did what?" she said. "Punched you on your ear? Let me see."

I turned sideways so she could do a proper examination.

"It looks a little red."

"I iced it so it wouldn't swell, but it still hurts."

"It seems you've got a real problem," she said.

"I think so, too. That's why I wanted to talk to you. What do you think?"

"Is this Cynthia a Clairol blonde with a dynamite figure?"

"She's a chemically-enhanced blonde with a great body. What about it?"

"She was at Toby's yesterday."

"You sure?"

"How many blonde Cynthias are there around here? Of course I'm sure. Toby introduced her to me. I got the impression that she and Toby are good friends."

"How good?"

"They went into a room together and talked for quite a long time. When she left, Toby just made some offhand remark, but I got the feeling they had been talking about something serious."

"So where does that leave me?"

"I don't know. Why don't you just drop the whole thing? Tell her that you got beat up on, and that was more than you bargained for."

"How would you feel about me if I did that to you?"

She stopped walking and looked at the waves rolling in.

"Okay. You can't do that. What about the police then?"

"That was the first thing I thought of, but it wouldn't work. I'd have to sign a complaint, and you know what would happen next. A lot of red tape, and in the meantime they could do a worse number on me. No, I have to come up with something better than that."

"Maybe you ought to have another talk with Cynthia. Tell her what happened. Maybe she'll think again about making some kind of arrangement with this man. After all, I don't think she'd want to see you hurt, would she?"

"I don't think so. In any event, I certainly don't want to see me get hurt."

We walked back to the cars. "I'm glad we talked," I said. "As usual, you make sense. I'm going to have a talk with her. See if I can get her to negotiate."

We were back on the road. Rosalind slipped her sandals back on. I leaned against her car and brushed the sand off the soles of my feet.

Rosalind straightened suddenly. "You know what, Jake?" she said. The sun was in her eyes, making her squint. She put a hand up to shade them. The gesture was familiar. I thought of how many times we'd lain stretched out side by side on this same beach, and how we'd both get hot, and I'd lick the salt on her skin, and later, other parts of her. "I just realized something."

"What's that?"

"I don't think you want it to end so simply. I think you want to get involved even more than you are now."

"What are you talking about?"

She came closer, searching my eyes for clues. Then she laughed. "Of course. You want to do this even though it's dangerous. In fact, you're even more intrigued because it *is* dangerous. You always did have this intractable streak in you.

Right? Although you always thought of it as *adventurous*. All those stories you used to tell me about hiking alone, hoping to spot bears and mountain lions. Then it disappeared. Why? You never said."

"I got older, that's all."

"But you missed it. Remember I tried to get you to go hiking again?"

"It wouldn't have been the same."

"Because I was there?"

"No, it just wouldn't have been the same."

"I just want you to remember something. If you do go ahead and get involved in this, don't forget whom you're dealing with. These people are probably criminals, racketeers, gangsters, whatever you want to call them. It's not a game to them. So be careful. Be very careful."

"I hear you."

"I'm glad. But tell me, am I right about this, the adventure, the thrill?"

"I don't know. I haven't been much into introspection lately. The only thinking I've done has been about you." I reached out and put my arms around her. She let me pull her close. The feel of her body in my arms was so right. I began to tighten my grip. Then she gently but firmly pushed me away. "Rosie," I said. "How long does this have to go on?"

"Until it's resolved."

"Let's resolve it then."

"How can we, when you don't even know what the problem is?"

"So tell me."

"I can't."

"Why?"

"When *you* figure out what it is, that will go a long way toward your straightening it out."

"So that's the way you want to play it?"

"I'm afraid so. But I have confidence in you. I know you can do it." With that, she got into her little VW and was gone.

That was the second time she'd disappeared on me like that.

Chapter 7

With Rosalind's words of advice firmly implanted in my brain, I headed for Morty's office. I had only a vague idea of where Cynthia lived, so it seemed like a good idea to get the address from Morty. It also wouldn't hurt to try and learn a little more about his friend Boris and what he was up to before he died.

I drove down Sag Harbor's Main Street, swung around, and squeezed past Fort Apache in order to get into the parking lot of the medical building. Fort Apache was a squat U of stores encased in red brick and plate glass, so named by the Harbor's denizens because of its devastating ugliness and because it rose up at the foot of Main Street, where it managed to obstruct both traffic and the view of the waterfront.

The waiting room had three people in it. On one wall was a reproduction of a Cézanne still life, but I knew there was a real one in his office. Morty's wife, Sherri, had personally installed it. I waved to Sylvia, his receptionist. "Ask if he can fit me in for a minute."

Sylvia was a motherly-looking woman, with a double chin and a bosom so large you could stack books on it. Morty's previous receptionist could have been a stand-in for Michelle Pfeiffer, but she lasted about as long as it took for Sherri to come into the office after-hours and find Morty's hand where it shouldn't have been.

Sylvia picked up the phone and spoke. "Go right in," she said.

I walked back along the corridor past two examining rooms and found him in his office in the back. He had another visitor.

"We were just talking about you," Morty said. "This is Agent Mackleworth, FBI."

The FBI man extended his hand. "Justin Mackleworth," he said, his voice flowing like Southwestern molasses. The accent suggested a ten-gallon hat and boots, but he was hatless and wore black wingtips with the thick soles the FBI was famous for.

"Jake Wanderman. Why were you talking about me?"

"Mr. Mackleworth seemed to know that Mr. Organ and his wife were friends of mine," Morty said. "He was asking me about Cynthia when Sylvia called to tell me you were here, so it seemed natural to mention that you offered to help her with her finances."

"Natural," I said.

"And did you?" FBI asked.

"Did I what?"

"Help her."

"Yes."

"And, if you don't mind my asking, how were you able to help her?"

"I began to straighten out her bills, for a start."

"In the time you were with her, did she say anything about her husband? Or anything that you might consider . . . unusual?"

"She told me her husband was dead, if that's what you mean."

"Anything about her husband's business affairs?"

"No."

"Nothing at all?"

"No." Then I said, "Who are you more interested in, Mrs. Organ or her dead husband?"

The FBI man looked at his fingernails as if deciding whether or not to have a manicure. From what I could see, a manicure would have been impossible because his nails were bitten down to the quick, leaving squiggly dark lines at the end of his fingers. I wondered what old J. Edgar would have made of that. "I'll be honest with you," he said. "It's the husband we're mostly interested in. I'm out here seeing the wife strictly as a matter of routine. This is confidential, you understand."

Morty and I both nodded.

"Boris Organ's death left some open files unresolved. I learned nothing of interest from his wife, but she did mention that Dr. Adler and her husband played a great many rounds of golf together. So I came over here to see what I could learn from Dr. Adler. It's only natural, you understand?"

"Sure, natural," I said.

"Now Dr. Adler, I'd appreciate you thinking carefully . . . did Boris Organ ever say anything to you about his business? His partners? Anything like that?"

"*Nada,*" Morty said.

"What about you, Mr. Wanderman? Did the wife indicate in any way that she might be afraid of something or someone?"

"Same answer," I said. "No."

"That's too bad. By the way, do either of you know how Boris died?"

"Is it important?" I said.

"They found his body behind the wheel of his Cadillac at

three o'clock in the morning on a side street in Brighton Beach."

"You mean he was murdered?"

"The official report was heart attack."

"But you think otherwise," I said.

"Let me tell you a little more about Boris Organ. Then maybe you'll understand."

"Fine," I said.

"He came here with that big load of Russkies who emigrated back in the seventies and eighties. Mostly they settled in Brighton Beach in Brooklyn. By and large they had a mind to be law-abiding citizens, but not all of them, if you get my drift."

"And our friend, Boris, was one of the non-law-abiding citizens?" I said.

"Exactly. He started out with extortion. It's easy and it pays off. He left extortion and went into credit card fraud. He was part of a team that swindled American Express to the tune of almost three million dollars. They went on to steal diamonds out of the diamond district, made connections with the mob, and got into gasoline bootlegging and tax evasion. Big time stuff."

I looked at Morty. "Did you know any of this?"

He shrugged. "Of course not. He was a perfect gentleman, as far as I could see."

Agent Mackleworth took two cards out of a plastic case, handed one to Morty and one to me. "I won't take up any more of your time. But if you think of anything, or if you hear anything, call me."

After he left, I said to Morty, "You had no idea the guy was Russian Mafia?"

"Not a clue. He joined the club without a problem. In fact, he was sponsored by Tom Gillian, president of the South

Fork National Bank. It was only after Boris died, I heard the rumors."

"What rumors?"

"That he might have had some mob connections."

"And you didn't bother to tell me before you got me involved with his widow?"

"What's the problem? You're only helping her with the checkbook, right? That can't get you into any trouble."

I was dying to tell him that I was in a lot of trouble but I couldn't bring myself to do it. Our M.O. had always been that I was the one who helped Morty out of a jam, not the other way around.

Sylvia knocked and opened the door. "Your patients are getting edgy, Doctor."

"Send them in," I said. "I'm gone."

Chapter 8

I pressed the intercom button at Cynthia's gate. There was no answer. Now that I knew about her husband, it was more important than ever that Cynthia and I have a heart-to-heart. I jammed my thumb against the button over and over again. Still no response. I called her number from the cell phone and got a recording. There was nothing else to do but try later.

I went home, did my sixty push-ups and a hundred sit-ups. I knew gym rats who could do more than two or three times that, but I wasn't out to prove anything, I just wanted to stay in shape. That's what I told myself anyway, but deep down I thought that if I ever did give myself over to introspection, I might come up with a different answer.

I put some water on to boil for the long grain wild rice I had in the pantry. I poured safflower oil into a skillet and sliced red and green peppers, a Vidalia onion, and a half-dozen mushrooms, then peeled four garlic cloves and minced them. While the vegetables were sautéing, I added kosher salt, black pepper, a dash of red pepper, oregano, a touch of coriander, freshly chopped parsley, and a generous shot of a Pinot Grigio I had bought at the liquor store next to the 7-Eleven.

I wondered about Cynthia. Was it possible she knew

nothing of her husband's business? Sure it was possible—she didn't strike me as the brightest of bulbs—but what could she think when she came across a closet filled with treasure? She had to suspect something.

When the rice was drained, I tossed it directly into the skillet, stirred everything together so the flavors would meld, and ate it out of the pan, accompanied by more of the Pinot Grigio. If the wine had a nose, I wasn't aware of it, but the cold tingle in my mouth when I drank it was good enough for me.

Rosalind loved my cooking, especially when I made something like this for the two of us. She used to say, "You have a great touch with a spoon, handsome, as well as with other, more valuable things."

I couldn't help but wonder what Rosalind was having for dinner that night, and whom she was having it with.

I called Cynthia again. This time she answered. "I just walked in," she said.

"I have to talk to you."

"You mean, now?"

"That's right. Now."

"I've been out all day. I'm really tired. Couldn't it wait till tomorrow?"

"No."

"Well, all right," Cynthia said. "Could you give me an hour? I need a drink and a hot bath."

An hour later, as darkness settled in, I was again pushing the intercom button. The gate swung open and I drove to the house.

Cynthia opened the door. "The housekeeper's off today, so I have to do everything myself." She was wearing a kelly green robe. Her feet were as bare as I imagined the rest of her to be under the robe. Her face was made up and her eyes looked like traffic lights signaling *Go*. I couldn't help flashing back to her hot hand on my chest, her lips pressed against mine.

She led me along a corridor and into the kitchen, where we sat at a small table. There were gleaming stainless steel pots on hooks above us, but I had the feeling that Cynthia didn't have much interest in their appearance or their function. "Would you like a drink?" she asked.

"No thanks."

She pulled a pack of Marlboros out of a pocket and lit one. "Okay. What's up?"

"A lot. I met a guy from the FBI today."

"Did he have a real Southern accent?"

"That's the one. Name's Mackleworth. He said he talked to you. What did he ask you about?"

"People Boris did business with. I told him I didn't have a clue."

"What about Solofsky? Your husband's partner?"

"He mentioned his name among others."

"Did you tell him anything?"

"Of course not."

"Did he say anything about your husband?"

"No. Why?"

Suddenly I was stumped. How could I just blurt out that her husband was a gangster? I didn't know if she knew it or not. And if she didn't, why should she believe me? Why should she even believe the guy from the FBI? As a matter of fact, I thought, why should *I* believe the guy from the FBI? With their history, going back to J. Edgar and his illegal activities, the FBI had to be looked at with a lot of skepticism.

I decided to deal with the one thing I knew for sure and that concerned us both. "Never mind. Ever since you showed me that case yesterday, and what was in it, I've been doing a lot of thinking."

"I'm glad you brought that up. To tell you the truth, I'm kind of sorry I got you into it. But you won't have to worry about it anymore. It's all been taken care of."

"How?"

She tilted her head back and blew smoke at the ceiling. I watched the smoke gather in a soft cloud and drift toward the hanging pots. "I think it's better if you don't know."

"It's too late for that, Cynthia. I have to know. There's someone breathing down my neck, wanting to get his hands on that stuff. If I don't tell him something, he's not going to breathe down my neck, he's going to break it, or have someone else do it."

"Who's that?"

"Your husband's partner, Jascha Solofsky. Remember him?"

Instead of answering, she tapped ashes into a glass ashtray.

"He wants to make a deal," I said.

"Fat chance!"

"He claims that if you give him the eggs, he'll take care of everything. You'll get your fair share."

"Do you believe that? I don't."

"Maybe not, but Solofsky has a bodyguard who looks like he'd enjoy pulling out fingernails."

I watched the end of her cigarette glow as she drew on it. She brushed some stray hairs away from her glamorous cheekbones. I looked up at the clock on the wall. It had gotten dark and we had not turned on the lights. I could just about see the second hand moving in steady jerks around the dial.

"You asked me to help you, Cynthia," I said. "And I promised I would. Now I think you better tell me what you

54

did with that attaché case."

Suddenly, there was a noise in another part of the house.

"What was that?" Cynthia said.

"It's glass breaking. I think we've got visitors."

"Omigod!" Cynthia said. "I shut off the alarm when you got here. I forgot to turn it back on."

There was more noise. More glass breaking.

"Where do you think they are?" I whispered.

"My guess is the living room," Cynthia whispered back. "They probably broke in through the French doors."

"Are there lights on in there?"

She shook her head.

"Good. If the whole house is dark, they'll think it's empty. But we have to get out of here."

Now low voices were distinguishable. One of them said, "I'm bleeding. I must have cut myself."

"Idiot."

I did not recognize the voice, but the accent was familiar.

"Let's move it," I said.

We sneaked into the foyer, where I could just make out the stairs leading to the second floor. We ran up as fast as we could, trying not to make noise. A couple of quick steps and we were in her bedroom. She fiddled at the bottom of the pink Gainsborough. The secret door opened.

"Get in," she said.

We both got inside. I saw right away that the attaché case was no longer there. Then she reached under a shelf, did something, the door slid closed, the light went off. We were alone in that small, dark closet.

Chapter 9

The closet was really small. We were pressed together about as tightly as if we were tied, Cynthia facing front, me in back. I could hear nothing but the sound of our breathing.

"What do you think's happening?" Cynthia whispered.

"They're looking for what used to be in this closet is what's happening."

I tried to hear something, but there was still no sound except our own breathing.

While we stood there, unable to move, I could not help becoming aware of Cynthia's body pressing against me. The robe she had on was a light one that did nothing to obstruct the contact between our bodies. There was a certain lushness about the parts of her that were impinging upon me, a round kind of succulence that was making it difficult to concentrate on what might be going on outside.

"Did you hear that?" Cynthia whispered.

"Sounds like they're running up the stairs. They'll be in here any minute."

Cynthia turned her head and put her lips against my ear; her breath tickled. "We're okay. This closet is better than a safe in a bank. They'll never find us in here."

"I hope you're right," I said.

Now there were additional noises, thumping, grinding, and voices, but they were so muffled it was impossible to make out what they were saying. Suddenly there were loud rapping sounds. They were hitting the walls. I could feel the vibrations. They must know about the secret closet, I thought. They're looking for it. The knocks continued a few more times. The voices were still there and still unintelligible.

I could feel my heart pounding away in my chest, driving the air out of my lungs. I think I might even have been praying. At the same time, Cynthia's body was still there. And in spite of the situation we were in, my body was beginning to do something that I did not want it to do. I couldn't believe this kind of thing could still happen. It took me back to a classmate's thirteenth birthday party, when I was dancing with a girl I liked and suddenly there was something between us. I was too young to realize that was simply puberty paying its respects. My only thought was, what could I do to get out of this quandary? My brilliant effort was to suddenly stop dancing and sit down. My dancing partner looked disappointed. It never occurred to me that she might have been enjoying it.

But now there was no place to sit down.

"What's that?" Cynthia whispered.

"I think you know."

"I know, all right. But your timing sucks."

"I understand. Believe me, I'm trying my best."

Our conversation managed to produce the effect we both wanted, and I could once more concentrate on what was happening outside our little space.

The noises seemed to have stopped.

"What do you think?" Cynthia asked. "Did they leave?"

"Sounds like it. But we better wait, just to make sure. We don't want to go out and find someone waiting for us." I began counting slowly. When I reached a hundred, I said, "I think we waited long enough. Are you ready?"

"Am I ever. I'm dying to get some fresh air."

"Then get us out of here," I said.

The room looked like T.J. Maxx after a fifty-percent markdown. All the lights were on. Drawers were pulled out of bureaus and the contents spilled out. The bed was ripped apart, the mattress and box spring slashed open. Dolls were scattered everywhere, some of them cut open as well.

"Those rotten bastards!" Cynthia cried.

"Now you know what I mean."

Cynthia picked up a doll from the floor and sat on a chair, holding it in her lap. It had been clothed in a tartan plaid outfit, so apparently it was a Scot. But this was one that had been badly slashed, the body shredded. "Marijane was my favorite." Tears rolled down her cheeks. "Look what they did to her."

"Better her than us." I went to the door. "I'm going to check downstairs. Make sure they're gone."

I went slowly down the stairs, trying not to make any noise. At the foot, I stopped and listened. There was no sound except for the refrigerator's compressor running in the kitchen. I went in there and took down one of the omelet pans hanging on the rack. It felt heavy and solid in my hand. There was a meat cleaver that looked as if it had been hung for decoration. I took that, too. Then I moved slowly out of the kitchen, pot in one hand, cleaver in the other. I was armed and dangerous. The next room was the dining room. Drawers were pulled out of a server and also from a cupboard. Broken glass and china were on the floor. King Lear had nothing to do with this situation but Edgar had said something appropriate:

> The worst is not
> So long as we can say, "This is the worst."

I went on into the living room. Paintings had been taken down and tossed to the floor, along with cushions from the furniture. The rugs had been pulled aside. The French doors Cynthia had mentioned were open, one of them with the pane near the handle broken, pieces of glass scattered about. I breathed more easily. The raiders were gone.

I returned my weapons to the kitchen and went back upstairs. Cynthia was sitting where I had left her, staring at her doll. "I'm really sorry about this," I said. "They broke a lot of stuff downstairs, too. But you're okay and I'm okay. That's what's important."

"I guess so."

I kneeled down in front of her. "Cynthia, look at me." She raised her eyes to mine. Their color had dulled and they were wet. "You owe me something. The truth. Now is the time to tell me what you did with that case."

"I guess you're right. I gave it to a friend of mine. I thought that was the best thing to do. She said she would know what to do with it."

"And just who is this friend?" I asked, although I was pretty sure I already knew.

"Toby Welch," she said.

Chapter 10

I tried to pry more out of Cynthia, but all she would say was that Toby was a dear friend, and that her dear friend assured her she knew a lot of important people, would take care of everything, and that Cynthia had absolutely nothing to worry about.

If Cynthia believed that, good for her. I wasn't so sure. Toby was rich and powerful, but was that enough? Besides, that didn't help me. I still had Solofsky to deal with.

I looked at her. She was biting her lip but the tears had stopped. "Are you all right?" I said.

She nodded.

"You sure?"

"I'm sure. You go on home. I just want to sit here and be miserable by myself."

"What about being in the house alone?"

"I'll set the alarm. I'll be okay."

I didn't argue. I went home and tried to think. What was Toby's role in this? Why would she want to get involved? And who had engineered that break-in? I was sure the accents I'd heard were Russian, but I couldn't swear they belonged to either Solofsky or his bodyguard. But if it wasn't them, who was it? Some other Russians trying to get into the act? Maybe the KGB trying to get their treasure back?

The adrenaline was pumping but it wasn't helping me to think clearly. The only clear idea I had was to speak to Toby Welch. Rosalind was her friend and living in her house, so I had access. I would call Rosie and ask her to set it up. Besides, I wanted to talk to Rosie again. A lot had happened since I'd seen her. It was hard to believe it had been this very same day. But as much as I wanted to talk to her, it was already after ten. I decided to wait until morning.

Chapter 11

The night was long and tedious. I was glad to see daylight. I got dressed, made a pot of coffee. The smell of freshly brewed coffee made me feel a lot better. To go with it, I micro'd a croissant I had in the freezer.

I phoned just before nine. The sound of Rosie's voice let loose a cockamamie mixture of yearning, remembrance, and guilt. "I'm glad you answered," I said. "The last time I called, I had to speak to two flunkies before I got to you."

"One of them is gone. I'm the replacement."

"What do you mean?"

"Since I saw you, Toby fired her secretary and hired me. So now I'm sort of her Girl Friday. I spent the day doing all kinds of interesting things. It was so much fun. Tomorrow we're going to L.A. Out in the morning, back in the evening."

I was instantly jealous. Also threatened. A glamorous life would take her further away from me, maybe to the point where I would never be able to get her back. I tried to be enthusiastic: "That's great. Sounds very exciting."

"Yes, doesn't it?"

"I already said it does. Now a change of subject. I need a big favor from you."

"What is it?"

"Get me together with your new boss. I have to have a talk."

"Why?"

"You're not the only one things happened to yesterday. Remember what I told you on the beach?"

"Of course."

"Well, I've learned a few things since then. One item of importance is that Cynthia must be very tight with Toby, because she gave her that stuff I told you about."

"Are you sure? Why would Toby want to have anything to do with it? She's got more on her plate than she can handle now."

"That's what I was thinking. Also, this is not exactly your usual business deal."

"It doesn't make sense," Rosie said.

"That's why I need to talk to her. Do you think you can arrange it?"

"It won't be easy. Every minute of her day is booked."

"See what you can do."

"Okay. I'll get back to you."

She was about to hang up, when I said, "I really enjoyed our walk on the beach."

A few beats went by. Then she said, "So did I."

An hour later, she called back. "She won't see you. She said Cynthia Organ is a friend and what she and Cynthia do is nobody else's business. She was very definite, even when I told her who you were."

"Please, Rosie. You've got to do something. I need answers."

"I guess it's really important, huh?"

"You know it is."

"Okay. Here's what I'll do. Tomorrow night, she's going to be at a charity function at Hay Street. It's for HARP. Toby is one of the Board members. I'll put your name on the guest list. Then, when I think the time is right, I'll give you the high sign, and you can go over and talk to her."

"Great. What time should I be there?"

"Between eight and nine."

Shortly after talking to Rosie, the phone rang. It was Solofsky. I wasn't surprised. It was a sure bet I was going to hear from him sooner or later. "What are you accomplishing?" he asked.

I tried to find out if he was the one who broke into Cynthia's house by making myself come across like a New York guy in the know. "Don't give me that horseshit. If you wanted to do it yourself, what did you get me involved for?"

"Explain yourself. I do not understand you."

"You want to play dumb, is that it? You want me to believe you don't know anything about the break-in?"

"I do not want to play anything. Just tell me what you are talking about."

I told him.

"*Moy tvoyou mat!* This is not my doing. I am one hundred miles away in Brooklyn, where other matters require my attention."

"Whose doing is it then?"

"There are many who are jealous of my success. They want to take from me what is mine. But they will not succeed. I shall return to your area as soon as I finish my business here. You can count on it."

"You made my day."

He ignored my sarcasm. "You will continue to do what you are doing. You are understanding me?"

Even though I knew he was a gangster, and I knew he could be dangerous to my health, I still was dying to tell him to fuck off. Out of prudence, I resisted. I'd wait for the right time. It would come. "I am understanding you," I said.

Chapter 12

Hay Street was the regional theater in Sag Harbor. It was situated on Long Wharf, the main docking facility in Sag Harbor, in what had once been a nightclub. Plays were presented, as well as readings and concerts, and in addition, charity benefits. These events were held on the wharf in a huge tent. Hundreds of people paid exorbitant amounts of money for tickets. Slathering sycophants that they were, they did so willingly because of the chance to "ooh" and "aah" and perhaps even be photographed with the few celebrities who showed up. Predictably, the photos would then appear in *Sam's Paper*, the celebrity gossip rag that was distributed free and in such quantities that it flowed across the land like toxic waste.

The party was held on Saturday night. At eight o'clock it was still daylight, although shadows were beginning to close in. I had to stop at a table that was set up on the wharf in front of the tent where guests had to present their tickets before being admitted. Seated behind the table were Morty and Sherri Adler: he in a dinner jacket, she be-gowned and bejeweled.

Morty looked up at me in surprise. "What are you doing here? You don't usually show up at these things."

"You'll see my name on the guest list. But before you ask, I'll tell you. I didn't pay for a ticket any more than you did."

My comment was out of line. The Adlers were major benefactors of the Sag Harbor Theater, and in addition, did volunteer work for it. It was Sherri who brought out the worst in me. From the day Morty introduced her, lo those many years ago, there was an instantaneous spark between us. Of hatred. We both recognized it at the time, but since she was going to marry him, and I didn't want to lose him as a friend, we made the necessary accommodations. We'd lived with them ever since.

Sherri gave me a look that would have frozen a hot pepper. "It wouldn't hurt *you* to volunteer for something once," she said.

"You're right," I said, as humbly as I could. "If I could sit next to someone as glamorous and as beautiful as you, maybe I would volunteer." It wasn't a total lie. She did look terrific: all creamy skin, décolleté, and black eyeliner.

I went in, leaving Morty with a puzzled expression, and Sherri with her mouth open, but speechless.

This affair, Rosie had told me, was to enrich the coffers of HARP, which stood for HOW ANIMALS RESCUE PEOPLE, an organization devoted to the rights and well-being of dogs and cats. They were also known to offer hospitality to any other non-human creature God, or nature, may have created.

The crowd surrounding the tables of food was swarming like maggots on animals that hadn't made it to HARP, so I got on a smaller line at the bar. Drink in hand, I wandered through the crowd, looking for Rosie. While looking, I thought I saw someone I recognized, someone who seemed out of place. It was only a glimpse, so I couldn't be sure. Then I saw Rosie near the bandstand. She was wearing a low-cut dress that showed off her great cleavage. It had been a long time since I'd had my nose in there, a long time since I'd had my nose anywhere close to where she liked it. I wondered if she was missing it as much as I was.

"You look fabulous," I said. "Almost as good as the day we were married."

"Cut the blarney. Right now, Toby's in the theater with a bunch of VIP's. I don't know what they're discussing or when she'll be coming out. But she should be here any minute." She was looking past me. "There she is. She's heading in this direction."

Toby Welch was coming toward us, trailed by a retinue. I was surprised to see Cormac Blather among them. What was he doing here? I wondered, then realized that in his business, contact with the super rich was the key to success. She was a presence, no doubt about that. More than six feet tall, she seemed to be looking down at me with an expression of benign enlightenment, something like a female Chuck Heston descending from the mountain after a talk with Jehovah. She wore her hair swept away from her ears, each of which had an earring attached to it as long as a telephone pole. "And just who is this?" she asked Rosalind, not taking her eyes from mine.

"This is Jake, my husband."

"You're a persistent sort of fellow, aren't you?" She held out her hand.

"I want to thank you for being so good to my wife."

"She's the one being good to me. She's a godsend. I don't know how I ever got along without her."

"That's exactly what I always said."

I became aware of movement and looked around. Several people had formed a circle around us. They were gawking at Toby. Some of them were holding papers and pencils, waiting for a chance to ask for her autograph. "Can we find a spot that's a little more private?" I said. "I have to talk to you about a serious matter."

"I'm afraid I can't. Duty calls. I have to hand out some awards. Best this. Best that." She paused. "Tell you what. Only because you're Rosalind's husband, mind you. This fracas is going to break up in about an hour or so. You come by my place sometime around eleven. We can talk then. Do you know where I live?" Before I had a chance to answer, she said, "Rosalind will tell you."

Dismissing me, she turned with a smile to face the autograph fiends.

Chapter 13

I hung out at the party for a while, had a bit more to drink, a few canapés, watched some people dance, saw some of our local celebrities. Alec Baldwin was there, known for his many letters to the *East Hampton Star* pitching various issues. Jerry, the columnist, was there. He was obviously an astute man, evidenced by his investing in a newspaper so he could have a column all his own.

By the time eleven p.m. showed up on my watch, most of the people had gone home. The band was still playing. A few couples revolved slowly in front of them. But the fat lady had sung and most everyone knew it.

Toby lived in the Georgica section of East Hampton, another of the many areas of the Hamptons occupied by the rich, the super rich, and the ultra rich. High hedges, dense landscaping, stone walls served well their purpose of keeping the ordinary citizen's eyes on the road or risk crashing into a specimen tree while trying to sneak a peek at the mansions behind those barricades.

I found Toby's driveway with little trouble. I was not surprised to find the inevitable iron gate. I pushed the call button. Nobody answered. I hit the button again and waited. There was still no response. Then I noticed that the gate was not in the locked position. I didn't like the circumstances, but I got out of the car anyway, shoved it open, and drove in.

I went a good distance before coming to the house. It looked like Tara, gleaming white in the moonlight. There was no Scarlett to greet me as I got out of my car, but all the lights seemed to be on and the front door stood open. In spite of the racket the cicadas were making, there was an eerie sense of silence. It was obvious something was rotten not only in Denmark but right here in East Hampton.

I went slowly up the front steps, across the landing, and into the house. I had seen this happen in a thousand movies and each time thought, shmuck, why are you going in there? This time I was the shmuck. I went past the marble-floored entrance hall into a large room with an enormously high ceiling studded with floodlights, all of them on. Opposite me was a fireplace that looked as if it had been transposed from a sixteenth-century palace. A large abstract painting almost totally black hung on the wall above it. There were clusters of sofas and chairs about the room, but no people. To my right, I could see into a kitchen, and beyond that, a dining room.

Not a sound.

Off to the left was a corridor with multiple doors. Carefully, I opened the first door: an office with desks, file cabinets, a computer, fax machine, copier.

Nobody.

Behind the next door was a room with a leather sofa and recliner, a wall unit containing several TVs, a VCR, and a stereo.

Again, empty.

The third door led into a room with floor-to-ceiling bookshelves. There was a library table in the center of the room, around which were straight-backed chairs. Each chair held a person tied with loops of clothesline, eyes open wide and head rocking back and forth. They were making grunting noises instead of talking, because their mouths were covered with duct tape. Toby was in one chair, Rosalind in another, a woman and a man, neither of whom I knew, in the other two, and in the last was Cormac Blather.

I rushed toward them. "What happened?" I said, even though they couldn't answer. Rosalind was nearest to me. I tried to untie her, but the ropes were knotted too well.

"I'll get a knife from the kitchen," I said.

"Ugh, ummm, ugh," Rosalind grunted.

"Oh, sure," I said. "Sorry about that." I pulled the tape off her mouth as gently as I could.

She took several deep breaths through her mouth. "Oh God," she said. "It was awful."

Then I did the same for the others. They, too, breathed heavily and began making moaning and muttering noises.

"Could you hurry up with the knife?" Toby said.

I ran into the kitchen and found a wooden block on the counter with a set of knife handles sticking out of it. The handles were made of a lustrous walnut. I noticed one of the slots was empty. I pulled a large knife out of the block, went back, and began cutting them loose, beginning with Rosalind. When Rosalind's hands were untied, she began massaging her wrists and crying.

Cormac was rubbing his temples. His complexion was gray.

The man and woman were speaking to each other in Spanish.

Toby seemed to be the most composed. When I got to her I asked, "What happened?"

"Well first, this man showed up," Toby said. "He said he was from the FBI."

"Mackleworth? Did he say his name was Mackleworth?"

"That's right."

What was he doing here? Then I remembered the familiar face I had seen in the crowd earlier.

"He announced himself on the intercom, said he had spoken to you. We buzzed him in, he showed his ID, began asking us questions. He wasn't here five minutes before the bell rang. Anita foolishly opened the door and these two men came in with guns in their hands."

"Ay, ay, ay," Anita cried.

"They didn't say a word. They took us in here and tied us up, then they went out with . . . what did you say his name was?"

"Mackleworth."

"They went out and shut the door," Toby said. "We could hear them moving around the house. I realized they were looking for the case. But I hadn't told anyone where it was."

"Where was it?"

"In my bedroom closet."

"Not the best choice for a hiding place," I said.

"Well, how did I know criminals would break into my house!"

"That's what I wanted to talk to you about. You were getting involved with bad people."

"Too bad you didn't tell me sooner," she said, ungratefully.

"In any event, we have to decide what to do now," I said. "Do you want to call the cops? We don't have to tell them anything about the case."

"No way. Do you know what kind of publicity this would generate? We'd have reporters and TV people swarming all over the place. Nobody's hurt. Let's just forget the whole thing."

Rosalind looked dazed. I went over and put my arms around her. "Are you okay?" I asked. She didn't answer, but I could feel how tense her body was. "I think we ought to have a look around. Anybody want to come?"

Toby nodded. She and Rosalind followed me up the stairs to the second floor. The others stayed behind.

We found Mackleworth in the first bedroom. He was sitting in an armchair, staring at us with an expression of disbelief on his face. His jacket was open, revealing a large red stain that had spread out in a circle around his heart. Projecting from the center of the circle was a brown walnut handle. I recognized it as one from the set of knives in the kitchen. It didn't take more than a look to figure out that he was dead.

Chapter 14

There was no choice but to call the cops. Toby did not object.

Luckily for her, no reporters were around at that time of night to learn what had happened. We were all interviewed. No mention was made of the attaché case or its contents. Toby told the detective there were two intruders. She gave him descriptions: medium height, medium build, white, sandy hair, one guy had a ponytail, no distinguishing marks. She guessed they had gotten in to steal but had no idea what was stolen, because once we found the dead body we no longer checked.

The detective was very polite to Toby. He suggested she try to get to sleep and when she was able, to please determine what, if anything, had been stolen.

When it was my turn, I told the detective who Mackleworth was and where I had met him. He raised his eyebrows but said nothing more about it. Before he left, he said we would be asked to come to the police station and give statements.

When all the technicians were finally gone and Mackleworth was rolled out in a body bag, the four of us—Toby, Rosalind, Cormac, and myself—were together in the living room. The servants had retired to their room. I sat next to Rosalind. For a long time, there was silence.

"I think somebody ought to see if the case is still in the closet," I said.

"I'll go," Cormac said.

"I'll go with you," I said.

Neither of the women said anything. They both looked as if they were about to throw up. I didn't feel so good myself. Seeing a dead man up close does bad things to your plumbing.

The two of us went into Toby's bedroom and opened her closet. It was large enough to house a family of four. We examined hanging clothes, the shelves, the specially-built compartments for shoes, belts, jewelry. There was no attaché case.

"What a pity," Blather said. "I never even got the chance to see the beauties."

"You don't seem very upset about it," I said. "Not the loss of the case and not the murder."

"You are quite in error. I assure you I am most upset."

We went back downstairs and told them the treasure was gone. I said to Toby, "How come you brought Cormac in on this?"

"Meaning, you want to know if I trust him? The answer is yes. Most emphatically. I've known him a long time. I've bought a considerable number of very good antiques from him. It seemed to me he would be just the person to know what to do with Cynthia's treasure chest."

"Well, it looks like it's gone, so that's that. But did you know Cynthia's treasure is probably illegal? In other words, stolen?"

"We don't know that for a fact, do we?" Cormac said. "I was going to send out discreet inquiries in that direction."

"It looks like it won't be necessary," I said.

It was four o'clock in the morning. I was beat. I was ready to go home. I asked Rosalind if she was going to be okay.

"Thanks for asking. I'll be all right."

"Are you sure?"

"Don't you worry about her," Toby said. "After you and Cormac leave, we're going to have a shot of brandy and go to bed."

"Yes," Rosalind said. "Don't worry. I'm going to be fine." She wrapped her arms around herself and shivered.

I knew she would have bad dreams that night. She always had nightmares after a traumatic event. An upsetting movie or something terrible on the news could do it. I wanted to hold her in my arms and comfort her, but all I could do was to plant a kiss on her forehead and go home.

Chapter 15

Early next morning the phone rang. I had trouble getting my eyes unstuck and my ears to work, but I managed enough to hear a voice asking me if I could come to the police station in Sag Harbor right away.

"You mean, now?"

The answer was yes.

The station was in a small building on Division Street, directly across from a hot tub showroom. I told the uniformed cop why I was there. He pointed to a door at the back with a sign that read: Vincent J. Mazzini, Chief of Police. I knocked and went in. It was a plain office with a cluttered pine desk, a row of dark green file cabinets that looked as if they'd been there since World War I, an American flag on a pole in one corner, the New York State flag in another corner, and some framed diplomas on the wall.

There were two men in the room. Behind the desk was the Chief. I recognized him from the pictures of him I'd seen in the *Sag Harbor Express*. He was about fifty, with thick black hair, olive skin, and a long, thin nose that could have come directly from one of the statues in the Uffizi. He wore a short-sleeved white shirt without a tie. "Mr. Wanderman?" he asked.

"Yes."

"Thanks for coming. Have a seat." He moved his hand in the direction of the other man, who was sitting on a folding chair at the side of the Chief's desk. "This is Bill Catalano. He's a detective from New York City."

I nodded and sat opposite the two of them. I wanted to tell them I didn't like being woken up and practically ordered to report to them, but I didn't see what that would accomplish other than pissing them off. So I kept my mouth shut.

"We asked you down to talk about the murder last night," the Chief said. "It's really an East Hampton matter, and that's where you should be giving your statement. But I spoke to the Chief and told him my friend Bill was here already, so he agreed to let us take your statement and fax it over to him. Is that okay with you?"

"Sure." I looked at his friend Bill.

"I can guess that you want to know what Bill is doing here. So I'll let him tell you." He leaned back in his chair and let Bill have his turn.

Bill Catalano looked exactly like a kid in my neighborhood who ended up in Attica. His body seemed to be a solid mass from his neck to his waist. His skin was darker than the Chief's and had an oily sheen. Someone had put a mushroom in the middle of his face for a nose. The surprise was his eyes, which were a light brown and as soft as a child's. When he spoke, the youth disappeared and became tough New York cop.

"I'll be honest with you, Jake. I'm not here to fool around. My specialty is the boys from Brighton Beach. Know what I mean?"

"I don't think so."

"You ever hear of the Russian Mafia?"

"Yes."

"Good. We got a Russian Desk in the department because these guys need to be watched. I'm attached to that

78

desk. Are you with me so far?"

"I'm with you."

"We got word that these guys have been operating out here recently. Soon after, what happens? A guy gets murdered and you happen to be the guy who finds him."

"I didn't find him. He was just there."

"Another interesting bit. That you just happened to know this guy."

"All I did was identify a body."

"You want to be cute, is that it?" His tone was noticeably unfriendly.

"I was told to come here and make a statement. That's what I'm doing."

"Don't you want to be on the side of law and order?"

"I am on the side of law and order."

"Then stop fucking with me and tell me what you know about the Russians."

"What Russians?"

"Start with Misha Bialkin."

Catalano was now grinning, his teeth a flash of white in his dark face. Chief Mazzini was frowning at me in disapproval. They obviously thought I knew this guy. "Who's that?"

"You don't know? He has a restaurant in Brighton Beach. But that's only a cover."

"Never heard of him."

"He's part of the *organizatsia*."

"The what?"

"It's what the Russian mob calls itself. Their version of the Mafia."

"Means nothing to me."

"So you say. Do you know any other Russians?"

"I know the wife of one."

"And who would that be?"

"Cynthia Organ."

"Boris Organ's wife. Ever heard of a guy named Solofsky?"

"Cynthia might have mentioned his name."

"And what do you have to do with Organ's widow?"

"I was helping her with her finances."

"What do you do for a living?"

"What does that have to do with anything? I'm retired." So far, they had not asked about the eggs. I didn't know if this was why Catalano was here, or if it was because an FBI agent had been killed. I only knew I did not like being in the middle of it. "Can I go now? I think I've answered all your questions. Unless you're accusing me of something."

"Take it easy, Mr. Wanderman," the Chief said. "Nobody's accusing you of anything."

"I'm glad to hear that. I'm just as sorry as you are about a guy from the FBI getting killed."

"Who might that be?"

"This guy I identified, Mackleworth."

"He was no more FBI than I am," the Chief said.

"What?"

"He was a two-bit hood from Dallas, name of Justin Midgely," the New York detective said.

I looked at him to see if he was doing a number on me. He wasn't. "Then what was he doing impersonating an FBI agent?"

"Somebody hired him to act the part."

Catalano gave me that malicious grin again. I didn't think he'd be satisfied until he had me sliced, diced, and boiled in oil. "And you know who we think that somebody was?" He didn't wait for me. "Misha Bialkin."

"I told you, I never heard of him."

"Maybe you will," he said.

Chapter 16

When I got home, there was a message to call my father.

"Hi, Dad. What's on your mind?"

"I have great news," he said.

There was a click in my brain. "Don't tell me."

"I'm telling you."

"Not again."

"Yes, again. But this is the last time."

"You always say that."

"I always mean it."

"Okay," I sighed. "Let's hear it."

"Don't sigh like that," he said. "You're not talking to a child."

"I'm sorry." I'd inadvertently let slip the sound of a sigh because the excitement in his voice had signaled what it had signaled on countless previous occasions: namely, that he had discovered his one true love. He was seventy-seven. True, he looked like forty-seven, but when was he going to grow up?

He went on with the established ritual. I must meet his new beloved. It was very important that I give my approval. (It always was.) "She lives in Brooklyn. Her father owns a restaurant in Brighton Beach. Not only that, he invited us to

81

dinner tomorrow night. We'll meet the whole family. It'll be fabulous! I'll get the name and address of the place and let you know."

"Brighton Beach, you said?"

"Yeah. Why?"

"Nothing." Was it too much of a coincidence that Brighton Beach was the home of the Russian Mafia and suddenly my father gets involved with someone in the same vicinity? Could that have been the reason for the New York detective's malicious grin?

"Good. The important thing here is not where the restaurant is located, but to bring your bride," he said. "I love you, but I love her more."

"Of course." I hung up without telling him that Rosalind might soon be my ex-bride.

Before I had time to think anything through, the phone rang again. It was Morty. "Did you tell me Rosalind was staying at Toby Welch's place?"

"Yeah."

"Did you hear what happened?"

"What do you mean?"

"Toby Welch's house. There was a murder."

"How do you know about it?"

"It's on TV. 'Good Morning, America.' Toby Welch is one of their network stars. They're playing it up big."

"Shit!" I shouldn't have been surprised. Toby was a rich and sumptuous feast. Once the story broke, every media vulture in the world would rush in to gobble it up.

"Do you know anything about it?"

"I know too much about it."

"So what's the story?"

"Not now, Morty. Not now." I hung up on him.

Again the phone. "Mr. Wanderman?" The voice was

smarmy, trying to be ingratiating, like the one in the middle of dinner that tells you you've qualified for a platinum VISA card.

"Who?"

"Jake Wanderman."

"Never heard of him." I hung up.

The phone immediately rang again. I hesitated. Maybe I should just let it ring, not answer. But it might be Rosalind. I picked it up. "Jake?" I recognized Cynthia's voice. "I'm scared."

"You heard about it?"

"On the news. I tried to call Toby, but I can't get through."

"I'm not surprised."

"My things. Are they safe?"

"I have bad news for you, Cynthia. The stuff is gone."

"No."

"Yes."

"Omigod. What are we going to do?"

"I wish I knew."

"Any ideas? Any ideas at all?"

"At the moment, not one."

"Then tell me this: do you still want to help me?"

Proudly, I did not hesitate. "A Wanderman never goes back on his word."

Chapter 17

The next call was from Rosalind. "I've been trying to reach you."

"It's a madhouse here," she said. "Toby's been on the phone all morning trying to figure out how to deal with this. Her network wants her to do an interview. Tell how they broke in, show how brave Toby was, let them photograph the house. They want to broadcast it on 'Good Morning, America' and their other news shows, especially on Peter Jennings. They figure it'll blow Brokaw and Rather out of the water."

"It must be tough being a celebrity. How are you making out?"

"I didn't sleep all night, but otherwise I'm okay . . . I keep thinking about that dead man."

"I know it was a shock, but it might make you feel better to know he wasn't from the FBI."

"What do you mean?"

I told her what I'd been told by the Chief and the New York detective.

"Do you think he was there to steal the case, too?"

"Seems like a good guess. The New York cop said he was probably working for another Russian guy. He's from Brooklyn, too." Then I took a deep breath, closed my eyes, and leaped. "Speaking of Brooklyn, I need to ask you something."

"About Brooklyn? I don't know much, but I'll be glad to tell you anything I know."

"It only relates to Brooklyn in that my father invited us to dinner there."

"How come?"

"He wants us meet his new intended."

Silence.

"Please say yes. He's expecting you to be there. He doesn't know you walked out on me."

"I did not walk out on you."

"What do you call it, then?"

"Okay. I guess you're right. I suppose you could say I walked out on you. But I had a good reason."

"I never heard it."

"You know why," she said.

"No, I don't. I can guess, but I don't think I should be guessing about something this serious."

"Think," she said.

I had an idea in what direction she was pushing me, but I resisted going there. Perhaps because I knew what I might learn when I got there. I knew it began when I decided to quit teaching. I had nothing left to give. Twenty-eight years had burned me out. Rosalind was still working, but she had made some remarks that indicated quitting would not be a hardship. I reasoned we would give up our apartment in New York, move out to our summer place in the Hamptons, and live there full time. My friend, Morty, thought it was a great idea. Naturally, since he already lived there. I told Rosalind what I had in mind.

"We can take a trip around the world. We can do anything we want. Within reason, of course."

85

I didn't recognize the lack of enthusiasm in Rosalind until much later, when it was already too late.

"Are you sure you want to do this?" she'd asked.

"Why not? No more school politics, no more pimply kids who don't give a damn. I can read Shakespeare, play golf and tennis. And you can do whatever you want. What could be bad?"

So I got my way. We went on a month-long trip to Europe: London, Paris, Rome, super-deluxe all the way. We stayed at the Claridge, the Ritz, the Excelsior. Before the month was over, we were both dying to get home.

I bought a new leather chair for my desk. I read *Hamlet*, *King Lear*, and, of course, *As You Like It*. Rosalind, Shakespeare's greatest heroine, is the star of that play. I joined the health club, rode a bicycle, played all the outdoor games. We went to every restaurant within fifty miles until we were both sick of going out.

After a while, I began to have the feeling that Rosalind was not happy. I didn't think it was anything serious, just a little bit of mope, I thought. So I tried cheering her up. "Would you like to go into the city more?" I asked.

"Not particularly."

"What would you like to do?"

"I don't know."

"Is something wrong?" I asked.

"I have to tell you, this retirement thing is not working out too well."

"Why not? I'm having a great time."

"Well, I'm not."

"What's the problem?"

"You really want to know?" She was grim.

I was blithe. "Sure."

"You comment on everything I do."

"What do I say?"

"Do it this way. Or do it that way. You follow me to the market and tell me what to buy or not to buy. I can't stand it!"

"I'm only trying to help."

"Help yourself and leave me alone. You do your thing and I'll do mine."

Rosalind's voice in my ear brought me back to the present. "Are you still there?"

"You told me to think, so I was thinking," I said. "We have to talk."

"Yes."

"But first, will you go to the dinner and not say anything about our being separated? It's tomorrow night."

"You know I wouldn't let your father down."

I told her I didn't know the address as yet, but that we had better allow plenty of time to get there. "And thank you, thank you, thank you."

"Don't overdo it," she said.

A while later, I heard the sound of a car crunching the gravel in the driveway. I looked out and saw sun bouncing off the surface of a black Lincoln. I put my hand to my ear and touched it carefully. It didn't hurt anymore, but I wasn't taking chances. I hurried down to the basement and picked up a short length of pipe I had prepared. I slipped it into my back pocket. Then I went upstairs to greet Mr. Solofsky and his friend, Crab.

They were out on the deck same as last time, Solofsky in a chair next to the table with the umbrella, and his bodyguard leaning against the rail with his arms crossed.

"Tell me what happened," he said.

"You saw it on TV, didn't you?"

"Tell me what I don't know."

I decided to stop pretending. "You mean about the eggs?"

There was an instant of recognition in his eyes, so now he knew that I knew. "Are they still in the widow's possession, or are they gone?"

"Gone."

His fist crashed down on the metal table. He said something in Russian that sounded vicious, then jumped to his feet and said something else in Russian to the bodyguard. I moved my hand behind me near my back pocket. If he thought I was going to stand still for another boxing lesson from the Crab, he was in for a big surprise. Instead, he surprised *me*. "All right, Mr. Wanderman. The events of the past few days have changed everything. You are out of the picture as of now. Your services are no longer required."

It took only a second to realize that Solofsky was signing me off. What a relief! Here was my chance to walk away and get back to my life, such as it was. "Okay," I said. "I can deal with that. From now on, I never heard of a Fabergé egg."

"Very wise," Solofsky said. "And you are not hearing of me, either."

"That, too."

"Pyotr," Solofsky said.

Crab stood up and walked in my direction. I gripped the pipe. The dog put his hand out and said, "We are friends?"

I had no choice. I left the pipe in my pocket and put my hand out. He grinned and squeezed, but I was ready. I squeezed back. He tried to outdo me, but his grin gradually changed into a scowl. I squeezed harder, until he finally let go.

"Come," Solofsky said to him.

They walked off the deck, Crab flexing his hand.

I couldn't resist. *"Dosvedanye,"* I called after them.

Chapter 18

The next day, my father called. "The restaurant's on Brighton Beach Avenue. It's called *The Golden Onion*. Be there about eight o'clock."

I almost cried when I picked up Rosalind, she looked so beautiful. She usually wore her hair pulled back, but now she had let it loose to fall around her shoulders like a brown waterfall. She wore some kind of gauzy stuff in a coral color that showed off her summer tan. I didn't recognize the white and gold earrings, but I was pleased to see the necklace she had on was one I had given her for a birthday present, a gold medallion with a woman's head in bas relief suspended on a chain of white stones.

"You look very beautiful."

"You don't look so bad yourself."

I was wearing my Ralph Lauren blazer, checked shirt, no tie, tan cotton slacks, loafers. You could have lifted me right out of a Land's End catalogue. No apologies. I felt comfortable dressed like a preppie.

I was dying to talk about a lot of things, mainly us, but the drive was going to take a good couple of hours so I didn't rush it. Besides, Rosalind didn't seem ready for an intimate discussion. I put the radio on and breathed in the perfume she wore. It went up my nose, into my bloodstream, and straight to my heart.

I thought back to the first time I'd ever seen her. I was moseying around the Strand bookstore, looking at books and women. I'd found bookstores great places for meeting the opposite sex. I glanced in her direction and immediately felt a rush. I wandered over and stood near her, not speaking; she turned around and looked up at me. My heart lurched.

Her eyes were so dark. I learned later that what she wore affected their color. And the sound of her voice was a symphony. I asked if she was free for a drink. She said yes.

For a long time the only sound in the car was the music of Mozart, Prokofiev, and selections from Verdi's *Aida*. When the music began to fade, which meant we were driving out of range of the East End FM, I shut off the radio. "I think I know why you left me," I said.

"You finally figured it out?"

"Just a hunch. Part of it has to do with my quitting work. I'm pretty sure about that. Am I right?"

"So far."

"I was getting on your case too much."

"That's right, too."

"I was becoming a boring son of a bitch."

"Again, right."

"There's more?"

"Keep going. You're doing fine."

"I had turned into a self-satisfied, self-indulgent, selfish man, the kind who thinks of nothing more than the pleasuring of mind and body, his own, first and foremost, and let the rest of the world and its humanity be damned. Is that close?"

"That's about it." She stared ahead through the windshield. Then she said, "Jake . . ."

"Yeah?"

"It's not just you. You're not the only one who's changed."

"What do you mean?"

"I mean, I've changed, too. Ever since we moved out here full-time, our lives are different. I'm not the same person, either. And I don't like the person I've changed into any more than I like the person you changed into. I probably never should have given up my job, even though it seemed the right thing to do at the time."

"You said you were getting tired of it."

"I know I did. I'm trying to explain why I left you. I didn't like the way our life was going. I felt I needed to do something about it."

"That's what you call doing something? Taking a hike? I'd say that was a little drastic, wouldn't you? Why didn't you just tell me something was wrong?"

"I tried, Jake. Believe me. But you were so wrapped up in your new way of life, you weren't listening."

I guessed she was right about me not being aware. She had gotten herself involved in conservation projects and was doing a lot of work for battered women. I thought that was good, she was involved. I thought she was okay. But I'd obviously missed something. "So now that you've had a chance to be on your own, what do you think? Are you glad you did it?"

"I'm not glad. But I'm not sorry, either."

"Well, *I'm* sorry," I said. "I was hoping you were going to tell me you'd had enough, that you wanted to come home."

"Just the opposite. I'm enjoying myself for the first time in a long time."

"Good!" I spat out the word. "I'm really glad to hear you're enjoying yourself for the first time in a long time."

"That's not what I meant, and you know it."

"Forget it," I said. I'd been on the brink of telling her how much I missed her, how much I wanted her back, how I needed her body next to me in bed, how I wanted to sit across from her and have a cup of coffee and read the paper together. Instead, I turned the radio back on and squeezed the wheel as hard as I could.

We didn't speak again for a long time, while the atmosphere was thick with tension and the miles added up on the odometer. But, as it always had in the past after a fight, the tension gradually dissipated and I began to breathe normally again. I glanced at Rosalind and saw her staring straight ahead and biting her lip. When Rosalind did that, I knew immediately what it meant: she was fighting the urge to tell me something. And it probably did not have to have any connection with what we had just been talking about. In fact, it was more likely that it didn't. It was also more than likely that it was something she was probably not supposed to tell me. Secrets were tough for Rosalind; she just couldn't keep them.

"What?" I said.

She was hesitant. "I wasn't going to tell you. I thought it would be better if you didn't know. Especially since it looks like this is all pretty dangerous. I tried to tell Toby to drop the whole thing, but she wouldn't listen."

I didn't say anything because I knew how Rosalind's thought processes went. The best approach was to just wait and let her get it all out in her own way. We were on the Southern State Parkway. I stayed in the middle lane, cruising at sixty, and paid strict attention to the road, because while the speed limit was posted at fifty-five miles per hour, the usual maniacs whizzed past me as if I were stuck in cement, some of them happily giving me the finger as they passed.

Finally, Rosie spoke. "Toby begged me not to say a word.

But I think it's only fair that you should know."

"Know what?"

"Toby still has the eggs. The people who murdered that man . . . they didn't get them."

I remembered searching that huge closet with Blather: dresses on one rack, suits on another, blouses on another, shoes stacked up like dominoes floor to ceiling, and Cormac complaining that he had not even had a chance to see the beauties. "It was all an act? The three of you were putting on an act for me?"

"When Mr. Blather came to the house, the first thing he did was to look in that case. 'My God,' he said. Then he took the case and hid it in the pool house. He said he would find a better hiding place later, but did not want to leave it in the closet."

"So where are the eggs now?"

"I don't know. Mr. Blather and Toby did something with them. But they didn't tell me and I didn't ask."

"I can't figure a few things out," I said. "One: Why does Toby want to get involved with this kind of thing? It can't be money. She must make millions. Is it because she wants so much to help Cynthia? Or is it something else? And two: there's something fishy about her and Cormac Blather. I just don't buy that story that she got him involved because she's done business with him in the past. I think there's something else going on."

"If there is, I don't know about it. She hasn't told me a thing. I didn't even know that stuff was in the house until Mr. Blather showed up."

"How come? I thought you were so intimate." I was looking at the road but I could feel the heat from Rosalind's stare. I knew I had stepped onto treacherous ground.

"Just what is that supposed to mean?"

"I only meant that I thought you two had gotten very close. I didn't mean anything sexual, although I do admit to having a prurient interest in her sex life, not having any sex life of my own."

"Her sex life and mine are none of your business."

"Is that because you're making it with her?" Even as the words came out of my mouth, I was sorry I'd said them. Not because I knew it wasn't true (I didn't know), but because it was a truly dumb thing to say.

I felt a sharp pain in my ribs, a result of Rosie's bony fist having crashed into them.

"I know you're a man, so you can't help being stupid sometimes, but this is the first time I thought you were an asshole."

I didn't like being called an asshole, but there was a good side to it, because it meant Rosie had not crossed over. Suddenly, ludicrously, preposterously, there was a bulge in my shorts. My Little Jake had expanded and become as hard as he used to be in the good old days. All it took then was a glance, or a lean over the sink, or even a turn of phrase, to throw us at each other. Time or place didn't matter. As I remembered, the kitchen floor was an active spot. I became quite familiar with the black and white checked pattern in the vinyl tile. I reached for Rosie's hand and before she could resist, guided it between my legs.

"What are you doing?" she protested, but didn't wrench her hand away.

"Remember how it used to be, when we were driving someplace, we used to pull off to the side of the road and fuck?"

Her hand remained where it was. "That was a long time ago."

"Not so long. What do you say, want to try it now?"

"On the Southern State? At the side of the road? We'd make quite a show for the passing motorists."

"I'll take the next exit," I said eagerly. "I'll find a spot."

Rosie laughed. She gave my friend a squeeze and took her hand away. "I don't think so. We'd be late. I wouldn't want your father to worry about us."

My excitement instantly altered, shriveled, shrunk, and eventually disappeared. "You always were a very thoughtful person," I said.

Chapter 19

I found *The Golden Onion* without much trouble, but had to drive another three blocks before I could park. From the outside the restaurant was a disappointment, nothing more than a shabby storefront with a cheap metal sign. I couldn't read the name written in Cyrillic, but I knew it was *The Golden Onion* because of the picture on the sign. I guessed it was supposed to be a representation of one of Moscow's famous onion-shaped domes, but instead it looked more like a turnip that had been left out in the sun too long.

We were an hour early. "Let's take a walk," I said.

Rosalind took my arm as if nothing had changed between us, and we strolled down Brighton Beach Avenue. Her arm through mine felt good. I thought of where her hand had recently been. I was sure getting a ton of mixed messages.

When I was a high school kid, I only knew Brighton Beach as a summer place. In those days, I lived with Aunt Fanny in the Flatbush section of Brooklyn, a long subway ride from the beach. My father was between wives, as usual. My mother died of cancer when I was nine, so my father had a powerful motive to find a mother for me. Between the ages of nine and eighteen, when I went to college, my father found not one but five mothers. He was in love with all of them. "I can't help it," he explained to me many times. "Falling in love is my nature. I'm like the fabled Irishman who can't pass a bar without stopping in for a drink."

In the summer a bunch of us guys would take the subway to the beach, throw a blanket down on the sand of Bay 7, strip to our bathing suits, flex our pathetic adolescent muscles while glancing around to see if we had impressed any of the girls in our vicinity, then make a mad whooping dash into the Atlantic.

Now the avenue's sidewalks were crowded with shoppers and strollers. The writing on the windows and the signs above them were in Cyrillic. Fruit and vegetable markets had their produce out on the sidewalk and women in babushkas were squeezing the stuff, having items weighed, arguing, kibitzing with the vendors, all of it in Russian.

"No wonder they call it Little Odessa," Rosie said.

It was time to go back. A man appeared from a door in the rear of the restaurant. He spoke with a thick accent. "Vott can I help you vit?" Before I could answer, he said, "You are maybe Herruld's son?"

It took me a second to translate Herruld into my father's name, Harold. "Yes, and . . ."

I couldn't breathe. His arms were wrapped around me and my lungs were being squeezed. "I am Misha," he yelled into my ear. "I am soon your father's father." He laughed at the idea and kissed me on both cheeks. Then he got hold of Rosalind and kissed her too, but in her case, after two smooches on the cheeks he gave her another one full on the lips.

Misha?

He was so . . . *cuddly* . . . and *young*, a lot younger than me. He had a big head with thinning hair carefully combed across the top, a twenties movie star mustache, the kind that looked as if it had been drawn on with eyeliner pencil, and he was missing an ear, just the stump remained. "You are here early, *Boychik*," he said.

"I'm sorry. But we made very good time."

"Is good. You stay. Sit down and take a load off." He winked, proud of his knowledge of colloquialisms.

He led us to a table and hollered loud enough to be heard in Moscow. Almost immediately a woman appeared, carrying a tray on which were a bottle of vodka and three glasses. He pointed at us and said something in Russian. She put down the tray and smiled. She was a tiny woman whose clothing and skin seemed to blend into the same tawny color. "This is my wife, Lena." She actually gave a little curtsy and then, like the field mouse she resembled, disappeared. "She is shy. But don't worry. Nobody else is." He twisted off the cap on the bottle and poured the liquid into the glasses. *"Nazdorovye!"* he said, and tipped his glass back, swallowing it in one gulp.

I did the same. It went down as easily as water and left a pleasant, warm afterglow. Rosalind took a sip and made a face.

"You do not like?" Misha asked her, concerned. "You do not drink vodka?"

"It's a little strong," Rosalind said. "But it's good. Very good."

"Jake Wanderman," Misha said, his look examining me. "Your father admires you, *Boychik*."

"I like him, too."

The wife came back with plates of herring, hard-boiled eggs, cheese, and some other things I did not recognize. "Eat something while you wait," Misha said. "I must help them to get ready."

He got up and in a little while we saw waiters and busboys putting tables together, setting them up for the party. After the settings were in place, enough plates of cold food were brought out to cover the entire tablecloth. Bottles of vodka were put on the table, along with the old-fashioned blue bottles of seltzer with the squirt handles on top. While we were watching and waiting, I had another vodka and dipped into the herring.

"What do you think of your new relation?" Rosie asked.

"He's something, all right."

"I wonder what happened to his ear."

Then it came to me. Misha! Detective Catalano grinning while asking me if I knew a Russian mobster named Misha Bialkin. This was the Misha he'd been talking about. It had to be. No wonder he was grinning; he'd known all about it, my father and the mobster! "Guess what," I said. "I think my new relation is a gangster."

"What?"

I told her about the detective and his questions.

"Maybe that's another Misha. You don't know his last name."

"Maybe. But somehow I doubt it."

"What are you going to do? Are you going to tell your Dad?"

I didn't have a chance to answer. There was a commotion at the entrance. A bunch of people came in, laughing and talking all at the same time. There were about six or eight of them and in the middle, yakking away a mile a minute, was my father. I was surprised because this was not his style at all. He was more the cool man of the world type. It blended with his manner of dress, which was custom tailored everything: bespoke suits, bench-made shoes made in London by H. Smith, Jimmie Li of Hong Kong shirts, even his underwear, made by a contractor he found on the Lower East Side who ran a sweatshop for Calvin Klein and had my father measured personally by his sixteen-year-old niece. My father didn't start out that way. His lifestyle had evolved slowly through the years as he went from being a seller of life insurance to the middle class to being the high-flying operator of Central Park West, who traded oil leases, real estate, odd lots of anything that could be bought cheap and sold high.

My father—who looked more like my brother—was taller by a foot than the people surrounding him. His arm was around a girl with hair the color of summer corn. His eye caught mine and he waved. "Jake. Rosalind. I'm so glad you're here." He came over to our table, his arm still around the girl with yellow hair. "Say hello to Zeena Bialkin," he said.

That certainly clinched it.

This was nothing new for my father. He was always fond of surprises. Other than women, he loved bringing home un-usual presents. For my tenth birthday, he showed up with a pony he had bought from a man who gave rides to children. I had no interest in animals that were bigger than I was, besides which we then lived in a three-room apartment on Avenue K. I would have loved a puppy, but my father didn't think small.

"Gee, Dad," I said. "He's really great. But what are we gonna do with him?" My father arranged to board the pony in Prospect Park and said I could ride him on weekends. At the first opportunity, when my father was out of hearing, I told the man at the stable that if anyone was interested in buying a pony, they could have one for a good price.

Zeena looked to be in her twenties. She wore a sleeveless red dress that looked as if it had been spray-painted on her body. And the body it did little to conceal was a steeplechase course of winding curves, hills, and valleys. Her hair, on the other hand, looked as if it had been cut by a beautician either blind or demented. Clumps stood out from her head at odd angles. A gold circle sliced through one nostril, and a diamond stud glittered in her bottom lip. On her right arm at the shoulder was a tattoo of a bird. She saw me looking at it. "It's the dove of peace," she said.

People began arriving and we were soon introduced to cousins and uncles and aunts and sisters and brothers. There were lots of V's: Vyacheslav, Valeri, Vladimir. There were also Olegs, Pavels, Mikhails, Anyas, Linkas, Natashas. Then we were at the big table, my father and Zeena at one end, Rosalind and I a few chairs away. Misha Bialkin stood next to them and raised his glass. "To my daughter and her new husband soon," he said in English. He said more in Russian. There were joyful responses and everybody followed his lead, tossing the stuff down in one shot.

Following Misha, there were more toasts. I can't remember how many, but I do remember that I joined in a few of them and even made one myself. After I gave my toast, I sat down and Rosie said, "For a gangster he seems like a decent sort of guy."

"Very decent. Yes, indeed." I put a lot of food down my throat but have no recollection of what anything tasted like, because by that time, my mouth seemed to have frozen into one position, a wide smile with teeth.

The music began. The musicians were not very good but they were loud. There was a girl singer in a beaded dress who sang what seemed to be "Night and Day," but she had obviously learned it phonetically and her ear was not the best because it came out more like Borscht and Schav. But hey, it was still Cole Porter.

I was encouraged to dance. I danced first with Rosalind. The thought of holding her in my arms was very appealing, but it turned out to be unromantic because I was having a little trouble with my coordination. My legs were sort of moving on their own. Then Misha cut in. After that, I danced with a lot of people, men as well as women. Nobody seemed to care who was dancing with whom. Every time I looked for Rosalind, she was with another relative and seemed to be having a great time.

I was soon bouncing around the floor with Zeena, who had the moves of an acrobat and the wiggle of a stripper. Her energy inspired me to try to keep up with her. I thought I was in great shape but after a particularly hot zig and zag, I began to feel like a 5K runner in a 10K race. "Let's sit down," I said. I took her hand. We sat while I got my breathing under control. "Where did you learn to dance like that?"

"Acting lessons. I wanted to be an actor. Those lessons included dancing, singing, voice, body control, the works." She smiled. I wondered if the stud in her lip hurt when her mouth stretched.

"And are you an actor?"

"I'm a performance artist. That's how I met your father. He never told you?"

"Not a word. Not even a peep."

She laughed. "It was a year ago. I was doing a work on Houston Street. Part of it was floating red balloons in bunches so that they would look like blood. Then I was going to shoot them down with a bow and arrow. The idea of it was that the balloons symbolized the hearts of all the mistreated and abused people of the world. The arrows stood for the corrupt dictators, the military, and governments that were draining their blood.

"I had this friend with me who was helping me blow up the balloons, but he was having trouble tying them up so the air wouldn't escape. We started getting heckled by a couple of skinhead types. They were calling us morons, and shit-eating fairies. They didn't bother me a bit, but my friend Pete has a temper and he was all set to go after these guys when your father steps into the picture. He goes over and talks to these guys. I don't know what he said to them, but they shut up and disappeared. Then your father comes over and says, 'They won't bother you any more. Is there anything I can do to help?' 'Can you tie off a balloon?' I ask. He says he's an expert, and in no time he has all the balloons blown up and tied. He helps get them in the air, but I never got to shoot them down because the coppers showed up and chased us off. Your father asked if I wanted to go with him to have a cup of coffee. And that's how it all began."

"How old are you?" I asked.

"Twenty-four." She took one of my hands in hers, brought it up to her mouth, and held it against the stud in her lip. The diamond stud pressed into my flesh. Her eyes bit just as hard into mine. "I know how old your Dad is. He knows how old I am. We love each other anyway. And I'm not after his money."

"Okay."

"You don't believe me."

"My father is handsome. Sophisticated. A man of the world. But he's still seventy-seven years old. I can see him falling in love with you, but . . ."

"I don't need his money."

"You're making a fortune shooting down balloons on Houston Street?"

"I'm a systems analyst. I make a hundred twenty-five thousand a year. I do the performance art on my own time because I love to do it."

"I'm impressed. But how does *your* father feel about your marrying someone old enough to be his father?"

"You don't know my father. Show him the money and he wouldn't care if Hal was ninety." So she knew her father liked money. I wondered how much else she knew about him. She stood up, hands on her beautifully formed hips. "So whaddya think? Are you gonna be my stepson, or what?"

My father and Rosalind joined us.

"Isn't she wonderful, my children?" He held Zeena's hand. "She anticipates my every need. And she's smarter than a fox. I know she looks a little strange, but that's just temporary. I'm sure she'll grow out of it."

"I enjoy looking strange," Zeena said.

"Of course you do." He adjusted the Patek Phillipe watch on his wrist. I wondered if he had told Zeena his famous but no doubt apocryphal story of how the watch had been given to him by Aly Khan in gratitude for fixing him up with Rita Hayworth. "You both probably think she's too young for me."

"What could give you that idea?" we said at the same time.

"At my stage of life, I am thankful to take whatever good comes along and greet it as a blessing. After all, who knows how many years I may have left?"

Zeena laughed. "On what I've seen so far, my guess is, plenty."

"Zeena told me the story of how you met," I said. "All that stuff with the balloons and those tough guys. She said you got rid of them. How'd you do it?"

"I tried to convey to them the impression that I was a Mafia don. I told them I had two bodyguards with me who would break their legs. They looked a bit skeptical, so I handed them a hundred bucks and they happily took off. Now, do I have your blessing?" He opened his arms and we all held each other like sinners at a Baptist prayer meeting.

Meanwhile, I was wondering how to tell him his father-in-law was truly a Mafioso, although of the Russian persuasion.

Chapter 20

It was a little after midnight when we said our goodbyes. The party showed no signs of slowing down. More hugs and kisses from Zeena, my father, and Misha.

"Where is your car, *Boychik?*" Misha asked. "Is it far?"

"Just a few blocks."

"Is late. I send someone with you."

"Don't bother."

"Is no bother. Is necessary. I don't want you should have difficulties."

I didn't argue. It was Brighton Beach and after midnight.

The guy who came with us had wide shoulders and arms that hung down to his knees. He didn't speak. We got into the car and thanked him. He made a motion for us to lock the doors, then left.

I pulled out of the space and drove under the El to the end of the block. I stopped for a red light. In the rearview mirror, I saw a car coming up behind me. It was moving slowly and for some reason I watched it. It kept coming closer and closer and, as I watched, it ran into me. I couldn't believe it. I had noticed that a man was driving the car and he had a passenger. Didn't the guy see me? Was he drunk? True, it wasn't much of a crash, just a bump, barely enough to stir up the vodka fumes in my head. I looked at Rosalind. I could see she wasn't hurt. "Can you believe this? You think he didn't see the red light?"

The man had left his car and was approaching my door.

"Drive away." Rosalind's voice was tense.

I was too slow. There was a tap on the window. I saw a hand, and in the hand was something black with a hole in the end of it. I had seen plenty of guns in the movies. They didn't scare me. But two inches from my face was another matter. The man holding the gun motioned for me to roll down the window.

"Don't do it," Rosalind said.

"If I don't, he's gonna shoot me."

When the window slid down, the man with the gun reached in and pressed the button to unlock the doors, then got in back. "Drive. I'll tell you where to go." His voice had no trace of an accent.

"Listen, if you want money, I'll give you what I have on me. It's a little more than a hundred, okay?"

"Drive."

"I have credit cards, too. Take everything, but let us go."

"Drive."

He had me go straight, then right, then left, then straight again, the other car following. He had me turning and going back and forth in an obvious effort to confuse me.

After about ten minutes more of the back and forth stuff, he said, "Stop here." The block we were on was an ordinary-looking street of high-rise apartment houses. "Turn off the motor," he said. Then a piece of cloth was being slipped over my eyes. He tied it tight. "And one for your lady."

Rosalind said, "It smells."

"Tough shit. Now get out of the car."

"Take it easy," I said. "We're not giving you any trouble."

"That makes you smarter than I thought you was. Now move."

It was awkward with the blindfold on. I heard a car door slam behind us and the footsteps of the other man. "Lock it up and take the keys," our guy said. "We don't want any crooks stealing these vehicles."

There was a chuckle, then a hand on my arm was pulling me. We walked a while, then he said, "Stop. There's a step." I guessed the other man was leading Rosalind the same way. I was strangely calm. My one real worry was Rosalind. She was tough, but something like this could scare the shit out of anyone.

I heard metal garbage cans clatter, the creak of a door, then we were walking down a ramp. The air was damp, and smelled of piss and rot. We went through another door. I was pushed down onto a chair.

"Take off their blindfolds."

This voice I recognized. When the blindfold was removed, I saw that Rosalind was next to me. We were both sitting under a bare bulb on those flimsy white plastic chairs they sell by the millions in Kmart. The light glared down on Rosalind's pale face. I tried to make her feel less frightened by being cool. "Rosalind, let me introduce you to Mr. Solofsky."

He stood apart from us, partly in shadow. I saw Crab standing near him, and immediately next to the bodyguard, in deeper shadow, was a seated figure, smaller, familiar. The two goons who had done the hijacking stood behind us.

Solofsky couldn't resist playing the game. "It is my pleasure, Mrs. Wanderman. I am sorry to have to meet you under these circumstances, but as I am telling your husband, I am very serious when it comes to business." Solofsky moved into the light. His pointed black beard now looked particularly vicious. He turned to me. "I am thinking you are not a man of your word, Mr. Wanderman."

"Who says I'm not?"

"Did we not agree, I am sure of it, that you are going to stay out of this . . . this business?"

"I said I would and I meant it."

"Then how do you explain that you are so friendly with Bialkin?"

"Misha Bialkin?"

"Indeed."

"I just met him tonight. His daughter is marrying my father."

"I know about his daughter. I know about your father. What I do not know is what else there is to connect you with my dear friend Misha."

"Nothing," I said. "Absolutely nothing."

"Excuse me if I do not believe you. The eggs are in the possession of this lady here." With that, he pulled the person who had been sitting in the chair next to the bodyguard, and pushed her into the light. It was Cynthia, but not the way she usually looked. Her hair was matted to her head as if it were soaked; her face had black streaks on it from mascara that had run down from her eyes. She moaned and fell to the floor. "Pick her up," Solofsky said. One of the goons came from behind us and lifted her onto a chair.

She didn't look at anyone, but she spoke in a tired voice. "Tell them. Tell them everything they want to know."

"The eggs are with her," Solofsky went on. "Then they are gone. Where are they? You say you do not know. Mrs. Organ says she does not know. She tells us that she gives them to her friend, Mrs. Welch. Then Mrs. Welch is attacked, someone is killed, the eggs disappear. The people who kill do not get the eggs. They go away with nothing. So where is the treasure? I ask myself that question, but I do not have the answer . . .

until tonight when I learn from certain sources that my old friend Mr. Wanderman is going to visit with my other old friend, Misha Bialkin. I think to myself that this is very interesting. Misha Bialkin and Jake Wanderman."

Certain sources. I took that to mean he had a spy on Misha. "I told you, I just met him because of my father and his daughter."

"That is a wonderful convenience. It explains nothing."

"It explains everything. That's the only reason I was there."

He took a step closer to me. "You are at the house of Mrs. Welch the night of the attack, are you not?"

"Yes. But I got there after it was all over."

"What better time to take away the eggs of Mr. Fabergé?"

"I didn't. They weren't there."

"I think otherwise. I think you take them from where they are hidden, and that you make a deal with Bialkin."

"No. You're wrong."

"You notice Bialkin, he is missing an ear?"

"It would be hard not to notice."

"He loses it in a knife fight. He thinks he is good with a knife, but he is not as good as the man he is fighting." He patted his chest.

"You? You took off his ear?"

"Correct. When I am young, I am very good with the knife. I still can be, if necessary. But to get back to Bialkin. He thinks he is a big man. He makes contact with the Italians. He deals in stolen credit cards, gasoline, anything he can get his hands on . . . even stolen icons. Oh yes, stolen artwork is becoming very good business. But there are lines, there are territories, and he is crossing over that line one time too many."

He motioned to Crab, who approached Rosalind with a

knife in his hand. The yellow light from the bare bulb reflected off the blade.

I looked at Rosalind. She had crossed her arms, holding herself for protection. Her eyes were open wide in fear. "Wait a minute," I said.

The guy who had pointed a gun at me took hold of her arms and pulled them back. For the first time I saw that he had a ponytail. *Ponytail.* Didn't Toby say something about one of the guys who broke in the other night having a ponytail? Crab took hold of Rosalind's dress and sliced it from the neck down to her waist. Her chest was now pushed forward, her breasts straining inside her bra. Crab used his knife to slice open the bra so that her breasts were exposed. He folded the knife into a closed position, then reached into his pocket and drew out a pair of pliers. A moan came from Cynthia.

"Would you like to see what pliers can do to those pink nipples?" Solofsky asked.

I started to move but felt a gun barrel on my neck. "No!" I yelled. "Don't do anything to her!"

"Tell me what I want to know."

"Okay, okay. You were right. I took the eggs." It was crazy, I knew, but I had to say something. And he was convinced I was in cahoots with Misha, so I gave him what he wanted. I didn't think about what it might mean later on, I just wanted to get out of there any way I could.

"Aha. How is it you are finding them and the intruders cannot?"

"Because my wife told me where they were hidden."

"Then what?"

"When my father told me about his new relatives, I made some inquiries. I learned that Bialkin was connected, so I got in touch with him. We made a deal. Fifty-fifty."

"And the eggs, where are they now?"

"Bialkin has them."

"How did he get them?"

"We arranged a meeting, and I delivered them to him."

"That is most interesting. I have had watchers. They detected nothing."

"Maybe they're not good watchers."

He looked at me closely. "Very well. Now that Bialkin has the eggs, what is he going to do with them?"

"Sell them. What else?"

"And who is he going to sell them to?"

"I don't know. It wasn't my business. All I knew was we were going to split the money."

Solofsky came over to stand in front of me. He took my chin in his hand and tugged at it so that I was forced to look up at him. He stared directly into my eyes as if he were trying to get inside my head, trying to figure out if I was telling him the truth. I stared back at him with all the hate I had in me. It must have convinced him because he said, "All right, Pyotr. You can put it away."

The bodyguard moved away from Rosalind and the man holding Rosalind's arms let her go. She tried pulling her dress closed in front of her but it wouldn't stay, so she held it closed with her hands. She was breathing heavily.

"Now what?" I asked.

"I have to think," Solofsky said. He retreated into the back of the room out of the light. Minutes passed. Rosalind's breathing was still heavy. Cynthia was making whimpering noises.

Solofsky came back into the light. "I decide that keeping you while I check out your story is more trouble than it is worth. Still, I trust you understand that you are accessible to me always. Please remember that I am previously telling you not to speak to the police, the FBI, or anyone else. Do not forget. You can go."

I stood and felt my knees wobble a little. Then I helped Rosalind up. "Are you okay?" I asked.

She nodded.

"Remember," Solofsky said. "If you are not telling the truth, I will soon know. Then the next time we meet will not be as pleasant a meeting as this one. Do you understand me?"

I didn't answer him.

"You can take her with you." Solofsky pointed to Cynthia, who sat in her chair like one of her torn dolls.

I helped Cynthia to stand. She almost fell as she leaned against me. I put my arm around her for support. Then the three of us began walking toward the dark end of the room where I assumed the door was.

"That's right," Solofsky said. "That is the way out." He motioned to the ponytailed man who had abducted us, who then handed me the keys to my car. "And do not bother trying to learn what building this is. It will be of no value to you. This is only a temporary use."

I took the keys and kept moving, holding Cynthia on one side while Rosalind held her on the other. As we were going out the door, ponytail said, "Hey, man."

I paused, thinking it had been too easy. Maybe they were not going to let us go after all. This goon of Solofsky's was going to take out that big black gun of his and shoot us down like animals in a trap. I held my breath, waiting for what was coming next.

"Your wife has nice tits," he said.

Chapter 21

I sat for a good while behind the wheel before I started the car. I didn't want to drive while my hands were still shaking.

The ride home was quiet. Cynthia fell asleep almost immediately, but not before telling us between sobs how she had been abducted by Solofsky and slapped around. He told her he had heard that she had been trying to get in touch with Boris's other associates, and that if she persisted he would have her throat cut.

"That son of a bitch," Rosalind said. "May he rot in hell."

"He probably will," I said.

"But not soon enough."

"Did you recognize the guy with the ponytail?" I asked her. "Could he have been the same guy who broke in that night at Toby's?"

"I'm not sure. I didn't get a good look at him that night. It all happened so fast. And tonight I was too scared to notice anything."

"But it could have been his men who broke in and did the killing. That would explain how Solofsky knew that the guys who murdered Mackleworth didn't find the eggs."

"I guess," she said. "I wouldn't doubt he's a killer. And that raises another question: what's going to happen when he finds out Misha Bialkin doesn't have the eggs?"

"He's going to come after me again. But it won't be so easy for him to find out anything. These guys are obviously bitter enemies."

"You might have started a war. And that's Zeena's father, remember."

"Don't you think I know that? I was trying to save your skin! You saw what he was going to do."

"Why didn't you just tell him the truth?"

"Because Solofsky was so sure I had made some kind of a deal with Misha. If I told him the truth, your friend Toby and Cormac Blather would be in trouble. At least, this guy Misha can take care of himself."

"What about you?"

"Maybe I'll catch the next plane to Zanzibar."

"This isn't funny. You better tell Misha what you did."

"Of course I will."

It was past three o'clock in the morning when we got to Cynthia's house. Her housekeeper let us in. She was obviously startled by Cynthia's condition but did not ask any questions. She helped Rosalind get Cynthia cleaned up, changed, and into bed. Rosalind insisted that Cynthia swallow some aspirin and a healthy shot of whiskey before we left. I asked Rosalind where she wanted to go next.

"I think it's too late to go back to Toby's. I wouldn't want to disturb her."

"You mean you want to come home . . . with me?"

"That's right. And stop thinking whatever you're thinking. I need to crawl into a bed and sleep. Nothing more. This isn't a James Bond movie."

"Give me a break, will you? I wasn't thinking anything like that." And I wasn't.

We went back to the house, where Rosalind still had

clothes. She got into one of her nightgowns, put on a robe, and offered to make us tea.

While we were sipping tea and nibbling on some butter cookies I'd made, Rosalind said, "I'm going to tell Toby what happened. She and Cormac have to know about this."

"Right. And she's got to lean on Cormac to get rid of those eggs. The sooner they're disposed of, the better. Once they're gone, the show is over."

It was five o'clock when we went to bed in separate rooms.

The next thing I knew, my eyes were open and sunlight was streaking through the window. The clock said it was after eleven. I'd slept about six hours but felt as if I needed six more. I got dressed and opened the door. The house had a vacant feel to it. I ran downstairs, hoping Rosie was in the kitchen preparing breakfast, but she wasn't. I hollered her name. There was no answer. I looked all over, but she was gone. My car was in the driveway where I had left it, so I guessed she must have called for a taxi or had someone come and pick her up.

I felt as desolate and empty as the house.

Chapter 22

I called information for the number of *The Golden Onion*. It wasn't going to be easy telling Misha that in order to get Solofsky off my back, I had set him up to be mauled, maimed, murdered, or possibly all three. There was no answer. Not a surprise. Restaurants that stayed open late usually reopened late. I would have to remember to call later.

I tried calling Rosalind, but was told she was out. I called Cynthia. The housekeeper said she was sleeping.

"How is she?"

"She sleep all the time. She not get up."

"When she wakes up, tell her I called. Jake Wanderman."

I thought about the death of Mackleworth, or Midgely, whatever. I had no proof that his murder was Solofsky's doing, but he seemed the most likely suspect. The question was, why? If he was really working for Misha, would that have been enough for Solofsky to get rid of him? A thought suddenly jolted me. Maybe Solofsky wasn't the villain here. Maybe it was somebody else altogether. If so, who else could it be? I ran over the list of the people who knew about the eggs. There was Cynthia, Mackleworth, Rosalind, Toby Welch, Cormac Blather, Morty Adler, Sherri Adler (if Morty had told her). I could not see any of these people committing murders, or having them committed. What about Misha? If Detective Catalano was right, and Mackleworth was his man, then Misha might also know about the eggs. Certainly, he was a possibility, even if he was going to be my father's father-in-law!

I didn't enjoy that thought. It did not slide neatly into the groove of what I planned to do next. I tossed the empty coffee container into the trash and went back to the phone. I tried the restaurant one more time. No answer.

I went on to my next move.

There was a man standing at Toby's gate wearing a uniform with a logo stitched inside a circle that read, "Peterman Security." The uniform was brown, which I thought made him look more like a UPS guy than a security guy, but he wore a holster on his hip with a big pistol in it, so he got my attention. He asked a few questions and made a call from a walkie-talkie before he let me in. I drove to the front of the house, where there was another guy in a similar uniform. Rosie's VW was there, as well as a few other cars, and a large van with ABC-TV on it. I assumed Toby's Range Rover was in her three-car garage, alongside her Jaguar and Mercedes.

Rosalind met me at the entrance. "Toby's doing her TV show from the kitchen today. They've been setting up for hours. I never saw so many wires in my life."

"I've got to talk to her," I said.

"The show's starting. You'll have to wait."

I'd been in Toby's kitchen the night I went there for a knife to cut the ropes. But that time I hadn't realized how big the kitchen was: white cabinetry, stainless steel appliances, refrigerated drawers, an island only a trifle smaller than Manhattan, topped with blue and white Mexican tiles.

Toby was standing behind the island facing the camera. An announcer with one of those ball-bearing-smooth voices introduced her as the premier decorator, designer, idea person, and all-around homemaker of the modern era.

She was wearing an efficient blue denim apron that covered all of her except for a froth of white ruffled blouse at her neck. She smiled and said, "Thanks Charlie, for that modest introduction." Then she looked at the camera as if she were talking to her best friend. "You know what I think is most important? Romance. Does that surprise you? It shouldn't. We all need more romance in our lives, especially in and around the home. And one of the best ways to get it is to do something romantic. Such as having breakfast in bed. You can serve breakfast in bed on a tray that you can make and decorate yourself."

She was good. She oozed sincerity. I began to imagine her serving me breakfast on one of her homemade trays.

"I am going to show you how to do that in a minute—but first I want to talk to you about healthy food. Over the past several years my eating habits have changed, and for the better. I've learned to trim fat and calories without sacrificing flavor. So now it's a natural thing for me to eat healthfully and enjoy myself at the same time. You can do the same thing by following my easy, elegant, healthy, and delicious recipes that are in my new book, *Toby Welch's Healthier Quickery Cookery.* I rely on fresh, rustic food like cipollines, baby turnips, celery root, parsnips, polenta."

Did people actually eat stuff like that?

"You don't have to use these. You can substitute whatever you like, just so it's fresh and, of course, rustic. For dessert I love to put together unusual combinations of fruit and spice, such as figs and mandarin oranges with a touch of cinnamon, or perhaps ginger. My book, *Toby Welch's Healthier Quickery Cookery,* is available in bookstores now, or you can order it by calling the toll-free number shown on the screen. The price even includes postage and handling, but I'm sorry, no COD's."

The camera must have gone off of her, because a makeup person ran over and dusted her face with a huge brush.

I went into the dining room and waited for Toby's highly-paid advice to come to an end. Her housekeeper came in with a mug of coffee and a plate of cookies. The cookies were good, tasted of lemon and had a filling of finely chopped almonds. I wondered who had made them. Probably not Toby. When would she ever have the time to actually cook?

Finally the two women arrived. Toby was tall, blonde, beautiful, very much the sun queen, in or out of an apron. Rosalind was a smaller sister, but did not fade because of Toby's brightness. Rosie had her special charm: that little gap-toothed smile, the clear, direct way she looked at you. For me, that was beauty enough.

Toby settled into a chair and gave me her TV smile. "I'm ready, Mr. DeMille."

"I'm not playing director," I said. "You need to hear this." I told her about Mackleworth not being FBI, the detective from New York and his connection with Misha Bialkin, Solofsky, and Cynthia's late husband, Boris. "What it boils down to is, there are lots of unpleasant characters looking for those eggs."

"That's why I hired security to keep an eye on my house," Toby said.

"It's a start, but not enough. I'd like to know why you took the eggs from Cynthia in the first place. What's in it for you?"

"She's just a very good friend who needs my help."

"Bullshit. There's got to be another reason."

She thought a moment. "You're right. But I can't tell you right now what the reason is. I can only assure you, my reason is legitimate."

"Not good enough," I said. "I need some honesty here. Trust."

Rosalind jumped in. "Jake. Why is that important? What matters is not why Toby is involved, but how to get her out of this situation. And us, too, I might add."

"So you're okay with it, if Toby wants to keep her reasons to herself?"

"Yes."

"Then I am, too. I just hope it's not something that's going to give us a headache later."

"I can assure you it will not," Toby said.

"Okay. Then please arrange a meeting with Blather. If we can get those eggs back into the right hands, the whole thing'll be over. No more Russian Mafia. No more New York cops. They'll be off his case, and ours too."

"I've already spoken with him. He won't see you," Toby said.

"Why not?"

"I can only guess. I'm pretty sure he was involved with Boris Organ, even though he wouldn't discuss it with me. When Boris died, I thought it would be over. But he says he can't just stop. He can't get out of it anymore."

"I don't know what that means, so you tell him this: he's not the only one at risk. We all are. If he doesn't care about himself, what about the rest of us? You tell him that."

"He's right," Rosalind said.

Toby moved her fingers through her hair and at the same time closed her eyes, working her way through some kind of thought process. Suddenly, her eyes snapped open. "Pokharam, of course."

"What's Pokharam?"

"Pokharam is my Tarot reader," Toby said. "I never make a major decision without consulting her. I wouldn't be where

I am today, if it weren't for her insight."

"Okay," I said. "If that's what it takes, do it. Get her over here."

"She doesn't leave her house," Toby said. "We have to go there."

"So let's go there."

Toby closed her eyes again. At least another thirty seconds went by. Then, once more her eyes opened. "All right. We'll go. But I must tell you something first. It is very important that you know that whatever may happen, Cormac Blather's safety is my primary concern. I know it may sound harsh to you if I put his welfare above mine, and yours, and Rosalind's, and everybody else's, but that is how it must be."

"I don't understand," I said. "Why?"

"The reason you asked about before. Why I'm involved in this. You may as well know. Cormac Blather is my father."

Chapter 23

While I was still reeling from the shock of the Cormac news, Toby called her Tarot reader to set up an appointment and I phoned *The Golden Onion* again. Someone finally answered, only to tell me that Misha wasn't there. I next got in touch with my Dad and told him I couldn't explain on the phone, but that it was urgent he get hold of Misha and tell him to watch his back. There were people out to possibly do him serious harm.

"What are you talking about, sonny? What people?"

"I can't go into it now, Dad. But your future father-in-law has apparently made a few enemies in his time."

"Haven't we all?"

"Sure. But ours don't usually come around and put bullet holes in us."

I hung up before he could ask anything else.

Toby told us this Pokharam woman would see us that afternoon. We got into her Range Rover and started out. On the way, I tried to get Toby to talk about Blather, but she refused. "Not now. I have to concentrate on what to do next."

I was sitting on the passenger's side in front, Rosalind in back. I caught sight of a green Ford Taurus in the side mirror. It was two cars behind us. I remembered that I had seen a similar car parked down the street when we pulled out of Toby's driveway. I'd checked before to see if I was being followed, but this was the first time I'd spotted someone. We were on the Montauk Highway headed west. I didn't say anything. I kept checking the mirror. The Taurus had dropped back, but I could still see it.

"Make a right at the next corner," I said.

"I was just about to do that. But how would you know where I'm going?"

"I don't. I just want to see something."

I was hoping not to see the green Ford again, but as we came up to a stop sign I looked back and saw it making the turn from the highway. "I think we're being followed."

"What!" Toby screeched.

"Are you sure?" Rosalind said.

"I'm pretty sure. There was a green car parked down the block from Toby's house, and I think that same car has been behind us since we came out of the driveway."

"So what do we do?"

"I've got an idea," I said. "When we get to the Mobil station, pull in and go around to the back where the mechanics are."

"Then what?"

"Just do what I say."

"Hear that, Toby?" Rosalind said. "The male voice. Just do what I say, because I know what I'm doing and you don't have to know."

"That's not what I meant," I said. Actually, her crack didn't really bother me, it made me feel connected. Like she at least cared enough to insult me.

Toby followed my directions and drove to the back of the station. I'd been using Mike's place for my repairs and oil changes for years. He was cynical but also an easygoing sort of guy. I thought I knew him well enough to ask a favor. I told him I wanted to leave her car there and use one of his for an hour or so. I didn't explain anything and he didn't ask, just gave me a look that acknowledged the eccentricity of man, and said sure. From inside his office I could see out front. Just as I thought, the green car was not in sight. It must have pulled over to the side of the road a ways back, in order to wait for us to come out. There was no way whoever it was could see what we were doing.

Mike gave me a battered old Chevy that didn't look like it would make it out of the station, but he assured me it would get us where we were going and back with no problem. I got the ladies to duck down, put a borrowed baseball cap on my head, and pulled out of the station slowly with only a glance back at the traffic and to see if the Taurus was there. It was. As I drove away, the Taurus did not move. I chuckled. "It worked. He's going to sit there an hour before he realizes we fucked him."

Pokharam's house was set back at the end of a long dirt road. It wasn't marked in any way. The road was not much wider than a path, and branches scratched against the side of Mike's Chevy, but I didn't think anyone would notice. At the end of the narrow road was a simple A-frame, comfortably settled in the midst of old firs, white pines, and birches, with saplings of all kinds growing between them. There was nothing other than natural landscaping, except for a fenced-in area off to the side where there were a variety of annuals in full bloom. A shiny, bright blue Mazda Miata, its top down, was parked next to the house.

We went up two wooden steps to a porch and a screen door, the door behind it open. Even though the house was in deep shade, what I could see of the interior was light.

A husky female voice said in an accent that was obviously English, "Do come in."

The room we entered was the living room, and I saw why it had looked bright from outside. One slope of the ceiling was all glass, and the room itself was yellow. The furniture, which included a couch, chairs, tables; the floor, covered almost entirely by a huge rug; and the walls, on which hung what appeared to be large sheets . . . all yellow.

The lady who had invited us in was tall and slender. She wore a yellow silk dress with a lace collar and yellow shoes. She stood at ease, with her hands clasped in front of her. On her hands were white gloves, which made me think of blue-haired ladies sipping cocktails. The light from above flowed over her, so that she seemed to be posed like a statue in a museum. "I am Pokharam," she said.

"These are my friends," Toby said. "Rosalind and Jake Wanderman."

"Dearest Toby. I am quite delighted you and your friends have come. I'm about to have tea."

She left the room and Toby motioned for us to sit. "This is her ritual," she said. "She has tea every day at this hour, whether anyone is here or not. When I come for a reading, we always have tea first. She says it helps her. While she is with me or with other people, she says she gets emanations from us that help her with her interpretation of the cards."

I told myself to keep my big mouth shut and to be open-minded. This wasn't the time to inform the world, and certainly not Toby, of my views on psychic phenomena, UFO's, Gypsy fortune tellers, palm readers, phrenologists, astrologists, soothsayers, and anyone else claiming to be an oracle.

Pokharam—what kind of a name was that?—returned with a wooden tray, yellow of course, on which she had the whole works: a yellow ceramic pot of tea, yellow patterned cups and saucers, milk, sugar, a plate of cookies, and another plate of tiny sandwiches with the crusts cut off. I wondered if they could actually be filled with watercress and cucumber, but I wasn't about to try one to find out.

"Shall I be Mother?" Pokharam asked.

The tea was poured with accompanying questions of how much milk and how much sugar. The cups were passed, along with the cookies and sandwiches. We sipped and said nothing while Pokharam smiled at us. She had a long oval of a face, in which her nose and mouth were as soft and yielding as a Dali watch. I put down my cup and watched the dust motes float in the light coming through the glass roof.

Finally, Pokharam spoke. "I suppose you need me."

"Very much," Toby said.

"It's as well you came today, then. I read for myself this morning, as I always do, unless I am distracted. It was extraordinary. I have never seen such an array of Trumps Major in one grouping. I therefore feel quite positive about providing you with the help you need. Of course, you know, as I have explained to you an endless and no doubt stultifying number of times, there are often situations where nothing of value results. Especially when there are others present. You must always bear that in mind."

Rosalind said, "We can go, if that will help."

"You are already here. Nothing can change that." She stood. "I shall go into the gray room and prepare. In five minutes, knock on the door and enter." She opened a door at the back of the living room and closed it behind her.

"Isn't she remarkable?" Toby said. "She's a duchess, or at least she was, but her brother inherited the estate, a sixty-room mansion on two thousand acres in the Cotswolds. Tarot has been in her family for generations. Her grandmother taught it to her but not to her mother, because she had the gift and her mother didn't. Her grandmother told her when she was a little girl that she would lose her fortune and come to the United States to make a new life. And it all came true."

"Where'd she get a name like Pokharam?" Rosalind asked. "It's not what you'd expect from an English aristocrat."

"She took it when she began her new life. She said she feels connected to the spirit of Pocahontas. Her real name is Sarah Montague-Vincent."

After five very slow minutes went by, we approached the door of the sanctum sanctorum. Toby tapped and we entered.

This room was a dramatic opposite to the one we had been in. It was small, not more than six by eight. And it was dark. The walls were painted a somber gray that seemed to swallow whatever light there was. A spotlight that lit the round table in the center of the room provided part of that light. Pokharam sat at the table in a throne-like chair. Around the table were three smaller chairs for us. There were other sources of light, minuscule halogens illuminating paintings which hung on the wall. Each painting was in full color and was a representation of what I guessed was a Tarot card. In the center of the table was a dish of potpourri that added a sweet scent to the air. Next to it was a narrow candle in a silver candle holder.

"Please be seated."

After we sat, Pokharam lit the candle. It produced another scent that, combined with the potpourri, made my nose twitch.

The only other furniture in the room was a narrow table with a glass top, the kind you see in museums. A small lamp lighted a display of Tarot cards. They glowed like illuminated manuscripts.

"Those were painted by Bonifacio Bembo in the fifteenth

century," Pokharam said. "They came into my family's possession in eighteen twenty-four by means of which I am not proud. My brother allowed me to have them when he came into his inheritance. It was very generous of him."

From a lacquered box, she withdrew a bundle wrapped in velvet and tied with gold cord. Untying the cord and opening the velvet revealed a deck of cards. Still wearing gloves, she removed the cards, carefully replaced the velvet and string in the box, and then proceeded to shuffle the deck. "I do not use modern cards, the kind one may obtain in stationery stores or joke shops. These were made in France in eighteen forty-five. They are of a high quality. Are either of you familiar with Tarot?"

"No," Rosalind said, living up to her namesake by answering for both of us.

"I'm afraid this is not the time for a lesson; therefore, I shall be succinct. The deck of Tarot consists of seventy-eight cards, of which twenty-two are the Major Arcana, the remaining fifty-six being the Minor Arcana. When I do a reading for myself, I make use of only the Major Arcana. It is more than sufficient. When four people are present, however, one must use the Great Pack, as the complete deck is known, because emanations from so many people will have an interfering effect upon the reading.

"Now Toby dearest, what is your problem, your question, that to which you must have an answer?"

Toby's eyes were closed again. I guessed that's when she did her serious thinking. She spoke slowly, as if she were in a trance. "A close relation is in possession of something which is very dangerous to him and to others. I know he is under duress. Should I persuade him to give up what he has? And if he does, will he then be free of all danger and responsibility?"

"Complex," Pokharam said. "Complex and difficult."

I thought that summed it up rather neatly.

She searched through the deck until she found the card she was looking for. "Here it is, Toby. Our Querent, our Significator. You are, as always, the Queen of Wands." She placed that card face-up on the table.

I was able to see that it was an illustration of a woman seated on a throne, holding a wand in her right hand and a sunflower in her left. On one side of the throne was an animal's head, on the other, the animal's feet.

Pokharam then shuffled and cut the deck three times before turning up the first card. She placed it on top of the Queen of Wands and said, "This covers her." She took the next card and placed it on top of the other two but sideways. "This crosses her." The next she placed above the others. "This crowns her." The fourth card went below. By now, I was getting it. "This is beneath her." The fifth card she placed on one side, saying, "This is behind her." The sixth on the other side, "This is before her."

I glanced at Rosalind, who looked up at me at that moment. I winked at her. She didn't wink back.

Next, Pokharam turned up three more cards, placing them one at a time in a row to the right of the Queen of Wands, the card that she had called the Querent. Pokharam studied each one of these cards as she placed them face-up on the table, one above the other. Before taking the next card, she took a deep breath. I looked at Toby, who was staring at the table as if it held the secrets of the universe.

"This is the tenth and last card," Pokharam said. "This is the card which will tell what will come. Please do not ask any questions when you see it. Please say nothing. I must concentrate all my faculties on this card, because it is the culmination of all the cards which you already see on the table."

I didn't believe any of this stuff, but there was something

about Pokharam that made me want to believe it.

She drew the card and placed it at the top of the row. The first thing I saw was the Roman numeral XVI at the top. Below it was a tall white tower out of whose windows shot orange and yellow flames. A man and a woman had leaped out of the building and were falling to the ground below. The title of the card was written at the bottom.

Pokharam stared at it for a long time. When she finally spoke, her voice was a whisper. "The Tower."

"And?" Toby said.

Pokharam said nothing, but the expression on her face would not have served her well in Happy Valley. She picked up the cards, leaving the Queen of Wands on the table. She mixed them and cut them a number of times. "We shall try once more." She then went through the same procedure as before. When she came to the tenth card, she paused and took another deep breath. She did not look at any of us. She laid down the tenth card. This time it was a picture of a woman. Her arms were tied to her body and she was blindfolded. She was surrounded by swords impaled in the ground, eight of them, expressed by the Roman number VIII at the top of the card.

"Swords, eight," Pokharam said. "I am afraid that what The Tower foretold is confirmed. What lies ahead is not good."

"How bad is it?"

"Crisis, difficulty, calumny, accident, treachery, perhaps even fatality."

That's all? I thought. How about plagues, boils, locusts, death of your firstborn?

"I am so sorry, my dearest Toby."

"What do you think I should do?" Toby whispered.

"What your heart tells you. Since whatever happens is inevitable, there is no other way." She placed her gloved hands on the table, one on top of the other, and bowed her head.

There was nothing more to do but thank her and say goodbye while Toby wrote a check. As we drove away, I looked back and saw a tall yellow figure, arm raised, waving goodbye.

On our way back Toby said, "She's a remarkable woman. I only wish she had better news."

"It's not so bad," I said. "She told you to do what you think is right. That's the best advice, because you know what that is."

"Do I?"

"Absolutely. Fix me up with Blather. I mean, your father. We'll get this all straightened out."

"I don't know," Toby moaned. "You heard what she said. All bad things. Maybe even death."

When we got back to Mike's gas station, the Taurus had gone. I thanked Mike and handed him a fifty. We climbed into the Range Rover and drove to Toby's place. I did not see the Taurus, but I knew that didn't mean they had given up. In the house, we went into her office. The answering machine light signaled. She punched the play button and we heard Cormac Blather's terrorized voice. "Toby, Toby. Help me. Please!"

Chapter 24

Toby paced back and forth, punching numbers into the telephone. "Oh my God. I hope he's all right." Cormac must have responded, because she said, "Father, it's me. What's the matter?" She listened, her shoulders hunched up under her ears. "What? How did that happen?" She listened again. "It's not possible. Don't tell me that." Listened again. "All right. I'll be there as soon as I can. I'll bring someone to help. But you know we have to be very careful. We have to make sure we're not followed. I don't know how long it's going to take. Be patient, that's all I can say." She hung up.

"What is it?" Rosalind asked.

She waved one hand in the air. "He's stuck in the bathtub. His back went out on him and he can't move. He's freezing because he ran the hot water to keep warm, but he ran it so long there isn't any more."

"How did he manage to call?" I asked.

"Portable phone. Takes it with him wherever he goes."

"Smart."

"I mean *wherever* he goes. I hate to say it, but I've talked with him when I just know he's sitting on the toilet. The toilet! It's at those moments when I wonder if he can truly be my real father."

"Speaking of which," I said. "Maybe now would be a good time for you to fill us in on this father business."

"Fine." Toby said. "But what are we going to do about him in the meantime? He might catch pneumonia or something."

"I hope not. But you're right, we can't just go there. They follow us, and your father is cooked. We've got to figure out another way of screwing them over."

Rosie said, "You came up with a great idea on the way to Pokharam. Maybe you can come up with another one."

"But now they know we're onto them. I have to give it some thought. While I'm doing that, why don't you tell us the father bit?"

"All right," Toby said. "It's simple, really. I grew up thinking my father was Throckmorton Welch. My mother divorced him when I was five and remarried three more times. She had no other children. Then, five years ago, my mother became seriously ill. She was dying and she knew it. She called me in and told me her secret, that I had been born in England, out of wedlock. She actually used that term, 'out of wedlock.' She told me then that Cormac Blather was my father.

"I did nothing about it until long after she'd passed on. Then I made a trip to London and did some investigating on my own. I learned he was in the antique business and had a shop. So I went there."

Rosalind said, "You did this all alone? You poor thing."

"It wasn't easy, I can tell you that."

"What was it like when you first saw him?"

"The hardest part was getting myself to open the door of his shop and walk in. My knees and my hands were trembling. I didn't know if I would even be able to speak. Then he came out from behind a hanging curtain and I saw this terribly fat man. I thought, this couldn't be my father. There must be another person in the shop. But it was him. He introduced himself right away, telling me his name and informing me that he was the owner. He invited me to browse.

"I spent an hour in the shop. His inventory was of very high quality and beauty. I think that helped to win me over. I went back every day for the next four days. I knew I had to decide what to do. I could not stay in London indefinitely.

"Finally, I made my decision. I did not know Pokharam then, or it would have been much easier. I told him my name. It made no impression on him. I learned later that he never watched TV, and of course did not read society columns in the newspaper. When I told him who my mother was and that I was his daughter, he was absolutely dumbfounded. He never knew anything about what had happened to her. She left England without ever telling him she was pregnant. He began to cry and told me I had made him the happiest he had ever been in his life.

"I invited him to come to the States and live near me. He never hesitated. He said as soon as he could settle his affairs, he would join me. We both understood that our relationship had to be kept secret. I knew the media would just love a story like that."

"Okay, I'm with you so far," I said. "But if the guy had a successful antiques business in London and then came here, and he had all your contacts, why should he want to fool around with stolen goods?"

Toby frowned. "What I didn't know was that my dear father had been dealing in stolen art for a long time. Against his will, he said. He told me he was blackmailed into it. That the blackmailer could have put him in jail anytime he wanted. When he came here, it continued. And once he realized how prominent I was, he knew the scandal would hurt me as well."

"Did he tell you why he was being blackmailed?"

"No. He would never say."

"Do you have any ideas?"

"None. Although I suspect it has to do with something that happened a long time ago."

We'd gotten back from Pokharam's late in the afternoon. I didn't have to check my watch to know evening was approaching because my rumbling stomach had already alerted me. Cookies and tea had not done much to stoke my tank. A big juicy hamburger with a thick slice of raw onion floated before my eyes.

"Is anyone hungry?" Toby asked.

I wanted to hug and kiss her in gratitude.

We had sandwiches of rare roast beef piled high on whole grain bread, accompanied by a dish of bread and butter pickles. There was strong coffee for a beverage. The combination made me feel a lot better.

I worked out my new plan. We would leave just before dark, so the follower would have trouble seeing who was in the car. I had Toby call Cormac again and tell him when we were coming. I also said to tell him that after a while there would be more hot water, so he could keep himself from freezing.

My idea was simple. Rosalind would dress up as Toby and drive out in Toby's white Range Rover. Whoever it was would follow her, while Toby and I went in my car with Toby dressed up to look like Rosalind. Using Toby's car phone, we'd call Rosalind and ask if she was being followed. If she was, all she would have to do was drive around for a while and lead them toward Southampton, which was opposite to where we were going in the Springs. Toby also wrote down her car phone number in case Rosalind needed to talk to us. Rosalind tied one of Toby's pink ribbons in her hair, and we put a pillow on the driver's seat to make her look taller.

The sun had set and darkness was slowly coming down when we waved to the security guards and drove out through the gate. I shot a quick look and thought I saw the outline of a car parked down the street, but I couldn't be sure. We drove to the corner, where Rosalind turned to the left and we went to the right.

Toby dialed Rosalind. "See anything yet?" Then she gave me Rosie's answer. "There are car lights behind her."

"Ask her where she is now."

"She's on Georgica."

"Tell her when she gets to the highway, to make a left. Drive slowly so she can see if the same car turns left also."

In the meantime, I had made a couple of turns and found myself on a street I didn't know. I looked in my rearview again and saw a set of headlights. "If somebody's following Rosalind, then they must have gotten somebody else to follow us. Unless that car behind us just happens to live here."

"It is possible. People do live in all kinds of places. I know where we are. Make a right at the next corner, then a left, then a right again. That'll take us out to the highway."

I concentrated on her directions while she spoke to Rosalind again. "What's happening?" A pause while Rosalind answered. "The car made the same turn. It's still behind her."

"Tell her to drive for another fifteen minutes, then turn around and go home."

I got to the highway and had to wait for traffic to pass before I could pull out. I saw the lights of the car behind me slow down and then stop. They did not want to come up close where I could get a look at them, but it confirmed that we were being followed, too.

"Shit! My great plan didn't work."

"What do we do now?"

"Where is this place he's at?"

She told me and said I could use Old Stone Highway to get there.

"Old Stone Highway has a lot of twists and turns," I said. "Maybe we can give them the slip up there. What do you say? Want to give it a try?"

"What would Pokharam advise, I wonder?"

"We don't have time for another Tarot reading. You heard her. Do what your heart tells you. What's it saying?"

I was looking at the road, so I couldn't tell if she had closed her eyes or not. "Go!" she said. "Goddammit to hell. Go!"

Old Stone Highway is a road that has to be taken slowly, even in the daytime. At night it is treacherous. I counted on the follower not being as familiar with it as I was. He trailed a good distance behind. At every turn, we were out of sight for a few seconds, but as we got farther along the road, I knew there were side roads I might be able to take if I got far enough ahead. When I came around one more curve and he was out of sight, I put my foot down and shot forward. I had to hang onto the wheel and concentrate and also pray no cars would come from the other direction, because I was all over the narrow road at every bend. Then I saw a lane that led off into the woods. I took it, fastened like a leech to the steering wheel, praying I wouldn't run into a tree. After about ten yards, I jammed on the brakes, shut off the motor and the lights. We were in total darkness. No way anybody could see us. A moment later, they came barreling past.

"How long do you think they'll go before they realize we turned off?" Toby asked.

"I don't know. But I'm not going to wait to find out."

I backed out faster than I ever thought I could go backwards, and drove the other way. Every few minutes I looked in the mirror but saw nothing. Toby gave me directions and at last we got there.

"You did it." Toby gave me a quick kiss. "Thanks."

"Don't mention it," I said, as I breathed a sigh of relief.

Chapter 25

The lights were on, the shades were down, and the front door was locked. "Do you have a key?" I asked.

"No. My father has the only one."

"I'll try the back. If it's locked, we may have to break a window to get in."

Before I had a chance to move, the door opened. A boy wearing ripped jeans and a tank top with rips to match said, "Come on in."

We stepped into a room that looked as if it had been thrown together for a summer rental. There were a few pieces of furniture on a bare wooden floor. The furniture was the kind that could generously be called Early Yard Sale. A window air conditioner was clattering like a freight train, but the room still seemed airless and hot.

Cormac sat stiffly in a chair in a bathrobe and slippers, his bare legs poking out. He looked like a potato with toothpicks stuck into it. His usually ruddy jowls were the color of ash and coated with a two- or three-day growth of bristle. His eyes were open, but his voice and manner had lost their customary air of superiority. "My dear. I'm so glad you've come."

Toby gave him a hug and kissed the top of his head. "Are you all right? How did you get out of the tub?"

Cormac raised a hand toward the young man. "Kevin. He got me out. Thank God he decided to pay me a visit."

Kevin jammed his hands into the pockets of his jeans. He was a scrawny kid, probably about seventeen, the cutout top displaying narrow shoulders and chest. His mouth curved into what I suspected was a perpetual pout that only seemed to emphasize the astounding perfection of his face. It was the kind of face that stared at you from the pages of *Vogue* or *GQ*. Pretty. Too pretty, every feature a cameo chiseled out of ivory.

"Thank you," Toby said. "What a wonderful thing you did. You probably prevented him from getting pneumonia."

"Yeah. Lucky I dropped in."

Toby attended to her father, wanting to know if he had had anything to eat or drink and would he like to have something now. They decided between them that tea was the appropriate beverage, along with some of Entenmann's chocolate doughnuts for which Cormac had a special preference. Toby vanished into the kitchen and I sat on one of the uncomfortable-looking chairs that turned out to be exactly as it looked.

"How're you doing, Cormac?" I asked.

"I've been better."

"Been getting lonely though?"

"As a matter of fact, yes."

"It must be nice to have a good neighbor like Kevin here."

"Indeed, yes."

I turned to Kevin. "What do you do, young fella? How have you been spending your summer?"

Kevin stared down at his torn unlaced sneakers. "I just been hangin' out."

"Doing a lot of swimming?"

"A little."

"Are you a surfer?"

"I got a board."

"What do you do for money?"

His eyes came up and met mine. Now something showed. I saw suspicion in those eyes, maybe even a flash of hatred. "Odd jobs. I don't take nothin' from nobody, not even my mother."

"Very commendable."

Toby appeared with a tray. Unlike Pokharam's tea service or her own self-adorned breakfast tray, there was no pot, just mugs with a tea bag floating in each one, and of course, the doughnuts. She put the tray down and handed a mug to Cormac. "I put milk and sugar in for you." She turned to me. "I don't know how you take yours."

"As seldom as possible. But milk and sugar is fine."

Kevin said, "None for me. I got to be goin'." He headed for the door.

"Well, thank you so much," Toby said.

Cormac sipped his tea and said nothing.

When the door closed behind the boy I said to Cormac, "Don't you think that was a little unnecessary, letting him have a key to the house?"

"What?" Toby said.

"The kid must have had a key, if he got in while your father was in the tub. The door was locked. Isn't that right, Mr. Blather?"

"It was more convenient for him to have a key." He spoke to Toby. "I see you've informed him of our relationship. Was that wise?"

"It was requisite," Toby said. "I'm sure Mr. Wanderman will be discreet."

"Of course I will," I said. "But what about you being discreet, Cormac? You're supposed to be hiding. It's not hiding if you take in stray kids and give them a key. Kids talk. Who knows who ends up hearing about it?"

"I couldn't help it," Cormac said.

"I know. You were lonely. And he's pretty as a picture, isn't he?"

"What are you talking about?" Toby said. She stared at her father.

Cormac sighed. "There are some things in life one cannot resist. Nor should one try to."

"I think I better sit down," Toby said.

As usual, Shakespeare knew what it all meant:

> *Love looks not with the eyes but with the mind;*
> *And therefore is wing'd Cupid painted blind.*

"Let's talk about what's important," I said, and filled Cormac in on all that had happened. I tried to emphasize the jeopardy element. "I don't want anybody to get hurt. So I'm willing to help."

Cormac closed his eyes. "I need to think."

Closing eyes to think must run in the family. He reminded me of a hippopotamus snoozing in the sun. After a long *long* time, his eyes opened. "As I see it, someone will have to go to Moscow."

"Moscow!" I said. "Why can't we just get in touch with the Soviets here in New York? We arrange for them to pick the stuff up, and that's the end of that."

"Do you know anyone in the Soviet Embassy?" asked Cormac.

"No."

"Then how do you know who you'll be giving the information to? How do you know that person isn't connected with someone who may have been involved in this from the very beginning? The answer is, you don't. And therefore it is most important to distance ourselves from those people, any one of whom may be part of the plot. Didn't you say you were being followed?"

"Yes."

"There you are," he said, triumphantly. "Besides, it's not just a matter of giving them back. There is a minimum price to be paid."

"I don't believe it. Your daughter's life is at stake and you're worried about how much you can get!"

"My daughter's life means a great deal to me. It is she whom I am thinking of foremost."

"Wait a minute," I said. "Does this have something to do with your so-called blackmailer?"

"So you know about that as well. Yes, the blackmailer is quite real. And the answer to your question is affirmative. There is a demand that I negotiate a price of at least seven million."

"Isn't there something you can do about this guy?"

"At this point in my life, the threat to expose me would no longer matter that much, although I am certainly not anxious to spend time in jail. And there would be a very strong possibility of that coming to pass. No, what I am most afraid of is the harm it would do to my daughter. The publicity would not only be embarrassing to her, it might threaten her career as well. I won't take a chance of that happening."

"Maybe you'd like to share with us who this guy is and what he's blackmailing you about?"

"It would serve no useful purpose. It is more important that we discuss Moscow. Are you willing to go on the journey?"

"I guess so. There doesn't seem to be anybody else in the room."

Blather chomped down on his second doughnut and in a moment it was gone. "There is a high official in Moscow with whom I am well acquainted. He has the ability to do whatever is necessary to arrange both the safe transfer of the assets and the payment for them. He will know the right people to contact."

"That's expecting a lot from one guy. How do you know you can trust him?"

"I have known General Pankov for a very long time. I met him in London when he was but a colonel. I would trust him with my life."

"You *will* be trusting him with your life, once we make contact with him."

"I am quite aware of that, but what other choice is there? As I see it . . . none." He put down his mug. "There are a number of things that must be done. One of them involves a Polaroid camera. Do you have one?"

"I have one," Toby said.

"Good. Mr. Wanderman will carry with him a photograph of one or two of the beauties as proof that what he tells the General is the truth."

"I hope you have them in a safe place."

"You may rest assured."

"I guarantee you I won't rest assured until this is all over."

"I understand your trepidation. I share some of it myself. But I am hopeful that with General Pankov's help we will bring this matter to a successful conclusion."

"You know what my Aunt Fanny used to say?"

"No."

"From your mouth to God's ears."

"Quite appropriate," said Cormac Blather.

Chapter 26

I realized I was actually excited about going to Moscow, with its onion domes and Red Square. Of course, I wasn't going as a tourist, but the idea of being there and doing something of value was exhilarating.

"I'm very concerned about Cynthia," Toby said. "She's still quite upset."

"After I finish the job in Moscow, she'll be okay."

When we got back, Rosalind was in the kitchen having a cup of coffee. There was still coffee in the pot.

"Mind if I have some?" I asked. While I poured myself a cup, Toby told Rosalind what we had worked out with her father.

"Why you?" Rosalind asked me.

"Mainly because there is no one else."

Rosalind was skeptical. "They say Moscow is the crime capital of the world."

"You mean it's worse than New York?" I said.

"Much worse. I read in the *Times* they're hijacking tourists right off the street. They take all their money and sometimes they beat them up, too."

"They're doing that now in all the great capitals of the world," I said. "It's a way of keeping up. If you don't do it, you ain't got it."

"You better be careful."

"It's sweet of you to care."

"You know I care," she said, her eyes suddenly filling.

I was surprised and pleased to see her tears, but I really didn't want her to worry. I tried to sound confident. "Hey, listen. This is not going to be a problem. I'm just going to deliver a message, that's all. There's nothing to worry about."

Rosalind came toward me. I expected a brief farewell kiss but instead, she pressed her lips hard against mine and pushed her tongue inside. "Good luck."

I had to take a breath. "If you promise to kiss me like that again, maybe I won't go."

Neither of them laughed.

Chapter 27

A trip to Russia wasn't like hopping a plane to France or England. In addition to a passport that I was lucky to already have, I needed a visa. In order to get a visa, I had to have a confirmed reservation on a hotel's stationery. That part was not too difficult. It meant calling the hotel Blather recommended and waiting for them to fax back a reply. The next step was to submit the application and a check for sixty-five dollars. The usual procedure was then to wait two weeks for them to decide if they would let me in. But the Russians had come a long way into the capitalist world. They let me know that if I wanted a visa faster, all I had to do was pay. For a hundred and forty-five dollars, I got the visa in one day.

While this was in process, I went to see Misha. He had a right to know that I had put him in harm's way. That didn't mean I had forgotten Detective Catalano's remark that Misha was not only involved in illegal activities, but that he might also be the guy who had hired the fake FBI man, Mackleworth. I hoped I might be able to find that out. I told him the whole story, including the bit about Solofsky's threat to Rosalind.

We were seated at a table in the rear of his restaurant.

Misha made a gesture as if he were grabbing someone by the throat. "That *pascudnyak*. He was always a low type."

"I hope you understand why I did what I did. I mean, telling him I gave you the eggs."

"I understand, *Boychik*." He was strangely subdued. "It is of no consequence."

"What do you mean? This is a bad man."

"I do not underestimate him. But neither does he underestimate me. I made it plain to him that if he wanted war, he could have it."

"You talked to him?"

"He got in touch with me two days ago. We arranged a meeting. He offered to give me a share of the profit, if I would turn over the valuables to him. When I turned him down, he made the usual threats."

"Did he tell you what the valuables were?"

"He did not have to."

"You already knew? How, from Mackleworth?"

"Who is this Mackleworth?"

"A guy impersonating an FBI agent. The cops said you hired him."

"On principle I deny everything. The man I hired had a different name."

"Midgely?"

He nodded. "At any rate, I do know a great deal about stolen art. So when there is a rumor that something of incredible value is on the market, it does not take too long to find out what it is."

"Do you know Midgely's dead?"

He frowned. "Poor bastard. I liked to use him for certain jobs, instead of the local traffic."

"Do you think Solofsky did it?"

"Perhaps."

"Doesn't that worry you?"

"No."

"If you don't want to worry, at least be careful. He told me he was the one who cut your ear off."

He did not say anything for a while. "Mr. Solofsky is thinking he can do anything he wants. We shall see." He touched his ear. "Yes. The missing ear is Solofsky's doing. But I was alone during that fight. He had others to help him. Besides, it was a long time ago. I do not think he would do as well today."

"And what about you?"

He laughed grimly. "I would make sure I was the one with helpers."

"I wouldn't mind a little help myself. I'm leaving to-morrow for Moscow to make a deal for the items in question."

"Moscow! So that is how it is to be handled. Do you speak Russian? No, of course not. Who is going to make this deal?"

"I can't tell you that."

"Why not?"

"I just can't."

"I understand. But you should be careful. I will not try to persuade you that I am someone you can trust. But I do not think you are aware how much risk there may be for you in Moscow."

"You think so? I'm just a messenger."

He wet a forefinger with his tongue and ran it along his mustache, first one side then the other. "Isn't there a saying about killing the messenger and then throwing him out with the bath water?"

"Something like that."

"Since you are soon to be a relative, I don't want to lose you. Will you accept aid, even though it is from me?"

Here he was being Mr. Nice Guy, and I wasn't very forthcoming. It was kind of embarrassing. Still, it couldn't hurt to accept an offer of help. "Sure. Be glad to."

"Good. I have friends in Moscow. You have a hotel reserved, yes?"

"Yes. The Ukraina."

He made a face. "Tourist trap. But never mind. When you arrive at your hotel, call this number and ask for tourist information." He wrote on a piece of paper and handed it to me. "You say what hotel you are at. They will contact you."

"Thanks, Misha. I appreciate this."

"You are my family now." He gave me a Russian bear hug and a kiss on each cheek. "Good luck, *Boychik*."

"You too," I said. "And watch your back."

He laughed again, louder this time, more like the Misha I'd met the first time. "They had better watch theirs."

On my way home, I couldn't help but wonder about Misha's friends in Moscow. Would they be there to help me or to help Misha? He had mostly put to rest my suspicions. I liked him, but I still had to consider the possibility that Detective Catalano might be right.

Chapter 28

The next night I was on a Swissair jet to the new Soviet Union. I tried to relax because it was going to be a long flight, but the seat was narrow, and there was a lot to think about. I was armed with Misha's phone number and another from Cormac Blather. Blather had already given me the same kind of instructions as those from Misha. It was possible that my phone in the hotel would be tapped as well, so it was vital to follow the procedures exactly.

Once on the plane, I suddenly had some doubts. I began to wonder how much trust I could put in Blather's arrangements. Was everything going to be as smooth as he had said it would be? And if it wasn't, should I put myself in the hands of the friends of Misha? Those questions were disturbing enough, but I was also going to a country where I did not speak the language and where I would have to do what people I didn't know told me to do.

For the next nine hours I breathed air that began to smell as stale as my breath, in a seat that pinched my elbows and all but scraped the skin off my knees. So when the flight attendants came around with unlimited offerings of booze, I was grateful. While I drank Stoli on the rocks, I thought about how Rosalind had kissed me goodbye, how much she seemed to care about me. I had spoken boldly about how this excursion was going to be a breeze, but deep down I hoped she wouldn't believe me. I guess what I really wanted was for her to think of me as a hero.

When we finally landed at Sheremetyevo II Airport, my head felt like a balloon straining to get airborne. I took my suitcase from the overhead bin and followed the crowd into a room lighted by an inadequate supply of flickering bulbs, which made everyone look as if they were taking part in an old Charlie Chaplin film. There were four booths at one end, and four irregular long lines in front of each. There was a sign in Russian, French, English, and German indicating passport control. I got on one line, knowing in advance that I would have the same luck I usually had in choosing a checkout line at the supermarket.

After I was finally stamped, I found myself on another queue, and a guy at the front of it who was everyone who ever worked at City Hall. His movements were as poetic as a mime winding an old-fashioned clock. The man moved so slowly, you had time to count the hairs coming out of his nose.

After that, I waited on another line so I could get rubles. When I finally got out to the front of the airport, where dozens of scruffy types were waving their arms and yelling "Taksi" at me, I was relieved to see a man standing next to a black limo holding a sign that read "Hotel Ukraina." I blessed Cormac for suggesting that I arrange this with the hotel when I made my reservation. I had to wait for some other passengers to show up, but this was not a problem. I stretched out on the back seat and promptly fell asleep. The other passengers woke me up. They were German businessmen from a Lufthansa flight. After introducing themselves in English, they ignored me and talked to each other in German while we rode into Moscow on the Leningradsky

Prospekt, a twelve-lane road full of trucks pumping black diesel smoke into the air.

The hotel looked like something out of a Gothic novel, with crenellated towers and tall spires, but I was too tired to even think about it. Jet lag had overtaken me and all I wanted was a bed.

I woke up a few hours later. It was four o'clock in the afternoon. I took a shower. The water trickled out of the showerhead as if it were coming out of a cracked hose. The temperature of the water was just a shade under lukewarm. This, for a room that cost three hundred dollars a night. The shower cleared my head anyway, and at least the toilet flushed.

I got dressed and poked around the room, looking for bugs. In spy movies, the rooms were always bugged. I felt foolish because I wouldn't know what one looked like unless it was obvious, and of course, if there were any, they wouldn't be obvious.

I called the number Blather had given me. I announced that I was at the Hotel Ukraina and asked for tickets to the Bolshoi. The person at the other end barked something in Russian and hung up. I thought maybe I had called the wrong number, so I tried again. I got the same response. For a moment, I thought about calling the number Misha had given me, but decided against it. Maybe I would use it if I needed help, but since I didn't need any help, why get involved?

All I could do then was wait. Of course I had my portable edition of the *Complete Works*, but my head was in no condition to read. I stretched out on the bed and turned on the TV and saw Larry Hagman wearing a cowboy hat and speaking Russian. I turned off the TV.

I was too tense to stay in the room. I went down to a lobby of red carpeting, chandeliers, and the aura of an old champion trying to make a comeback. It was kind of sad, but apparently made no difference to the customers. It was crowded with business types. Lots of suits and attaché cases. I saw the two Germans who had ridden in from the airport with me. One waved and walked over.

"Have you settled in?" His English was almost perfect.

"Yes. I'm feeling a little jet lag, though."

"Of course. It's only natural. Come have a drink. It will do you good."

After all that vodka on the plane, the last thing I wanted was a drink. "Thanks, maybe some other time."

"Of course."

I walked out to the front of the hotel, shook my head at the doorman who wanted to call a taxi for me, and looked across at the Moskva River. It didn't look like much, moving along at a slow pace, dark brown and probably toxic.

It was late in the afternoon and the sidewalk in front of the hotel was crowded with grim-faced humanity, all of them in a hurry. They rushed past me in all directions. I got bumped into a few times, but no one stopped to apologize.

I wandered down to the end of the block. Across the street near the corner, a group of people had spread various items out on the sidewalk to create a miniature flea market. I crossed over to look and saw a pitiable collection of junk: small picture frames, some with old photos still in them, spoons, knives, forks of all designs and sizes, none matching, some cups and saucers. Most of the sellers were old. Apparently they were desperate to get a few rubles to buy something to eat.

One old lady had spread out a rag on which she displayed a row of glittering buttons. I bent over to get a better look. They were beautiful buttons: iridescent, many-colored. Even though none of them matched, there was something about them, or maybe it was the old lady, that persuaded me I ought to buy them. I straightened up to see if I had small denomination rubles in my pocket.

Someone bumped into me again, this time almost knocking me down.

"Hey!" I said.

The guy who had pushed into me did not move away. Instead he grabbed my arm and began propelling me toward the curb. He was a short, stocky guy with a powerful grip. He wore a baseball cap turned backwards. His face was covered with a short black beard and mustache that made the cap incongruous.

I was off-balance and couldn't get my feet set to stop me from being moved. "What the hell are you doing?" I yelled.

A black car was parked at the curb with the back door open. The guy still had hold of my arm and was moving me steadily toward the open door. I struggled, but ineffectively, because while my head knew I was in Moscow, my body didn't know it had left New York.

I looked around desperately to see if anyone might be willing to help me, but all I saw were disinterested faces watching. I thought of that woman in Queens who was murdered while her neighbors listened to her screams and not only didn't offer help but did not even call the police. Was this going to happen to me?

"Go!" the Russian said, or something that sounded like it, and gave me a shove that sent me flying into the back seat of the car. He got in beside me and slammed the door shut.

I sat up and blinked a few times to focus my eyes. "Who are you?" I asked. "What do you want?"

He didn't answer. The driver was tearing through the streets of Moscow like a guy who had just broken out of jail. At each major intersection there was a traffic cop in a booth, but not one paid the slightest attention to our speeding vehicle.

155

After a while we left the major roads and drove through neighborhoods of high-rises: ugly, concrete blocks that went on mile after mile. Thousands of people must have lived in these buildings, but in contrast to the crowded scene in front of the hotel, there wasn't a person on the street. Finally, the driver stopped. The guy next to me got out and motioned for me to do the same. He opened a door and signaled for me to enter. The building's narrow halls looked as if they had not been washed or painted for decades. The smells hit me right away. I remembered my father once taking me along to show me how he sold insurance. We went into a building in lower Manhattan that was similar to this. Dark halls, overpowering odors of cooking (cabbage, of course), laundry, disinfectant, urine, others I couldn't guess at. I remembered wanting to puke from the smell.

I must have stopped walking, because the man pushed me from behind. We came to a door. He knocked once. It was opened right away and I stepped into a room that was different in character from the rest of the building. The floor was covered with an Oriental rug. There was a desk at the far end of the room, made of a lustrous wood glowing with mother of pearl inlays.

A man sat behind the desk. He was clean-shaven to the top of his head, which shone like a polished apple. He wore a dark suit of a soft material that had "custom made" stamped on the lapels. There were dark grooves under his eyes that somehow added to his elegance. He nodded at me. "Sit down, Mr. Wanderman."

"Okay." I did as he said. I was nervous and worried but tried not to show it. "You know who I am. Who are you?"

He bowed his head slightly. "I am General Nikolai Pankov," he said.

Chapter 29

He motioned for me to sit. "I must apologize for bringing you here, but it would not have been appropriate, nor intelligent, to have you come to my office in the Kremlin." His English was as upper-class and proper as a bowler hat and umbrella. "Would you care for some tea?"

I was so relieved I couldn't talk, so I just nodded. A door opened and a gray-haired woman wearing an apron appeared, carrying a tray with two steaming glasses of tea. Each glass was set in a metal container with a handle on one side. There were cubes of sugar in a bowl but nothing else. "I prefer to drink tea in the Russian manner. I cannot tolerate milk in my tea, despite all the years I spent in London."

Steam rose from the top of my glass like Vesuvius about to erupt. Even the handle felt hot. I took a tentative sip and, of course, burned my tongue.

The General inserted a cigarette into an ivory holder and lit it. "What did my friend Cormac tell you about me?"

"Only that you and he go back a long way."

"I would put it that we go back eons. It seems as if it were a thousand years ago. In point of fact, it was nineteen forty-four."

"Nineteen forty-four. I wasn't even born yet."

"I was nineteen, a lieutenant in the army but assigned to London as a clerk in the Soviet Embassy."

"And Blather?"

"A bit older, already involved with art and antiques. He worked for a man named Tommy Harris, a renowned art dealer. Since I, too, was a fancier of art, we met.

"I was acting as liaison between the NKVD, as it was known in those days, before it became KGB, and the GRU, which was army. Did you know that since the demise of the communists there is no more KGB? They fired a few of the top people and gave it a new name. It is now known as the Agency of Federal Security of the Russian Federation, or FSB. But we all know that names mean nothing. The vermin are still in place.

"Let me return however, to more pleasant days." His voice took on the sentimentality of reminiscence. "Harris had a magnificent house called Garden Lodge, just off the Earls Court Road. He and his wife, Hilda, entertained lavishly. The parties were mostly for agents of the British. Harris himself was MI5. He entertained them all: MI5, SIS, SOE. At one time or another, perhaps everyone in British intelligence would turn up at those parties. Naturally, the conversation at these affairs was quite specialized, quite intriguing. Cormac was there, of course. After all, he worked for Harris."

"What did all of this have to do with art?"

"*Doucement.* Patience, dear boy. What happened next was that Cormac and I became lovers. Imagine my surprise when he told me that Kim Philby, the master spy himself, had convinced him to work for us. Cormac's pillow talk became an excellent source of information."

"Did Cormac know you were a spy?"

"He knew I was Russian and that I would pass the information he gave me to the right people. I did not feel it necessary to bother him with details that were of no importance."

"Details?"

"What did it matter? Cormac helped contribute to the end of the war. The British were withholding important information from us about the Germans. They had established Ultra at Bletchley Park, a facility used to intercept and decode signals. Those rotters did not tell us anything, because they did not want us to know they had broken German codes. They did not trust us!" He removed the stub of the cigarette from the holder and plugged in a new one. "In gratitude for Cormac's endeavors, when the war was nearing its end and the Germans were in disarray, I made available to him various works of art that had come my way from Nazi plunder."

"You got hold of stolen art?"

"You have no idea how much the Germans looted. When we went into Germany, much of it was discovered. There were people who knew of my interest in art, and so it came to me."

"For a price."

"There is always a price."

"And this continued after the war?"

"For many years. I wanted to discontinue the operation a number of times, but Cormac always insisted that we do just one more deal. Just one more, he would say. For old time's sake. I thought I heard a desperation in his voice—perhaps he needed money—so I went along. This last one was not something I planned. This was entirely different. I would never be involved in the theft of anything from my own country."

"Who did the stealing then?"

"The new-old KGB, of course. No one else could have brought it off."

"Why would they do it?"

"To embarrass the army. To bring down those of us still in

power who oppose them. They want to bring the days of Beria back. The man who used terror and fear as weapons. KGB, above all. I have vowed to do everything of which I am capable to ensure that such an event never comes to pass." He blew a plume of smoke. "But something unexpected happened. The KGB themselves were hijacked and the booty spirited out of the country."

"Who was powerful enough to take on the KGB?"

"Criminals. Gangsters. The *reketiry*, as they are known, have become so powerful they are afraid of no one. The head of the gang that did this particular job is a man known as Putlezhev. Quite a droll name. It means eggplant."

"Why eggplant?"

"He has a purple birthmark that covers almost half his face."

"And this Eggplant was connected with Boris Organ and Solofsky?"

"That is so. They ran a gang together in Moscow. One went to the United States and the other remained here. They continue to do business."

"Not Boris anymore. He's dead."

"It doesn't matter. Putlezhev procures the goods. It could be anything: oil, machinery, weapons of all kinds. They have sold tanks, even jets, on the open market. Even art if it is valuable enough. What I do not understand is how Cormac came into possession of the objects."

"It's a long story."

"Some day you must tell it to me. At this moment I am delighted, because now that Cormac is involved, we can conclude this business in a satisfactory manner." The General leaned forward. "You have something for me?"

I had to unbutton my shirt to get at the money belt strapped around my waist. I removed four Polaroids from it.

The General took a magnifying glass out of the desk and studied the photographs. *"Incroyable!"* After a few minutes of studying, he said, "There are a great many forgeries of Fabergé circulating in the art world. They have been so well made that they have sold as genuine in Sotheby's and Christie's. I believe your Governor Rockefeller was known to have purchased at least one.

"As you may or may not know, the actual crafting of these eggs was done by a few master craftsmen who worked in the ateliers of Fabergé. This clover egg, for example." He held up one of the photographs. "It was designed by one of the most famous, Michael Perchin. The shell is *plique à jour* green enamel, with green gold and diamonds packed so closely together the settings are quite invisible. It was presented to Alexandra Feodorovna by Nicholas II in nineteen oh-two." He pointed. "You see this mark? It is his signature. All but impossible to duplicate because of where and how it is placed. I have seen the original in the Armory Museum. I would stake my life that this is the same."

"I'm glad to hear that. So, where do we go from here?"

He leaned back in his chair. "You go back to your hotel. I will see to raising the money. After I have it, we shall arrange the transfer." The General stood. "Our business for today is finished. Do not venture out from your hotel. You will hear from me very soon." He pushed a button on the desk.

We shook hands. The flunky who had brought me reappeared. I was driven back to the hotel without another word being spoken.

Chapter 30

All I had to do now was sit tight and wait to be contacted again. Then why did I feel unsettled? Maybe because it had all gone too easily, too smoothly. Was there anything about the General's behavior that wasn't right? Other than his doing a lot of talking, everything had seemed to be in order. So what was I worried about?

At any rate, I felt I deserved a drink. I went back to my room for a quick wash-up. I got the key from the key-lady who presided over the floor. My hotel was one of the old-fashioned kind that had a person on every floor who held your keys and observed what was going on. She had a parrot beak of a nose and hair that hung like a worn-out mop. I had heard from the bellboy she was there to make sure guests didn't bring any unauthorized persons into their rooms, but not to worry. He said if I brought a woman up, a tip would guarantee the old crone would see only what I wanted her to see. Then he asked if I wanted him to provide me with one. "Some other time," I said.

I went into the bathroom and splashed cold water on my face. I looked in the mirror and was surprised to see Misha scowling at me. *Moscow is dangerous*, he said. *I have friends in Moscow. Call this number.*

Scrambled Eggs

I thought I didn't believe in signs and portents, but the mirror changed my mind. Maybe the visit to Pokharam, the Tarot reader, had had some effect after all. I picked up the phone and dialed the number Misha had given me. A woman answered.

I said, "Is this tourist information? My name is Wanderman and I am at the Hotel Ukraina."

"You have the wrong number," the woman replied in English. She hung up.

The call made me feel better. I felt I now had a friend. I inquired at the desk and learned that the bar was located on an upper floor. By the time I got there, it was almost eight o'clock.

The place was packed. I guessed it was the height of happy hour, or its equivalent in Russian. The air was filled with the same energy found at bars in New York after the workday. People on the prowl . . . for sex or money, it didn't matter, as long as something paid off. There was a muted roar of conversations, occasionally an outburst of laughter. The cigarette smoke was as thick as an East Hampton fog. I sat at a small table and ordered vodka.

A voice said, "Hello." It was one of the Germans, with the other close behind. "May we sit down?"

"Sure."

The waiter came with my vodka, and also set glasses and a bottle of Jack Daniel's in front of the Germans.

"I hope you don't mind that I told the waiter to bring our order to your table. I thought you might like some company."

"Very nice of you," I said.

He poured for his friend and himself and raised his glass. "I like vodka, but Jack Daniel's is something special. It is the favorite drink of many in Moscow. Of course, one must have the ability to pay a hundred and seventy-five dollars for a bottle. *Na zdorovye,*" the German said.

I raised my glass. *"Na zdorovye."*

The vodka streamed down my throat like quicksilver. In an instant, I felt a warm glow.

"Another?" the German said. "This one is my treat."

"Very kind of you," I said.

The waiter brought another.

"Cheers," the German said. "We shall be international in our toasts."

Another silver stream ran down my throat. This stuff was good.

"So what are you doing here, Mister . . . what did you say your name was?" the German asked. He was a nice-looking guy, blonde and fair, except that with his brush of a mustache and hair parted on the side, he looked like a pale version of Hitler.

"Wanderman. Jake Wanderman."

"I am Hanscastorp and this is my friend, Ludwig." Ludwig was short and wide, with a weightlifter's neck.

"Hans Castorp? From the *Magic Mountain*?"

"Exactly. My mother was enamored of that book. So much so that she cared not that other children would torment me for it."

"For a name like Hans?"

"Hanscastorp. It is one name, my given name. Castorp is not my family name."

It struck me as funny that during Hitler's time this guy had a mother who admired Thomas Mann, an anti-fascist and a Jew, and who then had a son who turned out to look just like Hitler. Then again, maybe it wasn't so funny.

All of a sudden, my attention was caught by a woman a few tables away who was in the act of easing her body into a chair with the undulating rhythm of a snake. She wore a navy blue suit with a gray pinstripe and a skirt cut as short as it could indecently go, as well as a low-cut blouse that displayed almost all she had underneath it. As if to prove she meant business, whatever that was, she dropped a sturdy-looking briefcase on the table.

The German followed my look. He smiled. *"Valutnaya."*

"What's that?"

"For six hundred American dollars, you can find out."

"Is that what they get?"

"It depends, of course. If you desire, I could ask her to join us."

"No thanks."

"You are wise. There are other pleasures to be had in Moscow." The glasses were refilled once again. "So, are you a tourist, Mr. Wanderman? Or are you here on business?"

"Strictly a tourist."

"You are lucky. Moscow is extraordinary. There is so much to see, so much to do. The Kremlin, of course. St. Basil's, the Bolshoi, the Moscow Arts Theater, the Pushkin Museum, perhaps even the circus. The possibilities are endless."

"So I've heard."

"What have you done so far?"

"Nothing really. I got in this morning, when you did. I'm still trying to get over jet lag." As I said this, I could feel my tongue having trouble getting the words out. Jet lag and vodka were a potent combination.

"I have a wonderful cure for this malady. You come with us to an excellent restaurant. There will be music and dancing and good food and good wine. After that you will go to sleep, and in the morning you will wake up a new person."

"I don't know. I'm pretty tired. I thought I'd just eat something in the hotel and go to sleep early."

The German shook his head. "That is precisely what you

should not do. For one thing, the food in this hotel is abominable. What I suggest is much better, a sure fire method for defeating the jet lag."

Maybe it wasn't a smart thing to do. I had been told to stay in the hotel. But I was now relaxed and comfortable. I was aware that the deliciously smooth vodka had something to do with it, but so what? And just because the guy looked like Hitler wasn't a reason to dislike him. It wasn't his fault, after all. "You're on," I said.

We squeezed into one of those taxis called a Zaporzhet, a miniature tin can with an engine that could, but just barely. After about twenty minutes of careening through the streets of Moscow, we were dropped off in front of a building that looked like an abandoned warehouse. There was a man standing in front of the entrance who examined us, nodded, and said in English, "Welcome to *The Hungry Duck*."

Before we could go any farther we were looked over once again, this time by two men who were serious about it. Hanscastorp was at ease. He smiled and slipped something into the hand of one of them and we were allowed in.

The first thing that struck me was noise. It sounded like screaming at first but then I recognized it as music. The sound came from a series of loudspeakers situated in every part of the huge room. The volume was turned up to a level marked *pain*.

"What do you think of this place?" he shouted, as we sat around a glass table on chairs made of steel tubing. After five minutes on one of these, the possibility of lying on a bed of nails began to seem a better option.

In front of us was a dance floor jammed with a variety of people. The clothes and the jewelry were expensive. There were also a good number of heavyset men who looked heavier because of bulges in their jackets. Many of them were dancing with their daughters or their nieces.

Hanscastorp said, "This is where the swingers and the heavy hitters come. And the food is excellent. But first we must toast, yes?"

The waiter brought a bottle of vodka to the table and surprise, a bowl of ice. The German poured. "First, to your good health."

"And to yours."

Ludwig nodded, and as usual, didn't speak. We all drank. This time I didn't feel anything going down my throat.

Hanscastorp poured again. "Second toast. To good business, yours and ours."

We drank again.

"I am strictly a tourist," I said, carefully.

"Of course." He poured again. "To tourism."

My mouth was beginning to feel numb. I realized I had better get something other than liquid into me. "How about food?"

The waiter brought menus. Of course, they were in Russian. I suggested that Hanscastorp order for me.

"Good," the German said. "To begin, we shall have *pelmeni* and caviar. You will never remember that you had jet lag." After ordering he said, "Tell me, Mr. Wanderman, what made you decide to visit Moscow? A desire to explore museums or the Russian character?"

I concentrated hard before answering. It wasn't easy, but I managed to get the words out. "I don't know, I just wanted to come."

"You will not be disappointed. Russia is indeed a strange country, a formidable mixture of pragmatism and idealism, of poverty and wealth, of drunkards and ascetics, priests and hoodlums, *reketiry* and politicians." He laughed. "Although I am not so sure the latter group are very different from each other."

A young woman with hair shaved almost to her scalp approached. The others at her table—they looked like college kids—were watching and laughing. She said something to me in Russian.

Hanscastorp said, "She wants you to dance with her."

"Why me?"

They exchanged a few words. "She says you look like an American. She likes Americans."

"Tell her thanks, but no thanks."

"Go ahead," the German said. "You do not want to insult young Russian womanhood."

I managed to get to my feet and was pulled onto the dance floor. The floor was crowded but we squeezed in. The dancing did not include touching, just a lot of motion and contortion. The girl closed her eyes. I was vodka-loose, so I did the same and let myself go.

I was off somewhere, my head in the clouds, my body weaving and moving like a ballet dancer, or so it seemed to me anyway, when a voice said in accented English, "You must leave here immediately."

"What?" I opened my eyes and saw my companion still writhing in front of me. Right next to her, pretending to dance, was the beautiful hooker from the bar back at the hotel, the one with the low-cut blouse and the briefcase. And now I saw that she had violet eyes. "What are you talking about?"

"These people with you are not your friends. They are here to do you harm."

"How do you know? Who are you?"

"I am a friend of Misha's. Believe me. I know what I am saying. They are German but they work for Russians. They are very bad people."

"Misha? You're a friend of Misha? How did you find me so fast?"

"We've been keeping an eye on you since you arrived in Moscow."

The girl I was with kept on shaking, paying no attention to either of us. "Why should I believe you?"

"You do not have to. But I would suggest that it would be wise if you did."

My brain was struggling, like an engine filled with sludge. "Okay, I believe you. What should I do?"

"As soon as you can, go to the men's room. I will be nearby. Hopefully, we will be able to get out." She twisted away and vanished in the crowd.

I was suddenly a lot more sober. I made a motion to my partner of slitting my throat with my finger. She shrugged and continued to dance. I went back to the table.

The waiter appeared with food. I tried to appear to be interested. I pointed at what looked like dumplings covered with sour cream. "What are these?"

"Those are *pelmeni*. They are stuffed with meat. Delicious. Try one."

I forked one and popped it into my mouth. I chewed it vigorously, but it had no taste. "Where is the men's room?" I said. "I better go before I start eating."

"Excellent idea," the German said. "I shall join you. Better to eat with an empty bladder than a full one."

Did he really have to pee or was he keeping an eye on me? There was nothing to do but go along. I looked for Misha's friend but did not see her. The men's room was not much different from those back home, including the condom dispenser. While I washed my hands, I tried to figure out how I could get away from the German. I splashed cold water on my face in an attempt to get my head clear.

We came out of the men's room with me in front and the German behind. I had not come up with any plan, so I reluc-

169

tantly began to head back toward our table. Suddenly, Misha's girl appeared. She had her briefcase in one hand and a gun in the other. She showed it to the German. "Go down that corridor," she said. "Quick."

He didn't move. Almost casually, she said, "You will die if you do not do what I say."

He shrugged. "Please. I am not yet ready for my next life. I will go."

We walked until we came to a door. "Open it," she commanded him.

He opened the door. Suddenly, there were curious sounds: *pop, pop, pop.* A chip of wood flew out of the doorframe. I looked back and saw Ludwig at the other end of the corridor, a gun in his hand. He ran toward us.

The girl dropped down, held the weapon out in front of her, took deliberate aim. She was on one knee, holding the gun with two hands while Ludwig ran toward us, his arms and legs pumping wildly. All this seemed to be taking place in a slow-motion movie sequence while time seemed to have stopped. She squeezed the trigger. There was another *pop* and the smell of gunpowder. Ludwig reacted as if he had run into a wall. His body seemed to go up in the air and at the same time go backwards in a jerking motion. He fell flat on his back and didn't move.

"Go! Go! Go!" she told me. "Hurry."

In the meantime, the German had begun to run down a flight of steps. She put a bullet past the side of his head and he stopped. We followed him down. We were in a basement.

"Do you know where the exit is?" I said.

"No." She poked the gun into the German's back. He moved forward, us behind him, until we came to a door.

"Let me check it out," I said. Cautiously, I opened the door and looked around. It was clearly the back of the building, a litter-filled area with some light supplied from the glass windows above us. There was a Dumpster and a trio of dented garbage cans and, luckily, no people.

"Outside," she said to the German. "Turn around and face the wall."

"Are you going to kill me now?" He seemed to be amused by the whole thing.

"Face the wall and put both your hands on it."

She kicked at his feet so that he had to lean against the wall. She ran one hand over his body.

"I do not carry a weapon," he said.

"Check his ankles," she instructed me.

I bent down and felt both his ankles. "Nothing," I said. "Now what?"

"Hands behind your back," she told the German.

He pushed off the wall and did as she said.

She reached into her briefcase and handed me a pair of plastic handcuffs. "Lock him to the back door handle," she said.

I snapped one bracelet onto his wrist, then pulled him toward the back door and locked the other one onto the handle.

"That will keep him for a little while," she said to me. To him, she said, *"Auf wiedersehen."*

We went through an alley that led to another street. "Hurry," she said. "Walk fast, but do not run. There are always watchers."

"He thought you were going to kill him," I said.

"Did *you?*"

"I don't know. Maybe."

"I have never killed anyone without good reason."

We crossed several blocks before she stopped. She stamped her foot. "Shit! I made a mistake. My car is parked around the corner from the club. I do not think we should go near there at this time."

"That makes sense."

"The German will soon be out of his handcuffs. The police have no reason to keep him."

"What do you think he's going to do?"

"He will report to those he works for. They will look for you, of course. Obviously you cannot go back to your hotel."

"So what do we do?"

She reached into her briefcase once again and brought out a cell phone. She made a call, had a brief conversation, then put the phone away. "Someone will be here in a few minutes. We shall take you to a safe house."

"What good is that? I can't hide there forever."

"Do not worry. You are a friend of Misha's. We shall do everything possible to help you."

We waited on the corner, not speaking, but after a while I said, "Only a few people knew I was coming to Moscow. Misha was one of them. Is it possible that someone could have heard about it from him?"

She shrugged. "I cannot give you a definite answer. I was not there. But I will estimate that it is not more than a remote possibility. Misha is very experienced in these matters."

"So what's your guess? Who tipped these guys off? And just who are they working for, anyway?"

"I do not know the answer to your first questions. But I do have the answer to the last one. This German is known by us to be in the employ of a man they call Putlezhev."

"The guy they call the Eggplant?"

"Correct. And where the Eggplant is concerned, one can be sure trouble will follow."

Chapter 31

A black car drove up. Every car in Moscow seemed to be black. The driver was a burly guy in a leather jacket. A few words were passed in Russian and we took off.

We were soon in a part of Moscow filled with more concrete block apartment buildings. The Russians had put these up by the thousands to replace the rubble left over from World War II. Three out of four Russian men had been killed in that war, so most of the construction had been done by women.

"I'd like to know your name," I said.

"Anna."

"Mine's Jake."

"I know."

"I owe you a lot, Anna."

"You owe me nothing."

We had come to a neighborhood that had more of a high rent look than the one where I'd been to see the General. The streets were wider; the parked cars didn't look as if they'd been salvaged from a junkyard. While we drove, Anna and the driver spoke to one another in Russian. From the sound of it, they were not happy.

"We can't go in just yet. The resident *stukatch* is around," Anna said.

"What's a *stukatch?*"

"He is what you call a snitch, or an informer. Sometimes it is the police and sometimes it is the FSB who pay him to keep an eye out and report anything to them that looks unusual. Often, he will disappear for hours to get drunk, but recently he has been on the job all the time. Day and night. If we all walk in together, he will surely report that a foreigner has gone into the building."

"How would he know I'm a foreigner?"

She smiled. "It is obvious. Your clothes. The way you comb your hair. I am not exactly sure why, but even the shape of your face is different. It is a handsome face, but it is not a Russian face. And you are also taller than most Russian men."

"I might as well be carrying a sign."

"You are the sign." She and the driver spoke again. We cruised around a few blocks and then came to a stop. Anna and I got out. "There is another way to do this. Oleg will go back by himself. You will come with me. If anyone should speak to you, say nothing, just cough as if you have the bronchitis."

Oleg drove away and we entered another apartment house. The inside door was locked. Anna took a metal object out of her pocket. She inserted it into the lock and twisted it until the door opened. I followed her along a corridor and then down a stairwell into the basement. We walked rapidly through a long, dimly-lit corridor with walls that were spotted with sodden patches of plaster, and then we were outside facing the rear of another building. "That is where we are going," she said.

The door to the basement of her building was open. We went along a similarly damp corridor, up a flight of stairs, and then into a marble-floored lobby. "The elevator is just past here," she said. "I will go first." She ducked around a corner and in a moment was back. "Come. The coast is clear."

I followed her into the elevator, wondering if she had learned that expression from an old movie or a bad novel. The elevator took us smoothly up to the twentieth floor. We hurried along a carpeted hallway until we came to the right door. She pressed a bell button and we were let in by Oleg.

Once inside, Anna said, "Make yourself comfortable. Would you like something to eat or drink?"

I shook my head and flopped down on an overstuffed chair. Abruptly, the adrenaline that had been keeping me going vanished.

"It's almost one a.m. You must be tired."

"Yeah. *Come what may, Time and the hour runs through the roughest day.*"

"What is that, a quotation?"

"Shakespeare. The greatest writer who ever lived."

"I think there are some Russians who might dispute that."

I looked up at her. The light from a nearby lamp shone across her face. I saw now that her violet eyes were Asian, shaped like lotus seeds. Her hair fell straight as a curtain, black and lustrous, cut in low bangs across her forehead. Quite a woman, beautiful and a killer.

Anna showed me to a bedroom. It was small, had a narrow bed and a dresser with a mirror over it. She took a pair of pajamas out of a drawer in the dresser and handed them to me. "You should be quite proud of yourself. You did not panic. For an amateur, that is quite commendable." She kissed me lightly, then left me alone.

Sweat ran down my forehead and dripped off my nose. The room was stifling. I went to the window for air. In the far distance, two red stars glowed in the night sky. I thought I was hallucinating until I realized they were placed on top of

175

buildings in the heart of the city.

The next morning my mouth felt as if toadstools were growing in it. I brushed my teeth using my finger, splashed water on my face, and combed my hair. I looked in the mirror. My eyes, once described by an old girlfriend as "devastating," were streaked with red. I looked like Dr. Jekyll after Mr. Hyde had had a really rough night.

Anna appeared, wearing jeans and a black tee shirt. Her hair was pulled back and she wore no makeup, but she was still beautiful. More important, she had brought breakfast.

I was starving. I dug into the food: dense dark bread, rolls, butter, and jam. The coffee had the misfortune to be thicker than goulash, but it didn't matter.

When I finished, she said, "Tell me, what exactly is it that you have next to accomplish here?"

I told her about the meeting with the General, leaving out the details concerning the eggs. I explained about having to meet with him again, before I could go back to the States.

"It is good that you are circumspect, Mr. Wanderman, but it is not necessary. We know why you are here. That is one reason we are glad to help. Believe it or not, we, too, want our treasures back where they belong."

She picked up the telephone and had a long conversation in Russian. When she finished she said, "We have come up with the following plan. Let me know if it meets with your approval.

"I have a friend who is a secretary in the department where the General has his office. She will find a way to leave a note on the desk of the General's secretary. This note will be written and signed by you. You will inform the General that you were unable to return to your hotel, but you will meet him in front of the Pushkin house on the Arbat at twelve o'clock exactly.

"We have chosen this place and time because there will be many people there and we can observe from across the street that the person who comes for you is legitimate. Also, it is easier to conceal you in a crowd of tourists."

"You think this is going to work?"

"Yes," she said.

I wrote the note as she directed. She took it and left, telling me she would return as soon as she was able. I was not to answer the door or the telephone. "There is food if you get hungry. But I expect to be back quite soon."

I began pacing and thinking. My suitcase was back at the hotel. Would I be able to get it? Was it important enough to worry about? It was obviously more important that I was in hiding, because somehow Solofsky had learned of my Mission to Moscow and had put his colleague, Mr. Eggplant, on my case. Luckily, I had my money, passport, and credit card in my money belt, and that was securely wrapped around my waist. What I couldn't help wondering was whether or not their plan would work.

A lot of questions and no answers. For distraction, I got down on the floor and did my usual sixty push-ups. The last ten were a struggle, which suggested I was getting out of shape. Not surprising, since I had done nothing but booze it up since I arrived. Then it struck me that I'd been in Moscow less than one complete day.

Anna did not return for a couple of hours. When she did, she was all business. "The note has been given to my friend, who tells me she will have no difficulty in placing it where the secretary will see it. Then we wait."

"Tell me if I'm wrong," I said, "but it seems to me there are only a few things than can happen. One: Will the secretary show it to the General? Two: If she does and if the General reads the note, will the General believe it? Or three: Will he think it is some kind of trick? And four: Will the spy in the General's office read the note as well?"

"How do you know there is a spy in the General's office?"

"Just a guess," I said.

"More than likely you are right," Anna said. "If the General does get to read the note, I think he will send someone to see if it is genuine. He will have his own men in place, just as we will. As for FSB-KGB spy, who knows?" For the first time I saw her smile. "At any rate, it should be quite interesting."

"So what do we do now?"

She glanced at her watch. "It is almost ten o'clock. In one hour Oleg will come, and we shall go to the Arbat. There we shall wait to see what happens."

"One more hour," I said, walking back and forth. "Are you going to stay, or are you going to leave me alone again?"

"I will stay."

"That's good. I think you're the only reason I'm not coming apart."

She sat on the couch and crossed her legs. They were great legs. "I don't think that's at all true, Mr. Wanderman. You strike me as a man quite capable of doing what is necessary. You are strong, both mentally and physically. I do not see you 'coming apart,' as you put it."

"Thanks. That's a nice compliment. But I wonder if you'd mind telling me something?"

"What is that?"

"How did you get into this? Or, as we say back home, what's a nice girl like you doing in a place like this?"

"One reason is that I hate the FSB. They are the rats of our society. They will eat you down to your fingernails if you let them."

"What does that mean?"

"You know how children go into the business of the family? If the father is a farmer, the child is a farmer. If the father is an engineer, the child becomes an engineer."

"So what are you saying is your father is a gangster, and that's why you're doing it."

"Not my father. He is an honest man. He hates what I am doing. But the man you know as Misha is my uncle."

"Misha is your uncle? That's pretty funny."

"What is funny?"

"Because Misha's daughter is going to marry my father."

"Zeena?"

"That's right. Zeena, your cousin."

"That will make us relatives. That *is* funny."

"So how did your uncle get you into his business?"

"He didn't want me in it. But I was intrigued by what he was doing. Battling the system. There was something romantic about it. Also, I do not deny it, there is the matter of money. As I said, my father is an honest man. Because of his honesty and work ethic, we lived in a one-room apartment and ate cabbage every day. I decided that my uncle had a better idea. They both tried to talk me out of it, but they couldn't stop me once I made up my mind."

I had no problem believing that. "And the KGB or FSB? The hate?"

"They killed Yevgeny. We were going to be married. He had done nothing wrong, but he had gotten in the way of one of their operations, so they eliminated him."

"I'm sorry."

"Thank you. It was a long time ago, but the hate remains."

"I don't know," I said. "You're obviously intelligent. And beautiful. Don't you think you could find a better life?"

"What is better? I am a superior thief, burglar, entrepreneur. I know how to steal, I know how to kill. I know how to lie. What kind of job does that qualify me for?"

It didn't take me long to come up with an answer. "Politician?"

Chapter 32

There were two quick rings of the buzzer.

"That is Oleg. It means the *stukatch* has gone for the moment. Let us go now."

We drove across town and parked. "We will walk from here," Anna said. "The Arbat is closed to traffic."

We walked through a narrow lane and entered an open area crowded with pedestrians. The buildings had that restored Disney look: new-old, semi-authentic, pretty. The streets were cobblestoned and there were gift shops and little boutiques selling the usual tchochkes for tourists. We passed a theater, art galleries, a concert hall, and went into a self-service restaurant.

Anna spoke to Oleg, who nodded and left.

We sat at a table from which we could see the street.

"Across from us is number fifty-three, the house where Pushkin once lived. We have an excellent view. While we wait, you can have something to eat. We are early."

I looked at my watch. It was only eleven-thirty. "I'm not hungry."

"Have something. You may not get a chance to eat for several hours."

"I'll have what you're having."

She went away and came back with two bowls of soup. "*Akróshka.* Very good. Especially in warm weather."

When I finished eating, Anna said, "There is the General's man."

Across the street, lounging in front of number fifty-three, was the same guy who had taken me to the General, still wearing the baseball cap back to front.

"Wait here," Anna said. She left the restaurant.

I watched for her to cross the street but she didn't. She must have stayed on the restaurant side and was out of my view. I kept my eye on the General's guy, who behaved like a man exasperated by a late date. He turned this way and that. He stared into space. A couple of young women passed by wearing sleeveless tops and tight short shorts. He didn't hesitate to give them the same languid leer I'd seen on many New York street corners.

Then I saw Oleg ambling along like a casual sightseer. When he reached the guy he stopped, pulled a pack of cigarettes from his pocket, and appeared to ask for a light. The General's man took a lighter out of his pocket and put the flame to Oleg's cigarette. Oleg moved on. The guy remained where he was for about another minute, then walked away.

Anna came back into the restaurant. "Come."

I followed her down the street to a corner, where we turned and went down a side street; then another turn and there they were, Oleg and baseball cap, standing beside the same black car used to take me to see the General.

"Get in," she said.

I climbed in. Anna attempted to follow me, but the General's man held up his hands.

"*Nyet, nyet,*" he said. This was followed by a lot of Russian.

Anna answered forcefully. Oleg chipped in.

The response was more of the same, as well as a shrug which I couldn't fail to interpret as, "It's out of my hands, fellas."

More back and forth until finally Anna said, "I am not allowed to accompany you."

"Why not?"

"He says the General insists you come alone."

"Then that's what I'll do."

"I think it will be all right. He says that he, himself, cannot make any promises, but that if the General agrees, he will bring you to the front of the Bolshoi theater. We shall be waiting there for you. If he drops you anywhere else, take a taxi to the Bolshoi. You do not have to speak Russian. Just say 'Bolshoi.' Any driver will understand." She leaned in and kissed me. "Good luck."

Chapter 33

We drove for a long time. I remembered how I'd thought I was going to be just a simple messenger. Wasn't that the original idea? I hadn't counted on the guys in the nightclub, Anna to the rescue, and now this, riding off to somewhere in the hands of people I didn't know. The joke was on me.

I watched the broad avenue change to a macadam road. The guidebook described Moscow's roads as a series of rings. Abruptly, I realized we had passed what must have been the outer ring of the city, because traffic all but disappeared. We passed small villages consisting of little more than shacks. There were people working in the fields, a few melancholy cows, and the smell of manure.

The road narrowed. After a while the narrowness became one lane, then it turned to dirt. Here and there an outpost of tall trees had gotten together to make a small forest. Except for these occasional outcroppings, the countryside, even in summer, was barely green.

Ahead of us, I saw a small wooden house. This had to be a *dacha*, the upper-class Russian's country home. It looked a lot like a bungalow a friend of mine had in the Poconos, except this one had a metal roof. Another difference was that parked in front was a black sedan with two men in it, a radio

184

antenna jutting out of its rear deck. We got out and walked up a driveway bordered by a few scrawny pines and elms.

The old lady who had served tea the last time I had seen the General let us in. We went through a hallway and into what I guessed was the main room of the house only because there was a sofa and a few chairs. A fireplace held a scattering of old ashes. Above it hung a portrait of Lenin. The room had only two small windows, making it as dark and dreary as if it were a sunless winter day. A small breeze came in, preventing the room from becoming a sauna.

The driver pointed at a chair. I sat and waited. In a few minutes the General appeared. He nodded to the driver, who immediately left.

This time General Pankov wore a loose peasant blouse of white linen. He produced his cigarette holder, inserted a cigarette, and put a flame to it. "Much has been happening to you, has it not?"

"Too much," I said.

"It is well that you have good friends here."

"Very well."

"I shall not take a great deal of your time. A payment of nine million has been arranged. There will be no further negotiation. It has been decided that one million will be paid upon delivery of one egg only. It is being done based on my word. When that transaction has been completed and we are satisfied that the article is indeed genuine, the remainder will be paid in a lump sum and the balance of the Fabergés will then be delivered. If there is any attempt to deceive or defraud, my life will not be the only one forfeited. Is that understood?"

"Understood."

"Good. I assume you have all the necessary information for the transfer of the money. Correct?"

"Yes."

"From our end I shall tell you how to arrange for the delivery of the first egg, and then the rest. You must remember everything I tell you. It is most important not to have it on paper. Is that understood?"

"Yes." Cormac had told me the same thing back in New York. He had insisted I commit the method and code words to memory.

"All right then. Here is what you do."

He then told me that Cormac was to call the Russian Consulate in New York. He was to ask for Mr. Constantine. He was then to follow a certain procedure that would translate into when they should meet. There was a fallback procedure as well.

"What if this guy Constantine isn't there? Suppose he's on vacation or something."

"Just follow these instructions. It is most important that you repeat to Cormac exactly what I have said. Exactly. Is that understood?"

"Understood."

"The first contact is to establish that all is well. Mr. Constantine will then give you instructions as to how to make delivery. Is that understood?"

"Sure."

He sighed. "It must be exact. There can be no mistakes."

"I'll do it. Don't worry." Then I told him what Cormac had told me about how the money was to be delivered. More of the same kind of mumbo-jumbo. The money was to be sent to an account Cormac had set up in one of those tailor-made-just-for-swindlers banks in the Cayman Islands. I told him the phone number and the name of the contact. "Then all you have to say is, 'Big Mac.' "

"Big Mac." The General smiled. "That is amusing.

Cormac always loved food, but I cannot imagine him eating at McDonald's."

"Neither can I."

The General stood up and walked with me to the door. As I was about to leave, the General said, "Did you know that this man, Fabergé, was not only a superb artist, but an ingenious salesman as well? He went to Alexander III and offered to design a special Easter egg for the Empress. He said it would look like an egg but that there would be a surprise. He gave the Czar no further details. When the egg was presented, it contained a gold yolk, inside of which was a gold hen. Inside the hen was a diamond imperial crown, and within the crown itself was a miniature ruby egg. The Czar and the Empress were both astounded and delighted. From that moment on, Fabergé received the commission to make a new egg every year. It made him quite wealthy."

"Thanks for the history lesson," I said, then asked him to tell his driver to take me back to the Bolshoi theater as Anna had instructed. The General spoke a few words to him. The driver nodded and touched his cap in a kind of salute. "Done," the General said. He held out his hand. "I suppose we shall not be seeing each other again. I wish you good luck."

"Thanks," I said. "Same to you. I think we can both use it."

The men outside didn't look at me as I got back into the car. We left the dirt road behind and drove toward Moscow. We passed the peasants I'd seen before, still bent low over the earth, like figures in a nineteenth-century painting. One of them, a woman, straightened, and watched as we went by. I remembered reading about rampant starvation in Russia during World War II. There were rumors of cannibalism. It was said many a German soldier had contributed in this bizarre way to the peasants' survival.

The driver kept both hands on the wheel. I was glad because I suddenly realized we were traveling at what seemed to me to be a recklessly fast speed.

"What's the hurry?"

He didn't answer.

The scenery was going by in a blur. I could feel the speed continuing to increase.

"Hey!" I said. "Why so fast?"

Then he spoke. "A car is following us."

"You're kidding." I turned quickly and looked out the rear window. Sure enough, about a hundreds yards back was the inevitable black car.

"Who are they?"

"I do not know. I do not want to know." Our car surged ahead.

They stayed right with us.

I leaned forward and poked the driver on his shoulder. "What's your name?"

"Why do you want to know?"

"Just tell me your name, for God's sake!" I yelled. "What is it, a state secret?"

"Pasha."

"Listen Pasha, I have a feeling these guys mean business. Is there any way we can get off this road and ditch them?"

"There is no other road for fifty kilometers, except for those leading to small villages."

"Shit! They're no good to us. I guess the only thing to do is go faster."

"I cannot go faster. The car has reached its maximum speed."

I looked back and saw the other car beginning to edge closer.

Ahead of us was one of those small forests that appeared every once in a while. The road made a swing around it. I hoped that when we made the turn there might be a different road we might be able to take. When we came around the curve, what we saw instead of a road was another car up ahead parked crosswise, blocking the road and any chance we had of getting away. Two men stood on each side of the car with guns in their hands.

Pasha had to jam on his brakes to avoid a crash. Our car went into a long skid while Pasha fought the wheel. Eventually we came to a stop.

The doors were pulled open. A voice said, "Out!"

I slid along the seat and began to exit when a hand grabbed my arm and yanked me so hard I skidded on the gravel and fell to the ground. The tip of a shoe went into my stomach. A stab of pain went slicing through me all the way to my back and neck.

"Get up!"

I tried to stand but I couldn't move. A hand grabbed my shirt collar and pulled me up.

Suddenly a gun went off. The shot was loud and there was a burning smell. Pasha was on the ground, his hands pressed against his stomach. Blood flowed through his fingers.

"Jesus Christ! You shot him."

"He was a known criminal," the man standing next to me said. "He tried to escape. For that he was shot."

I knew it was reckless, but I couldn't hold back. "That's a lie and you know it."

He had the eyes of a ferret. His teeth were gray except for one in front, which was gold. He smiled at me and the gold tooth glinted in the afternoon light.

He continued to smile as he raised his gun and swung it

189

against the side of my head. The blow knocked me to the ground. I tasted bile in my throat. I sucked air and felt my eyes roll up into my head. I knew I was blacking out, but not before I foolishly remembered: *There's daggers in men's smiles.*

Chapter 34

When I opened my eyes, I found myself stretched out on a cot. Directly above me hung a naked light bulb. I blinked and heard a groan. I was about to look to see where it had come from when I realized it had come from me. I tried to sit up and stopped. The movement had caused a wave of nausea to roll over me. I did some slow, measured breathing until it finally went away. My head throbbed. I reached up carefully to touch it and felt a bandage. Then I remembered the son of a bitch with the gold tooth bashing me with his gun. I was more than stupid for having mouthed off at him. It hadn't helped Pasha for sure, and all it had gotten me was a major concussion.

I sat up slowly. My mouth was dry. I was in a cell, maybe five by seven. It had no furniture other than the cot I was on. A door at one end was closed. There was a sink and a toilet. A sink meant water. The thought of cool water entering my mouth, running in a delicious stream down my throat, gave me the strength to raise myself slowly, very slowly, to my feet. The blood inside my head began playing a Sousa march. My legs were wobbly, but by taking small steps I made my way to the sink and turned the faucet handle. Nothing happened.

I tried the other faucet and almost bawled like a baby when

the water began running. There was no glass, so I cupped my hand and funneled some into my mouth. Then I splashed it on my face.

The wall above the sink did not have a mirror. What it did have was graffiti. There were words, sentences, drawings. One drawing was of a cat on its back, its legs stiff in the air. I couldn't read the words but I could feel the anguish of those who had been kept here. The other walls had graffiti, too. They were done in pen, pencil, and magic marker, as well as scratched in with anything that had a point. I had read somewhere about the graffiti on the walls in the infamous *Lubyanka* prison, where people in Stalin's time were tortured and shot by the thousands. And now, here I was, maybe in that same prison.

I went back to the cot. I shouldn't complain. I was alive. I thought of Pasha on the ground, blood pouring from his guts. And for what? I tried to think of something good, something positive. I thought about Rosalind, whom I loved. I thought about my father. I loved him, too. And Zeena. I thought about Cormac. Did he know this was going to happen? Of course not. It was an unworthy thought. I thought about Cynthia. My meeting her had started it all. If I had turned her down, I'd be safe and sound back in my house in the Hamptons, happy as a hummingbird. Only I knew that wasn't true.

In the beginning, I believed I'd signed onto this so-called adventure because of too much vodka and a little bit of lust. But deep down I knew that was me bullshitting myself. What it really had to do with was Rosalind. I thought that my getting involved in helping Toby and Cormac, getting the treasure back to where it belonged, would show her I was a man worth respect and consideration. I was trying to revive the man she had once loved and ought to love again. And maybe, just maybe, I was out to prove something of the same sort to myself. I had come to Moscow to do something worthwhile. I had thought it would work out. If it did not work out—and right now that seemed more than a strong possibility—at least I would have the satisfaction of knowing I had given it a good shot.

I took a deep breath, which made my head throb even more. The one thing I was sure of was that now that I'd come this far, I was going to see it through to the end, no matter what.

Bold thoughts for a guy locked up in a Russian jail.

The room was close. There were no windows. Whatever air there was came through a small vent in the ceiling. Abruptly, I realized I was wearing a loose cotton shirt and baggy pants and on my feet were felt slippers. They had taken my clothes, and of course, my money belt with my passport and dollars. I was relieved that the photos of the Fabergé eggs were no longer in there, but I doubted it made much difference.

The door opened and three people came into the room. One was the guy with the rodent eyes who had shot Pasha and clubbed me. Another was a man in uniform carrying two plastic chairs and a tape recorder. The third was taller than both of them. He had a head full of curly hair, and a face you couldn't ignore. Spread out over one cheek and reaching down to his chin, in effect covering half his face, was a lurid splash of purple. Purple mark? Was this the guy they called the Eggplant? The guy the KGB was going to execute on sight? It couldn't be him, could it? Unless he had a twin, I didn't see how it could be anyone else.

The uniformed guard put the chairs down, carefully placed the tape recorder on the floor, and went out. Ferret-face sat in one of the chairs and motioned for me to get off the cot and sit in the other one. He had a file folder in his hand. He pulled a sheet of paper from it and began reading out loud. He was speaking English, but so heavily accented it took me a while to understand that he was reciting a long list of crimes I had committed. He read too fast for me to follow much of what he said, but I picked up on a couple, dealing in stolen goods and driving above the speed limit.

He finished and said, "What do you say to those charges?"

"They're ridiculous."

"They can bring you twenty years in the gulag."

"They're not true. Not one of them."

"Can you prove that?"

"Can you prove that they are?"

"Of course. We already have proof." He reached into the folder, held up a bunch of papers, and waved them back and forth the way Senator McCarthy used to when he was trying to get some poor shlub to admit he was a communist. "These are the testimonies of witnesses. They have testified that you are indeed guilty of all the crimes of which you are accused."

"They must be very reliable witnesses."

Ferret-face smiled, the gold tooth glinted, and I have to admit I flinched. The flinch was instinctive. I didn't want a gun banging me in the head again. But I was mad at myself for showing fear.

"Do not be afraid, Mr. Wanderman. I am not going to hurt you. That is, if you cooperate."

Now for the first time, the other man spoke. "It will be better for you, if you do as he says." His accent was also heavy but I understood every word.

"Who are you?"

"I will tell you because then I think you will better understand the position you are in. My name is Borodin. Pavel Borodin. I am, I was, an associate of Mr. Solofsky. So I know everything. I know why you are here. I know who you have been to see. I know that arrangements have been made. And because I know these things, now our friend here knows everything as well."

So he was definitely the Eggplant. "And who is your friend?" I asked.

"You are an intelligent man. I think you must have guessed by now that you are in the hands of the Agency of Federal Security of the Russian Federation."

"FSB, formerly known as KGB."

"Then you know the circumstances. So are you going to do what is necessary?"

"Is Pasha dead?"

"Who is Pasha?" the Eggplant asked. Ferret-face muttered to him in Russian, obviously explaining who he was. "The General's driver? Yes. He is dead."

In a flash I saw Pasha holding his stomach, blood seeping between his fingers. The words were out of my mouth before I could think. "You're nothing but a bunch of fucking killers. Go to hell!"

Ferret-face carefully put the file on the floor, leaned forward, and with an open palm belted the side of my head where the bandage was. There was a roar and a flash of light. I bent over and squeezed my legs with both hands, trying to keep from vomiting.

They had a brief conversation in Russian, then the Eggplant spoke again. "I do not think you understand, Mr. Wanderman. It is too bad about the driver, but we are talking about *you*. The threat of the gulag is not an idle one. They have the power to send you away for twenty years."

I was trying to breathe. He sounded far away.

"It would be the end of you. Your life would be over. Even if you did not die from the brutal conditions that exist there, you would never see or hear from your family and friends again. Listen to what I am saying. Is what you are protecting worth all that?"

Of course not, but I couldn't answer because I was doing all I could to keep the room from spinning.

"I am out of patience," Ferret-face said to no one in particular. "I will get Gregor in here. After ten minutes with Gregor, he will beg us to let him cooperate."

I didn't like the sound of that. Ferret-face was bad enough.

The Eggplant said, "Gregor will beat the shit out of you. He will also probably break several bones in your body. If that doesn't work, they will drug you. The drugs they have will permit you to tell them everything you know about everything. So in the end, all your foolish bravery will amount to nothing. Do you understand? Can you hear what I am saying?"

"I hear you."

"Then give them what they want."

"What's in it for you?"

"Nothing. I am a prisoner, exactly like you. I am alive only because I have agreed to help them."

"Enough," Ferret-face said.

"I don't care about the goddamn eggs," I said. "I'll tell you everything I know. My only condition is that none of my family and friends back home get hurt."

His gold tooth flashed. "We have no interest in your family or your friends, as long as they do not interfere."

"So you promise?" I said this even though I knew his promise wasn't worth shit. I just wanted to make him say it.

"I promise." He barked at the Eggplant, who then left the room. "Tell me about General Pankov." He pulled a chair next to mine and sat, his face almost in my face. He pulled the recorder closer and pushed a button to start it. "Proceed."

"Where do you want me to begin?"

"Tell me who you have met with since you arrived in Moscow and everything that was said."

"Could I have a glass of water?"

He looked at me as if I had asked for a bottle of Dom Perignon. He got up, opened the door, and barked. The guard brought me a carafe of water and a plastic cup. I drank, and set the carafe and cup on the floor.

"You have had your water. Now speak."

I began by telling him about Blather fixing me up with the General and their plans for the Fabergés.

He wanted details of the bank transactions and the specifics of the transfer. He wanted the codes. I told him everything Cormac had told me and everything the General had told me. He asked a lot of questions. They were often different ways of asking the same thing. I assumed this was skilled interrogation. It didn't bother me because I had answered all his questions truthfully.

It couldn't have taken long, but it seemed like hours. Just when I thought it was all over, he said, "Tell me what happened in the nightclub."

He had caught me by surprise. "*The Hungry Duck?*"

"You were with Mueller. You were having dinner. His partner was shot and he was found tied up with handcuffs. And you did not return to your hotel."

"Who's Mueller?" I guessed he was trying to find out about Anna. I had to stall, play dumb.

"The German businessman who invited you to the club."

"That guy. I didn't know his name."

"He was working for us."

"Is that right? I should have known he was too friendly."

He pushed his face so close I could smell his foul breath.

"You are trying to obstruct me. Do not do this. Tell me what happened."

I didn't have much hope he'd believe me, but I tried my best to bluff my way through it. "To tell you the truth, everything happened so fast, I'm not sure what exactly did happen. But I'll try to reconstruct the events."

"If you would be so kind." Sarcasm didn't go with his personality.

"I had to go to the john. Your German guy—"

"What is john?"

"Toilet. He went with me. When we came out, somebody jumped him. There was a lot of confusion and his partner was shot. That's about it."

The overhead light threw shadows across his narrow face. "I believe you have left out a few details."

"Such as?"

He stood up. "Look at me," he said. I had to look at him with the light glaring in my eyes. "Who was the woman?"

"Oh, the woman." I couldn't deny her because the German would have told them everything. "I don't know who she is." I tried to sound casual. "Maybe she's the General's girlfriend."

He shook his head. "I do not think so. The General likes boys."

"Really? In that case, your guess is as good as mine."

He leaned over and raised his fist as if he was going to hit me again. "Do not lie to me."

"I'm not lying," I shouted, trying to look scared. Since I really was scared, my acting was good. "Why should I lie?"

"We shall see." He went outside.

I took a deep breath and poured myself another glass of water. All along I had assumed he thought I had come to Moscow to meet with the General, and knew nothing about my connection with Misha's friends. I had forgotten about that fucking German. My only way out was to continue to stonewall, and deny, deny, deny.

He came back in a few minutes. "We have no knowledge of any woman other than his old housekeeper. I will ask you again. Who is she?"

"I'm telling the truth. I don't know. She showed up at the nightclub, hustled me out of there, and got me together with the General's driver. That's all I know."

His mouth twisted into a smirk. "You think you are being clever. But I am not a fool. Whoever helped you will eventually be found and dealt with. It is lucky for you that right now we have all the information we need."

I tried not to show my relief. "What happens next?"

"When it is necessary, then you will know." He came closer and inspected my bandage. He reached out and poked it with his finger. "Does this hurt?"

"What do you think?"

"Remember there is more where that came from," he said.

Chapter 35

A tray of food was brought in. I sat on the bed and put the tray on one of the chairs and began to eat. There was a bowl of cold borscht, a plate of kasha with a piece of unfamiliar-looking brown meat, a glass of tea, and for dessert, a cookie that almost broke a tooth. I ate it all. About a half hour later, the single light went out, leaving the cell in total blackness. I couldn't even see my body. There was nothing to do but go to sleep.

As soon as I closed my eyes, my brain filled with rapidly changing scenes. I didn't want to watch most of them, especially the ones that took place in the car with Pasha. I tried to escape by thinking of home, but I was too aware of the thin mattress, my throbbing head, the air in the room closing in on me. I rolled back and forth on the mattress. One of Shakespeare's sonnets came into my head. I remembered reading it to Rosalind when we first moved in together.

> *My mistress' eyes are nothing like the sun;*
> *Coral is far more red than her lips' red . . .*

I fell asleep trying to remember the rest of it.

A different guard woke me up, a woman this time. The

light was back on. She handed me a tray with hot cereal and a mug of coffee. The cereal was hot, but thick as glue, and so was the coffee. When I finished eating, the guard came back with my clothes. She gave me a towel and a miniature bar of soap and made motions for me to get dressed. She watched me while I washed and dressed, then handed me my money belt. I checked and happily found everything still in it. She then motioned for me to follow her.

We went out into a narrow corridor. There was a row of doors behind which I imagined rooms or cells similar to the one I'd been in. We must have been underground because there were no windows. We climbed some steps, went along another corridor, then entered an elevator. When the elevator door opened, another guard was waiting for us. I stepped out and followed the other guard down a hall that was a lot different from the one I had left below. Here was carpeting, windows, and light, none of which made me any less tense.

The guard knocked on a door. A voice inside said something. The guard opened the door. Inside was a large room with a high ceiling. The walls were hung with oil paintings in gilt frames. A crystal chandelier twinkled above me. At the far end of the room, behind an acre of Oriental carpet, a man in a business suit sat behind a massive, ornate desk. Standing next to the desk was my friend, Ferret-face.

He motioned for me to approach. When I did, he said, "This is comrade Barranikov, the head of our Ministry of Security."

The man had a head of white hair and a full white mustache to match. He did not get up.

"Sit down, Mr. Wanderman," he said. His voice had the same cultured accent as General Pankov's. "You came to our country as a guest, but I regret to say you have not behaved like one. You appear to have broken a number of our laws."

"That's bullshit and you know it."

He ignored me. "We have given you the option of being sent to a prison camp or of helping us. You have wisely chosen the latter course. It is most important that you understand that our interest is solely the recovery of our national treasure. It is for that reason alone that we are permitting you to leave. We are sending you back to New York, where you will follow your original instructions from General Pankov. After that first contact is made, we shall take over. If all goes well, we should have the items in our possession with little difficulty. We expect your full cooperation in this matter. You understand what will happen if you decide to change your mind once you are back on your home ground."

"Wait a minute! You never said anything about me doing anything else. I gave you all the information you wanted. You said you'd let me go." I stared at Ferret-face and remembered no such words were ever spoken. I'd made them promise not to harm my family and friends, that was all.

The comrade spoke again. "I think you understand that you have no choice in the matter. They are expecting a call from you, so that is what they will get."

"I don't think this is a good idea. You've got guys who are trained to do this stuff. I'm not experienced in this kind of thing. I might screw it up."

"Don't be foolish, Mr. Wanderman. You will do exactly what we tell you to do. In that way, all our objectives will be met. Then you will be free. Is that understood?"

They had me by the *cojones*. They knew it, and I knew it. "I expect you to stand by your promise that no one will be harmed," I said, trying to get back a little dignity.

"Absolutely. We are not inhumane people. If everyone cooperates, there should be no reason for injury to anyone concerned." He stood up. "You will be taken to your hotel now and retrieve your luggage. Then you will be taken to the airport. A plane leaves in two hours."

Ferret-face took me by elevator to a courtyard where we got into a limo, black of course. Sitting in the rear was the Eggplant. Ferret-face laughed. "We did not want you to be lonely on the flight back to New York. So Putlezhev will accompany you. He is delighted. Right, Putlezhev?"

The Eggplant's face was grim. He didn't answer.

We pulled up in front of the hotel. "I will go in with Mr. Wanderman. You will stay in the car," the Ferret said to the Eggplant.

We went past the tourists and businessmen in the lobby. I wished I could tell them what was happening. The whole thing was crazy, unreal. It was me in a movie but it was also me on the outside, watching the scene being played.

In the elevator Ferret-face was actually humming. I couldn't believe the son of a bitch was ever happy enough to sing. The worst of it was that I recognized the tune. "The Sound of Music." I hated that song. We got out on my floor and went to the key-lady.

Ferret-face barked at her and she handed him the key. He certainly had a way about him, because what little color she had left in her face disappeared. As soon as she handed over the key, she left her desk and disappeared through a door at the other end of the hall.

He pushed me ahead of him as we walked down the corridor to my room. He put the key in the lock and opened the door. As we entered, he said, "All right. Get your things together and be quick about it. I'll be glad to get you on that plane and out of Moscow. You Americans make me sick."

"I'm not too thrilled with you either," I said, heading for the closet where I'd put my suitcase. Then I realized that my suitcase was on the bed. Someone had already taken it out of the closet.

He said something in Russian. Even though I couldn't understand, it sounded like a curse.

That got me mad. It wasn't bad enough that he had shot an innocent man, split my head open, and caused me great pain, but now he was bad-mouthing me because I was an American. "Fuck you, too," I said.

I turned, startled to see him reaching into his pocket and attempting to pull out his gun. That was when Anna shot him.

Chapter 36

I watched the anger at this insult turn his rodent eyes red. He stood there for what seemed like forever, partially bent over. Then his legs gave out and he fell to the floor.

Her gun had hardly made a sound. I understood why when I saw the steel cylinder on the barrel.

"Close the door," she said.

I shoved it closed. "How'd you know they were bringing me here?"

"The rats are not the only ones with spies." She leaned over him and examined the wound. "Stomach. Not good for him, but he'll survive." She patted him down, removed his cell phone, and picked his gun off the floor. "Who else is with you?"

"There's a driver in a car in front of the hotel. And the Eggplant is there, too."

"What is *he* doing here?"

"They own him. To save his life, he's working for them to get the eggs back."

"And when they get them back, what happens to him then?" She answered her own question. "He's a cooked goose."

"Never mind about him," I said. "You shot an important guy. What do we do now?"

"Change your clothes. Put something different on."

I changed out of my grungy chinos and polo shirt, put on fresh jeans and a denim shirt.

"We will leave the hotel like ordinary tourists."

"Can we do that? What about my bill?"

"Your friends took care of it. The hotel is expecting you to leave, so that is what you will do."

"What about this guy? He doesn't look so good." Ferret-face was on his side, with both hands holding his stomach. He was groaning. I got a towel from the bathroom and placed it on his wound.

"They will find him soon after we leave. I am sure of that."

The wounded man said something in Russian to Anna. She said something back, then shrugged, took a roll of duct tape out of her handbag, tore off a strip, and pressed it over his mouth. "Hold that towel in place," she said to me. She pulled his hands behind his back and used more tape on his hands.

"Do you have to do that?"

"I don't want him shouting for help before we get out of the hotel. He'll be all right."

"I hope so. I don't like the prick, but he doesn't deserve to die for it."

"He won't die." She opened the door slowly and looked out. "Come now," she said. "There is nobody in sight."

I took my suitcase and we went hurriedly down the corridor to the elevator.

"Did you take care of the key-lady?" I asked.

She nodded. "She will say nothing."

The elevator rode smoothly down to the lobby. I had never believed they would send me to Siberia, even though the threat was a real one. I had confidence they were using that as a ploy, a way to get me to do what they wanted. But circumstances had changed. Now I could be accused of attempting to kill one of their own. If we were caught this time, I was pretty sure there would be no way out.

The lobby was busier than usual. There were people everywhere, moving this way and that, a lot of noise and confusion. It made me feel better. In this mob, I was a lot less conspicuous.

We went to the front and looked out. I pointed to the car. The driver was sitting behind the wheel, smoking. Putlezhev was in the rear, only a part of his head visible.

"What's next?" I said.

"They don't know me," she said. "I will go to the car and pretend I think they are selling rides to the airport. While I am talking to them, you walk out to the left and go around the corner. Oleg is waiting there. Do not look at us. Just act unconcerned. Move quickly but not obviously so. Okay?"

"They don't know you, but they know a woman got me out of that nightclub. Ferret-face was asking me a lot of questions about you."

"That doesn't matter. They do not know who I am."

"I hope you're right."

She took hold of my hand and squeezed. "It will work. They will look at me and see nothing else."

She was right. I was aware again of how young and beautiful she was. "Okay," I said. "I guess we have no choice. Let's do it. You go to the driver's window and start talking to him. That's when I'll move."

She stepped out onto the sidewalk and pretended to be looking for someone. After a moment of searching in both directions, she headed for the car. She walked slowly around the front of it into the street and approached the driver's side. I saw the Eggplant's head move forward as she leaned in. He was not a dummy. A beautiful woman behaving oddly would make him suspicious.

I headed away from the door, and without looking back, walked as quickly as I could toward the corner. My instinct was to run, but my brain was telling me to try and look as if I were strolling. I had just reached the corner when I heard a shout. I turned and saw Anna racing toward me, her gun out. Behind her was the driver. He was running after her and pulling at something under his jacket.

"Hurry!" Anna yelled to me.

I took off as fast as I could go. I saw Oleg in the middle of the block. I ran toward him and waved, trying to get him to understand. He understood immediately. By the time I reached him, he had started the car and had the back door open. I tossed my suitcase inside, looked back, and saw Anna running toward me.

The driver came around the corner. He dropped to one knee, a gun in his hand, and took aim.

"Watch out," I shouted foolishly, as if she could do anything about it. There were other people on the sidewalk. A couple standing not far away must have seen what was happening, because they threw themselves down on the pavement.

I heard the shot, like a cork being pulled from a bottle, heard a "ping," and saw a chunk of concrete come off the building opposite. Anna stopped, and fired off a couple of quick rounds. I ran toward her. There was another shot from the driver. I grabbed hold of her hand and ran back with her to the car. I shoved her in and followed, slamming the door.

Oleg tore out, tires squealing. He drove fast for a couple of blocks, turned a few corners, then slowed down. He called back to Anna in Russian.

"What is he saying?" I asked.

"He wants to know where we should go. We must get off the streets soon, because they will have radioed a description of the car. They will be looking for us."

I noticed that she was in an awkward position on the seat. I took her arm in an effort to help her move. She gasped.

"What is it? Did you get hit?"

"Yes. But I don't think it is bad."

I saw a bright rash of blood on her arm where it had come through her blouse. "Oleg!" I said. "Anna's been shot. We've got to get someplace right away."

He looked back, and stepped on the gas again.

I carefully rolled up the sleeve. There was a lot of blood. Either I had seen it in a movie or my Boy Scout training came back, but I knew what to do. I tore the sleeve off her blouse. Then, with the aid of my teeth, I ripped it into strips, using them to wrap the wound as tightly as I could. I hoped it would work.

After a series of turns, we came to an industrial neighborhood. The buildings were of crumbling red brick, old and dirty, windowpanes gutted. They had the look of abandoned warehouses and factories. Oleg stopped, jumped out, and pulled open a garage door, then got back into the car and drove inside, switching on the headlights. In the beam of the headlights, I could see cartons with markings on them stacked against the walls. He shut off the motor and closed the door behind us.

"Where are we?" I asked Anna.

She didn't answer. She had passed out.

I picked her up and carried her, following Oleg up a narrow flight of stairs, into an office, then into another room with a sofa and a couple of upholstered chairs. I put her on the sofa, which was just like my Aunt Fanny's, covered in a pattern that looked like cabbages. Oleg brought me a whole bunch of stuff: water, bandages, iodine, and of all things, Johnson & Johnson first aid cream. Talk about American know-how. He muttered something in Russian. I guessed that he was telling me to hurry up. "I'm moving as fast as I can," I said to him.

I carefully undid my homemade bandage. The blood had mostly stopped flowing.

Anna opened her eyes. "Have I been shot?"

"Looks like it. I'm trying to see where the bullet is."

"I do not think there is one," she said. "I don't feel anything."

"Let's hope you're right. Meanwhile I have to look. It may hurt." Blood had dried and stuck to her skin in clumps. I washed it off gradually by soaking a towel and dabbing gently. I could see that a chunk of flesh had been torn away, but I didn't see any sign of an entry wound. "It looks like your luck held."

I applied the first aid cream to the cut. Blood continued to seep, so I put the bandage on firmly. "This doesn't hurt too much, does it?"

She shook her head. "Do you mind if I rest a little now?"

Before I could answer, her eyes had closed and she was asleep. I turned around to tell Oleg the good news, but he was gone.

Chapter 37

One side of Stalin's face had a stain larger and more colorful than the Eggplant's. He was pointing at me and saying, "Shoot this dumb fucking American. At once!"

Before they could take me away to be shot, I woke up and saw Oleg and two other men in the room.

Anna was sitting up and talking to them. She had her hand protectively over the bandage I'd put on her wound.

"How are you feeling?" I asked. "How's your arm?"

"Not to worry. It will be all right. What is important now is that you tell everything that happened after you left to see General Pankov. It may help us in deciding what we must do."

I told her about the General in his *dacha*, then driving back and being ambushed. I told her about Pasha, about the interrogation, the plan to send me back to New York with the Eggplant as my guardian. When I finished, she translated everything for the others.

"After what has happened," she said, "there will be a massive effort to find you. All their resources will be used. A suggestion has been made that we to take you to the American Embassy and be rid of you."

"Why don't you?"

"It is not an option. For one thing, the Embassy will be watched very closely. We wouldn't get within a block without being picked up."

"And?"

"And what?"

"You said, one thing. What's the other thing?"

"The other thing is that I made a promise to help you. I won't go back on my word." She spoke to the others, and after some back and forth, and a few dirty looks thrown at me by the new guys, they left.

"How come they listen to you? Where's the head man, the boss?"

"I am boss," she said.

"You?" I couldn't hide the surprise in my voice.

"Why not? I am smarter than them and they know it. I am also better with a gun. Now, here is the plan. The most powerful man on our side is General Pankov. We will try to get in touch with him and see what he can do to help. We are asking him to call my cell phone." She walked over to the table. There were a couple of paper bags on it. Abruptly, I was aware of an aroma of cooked food. "Are you hungry?"

"I guess I am."

"Do you like Big Mac?" She reached into the bag and pulled out hamburgers, fries, and shakes from McDonald's. Curious, I unwrapped one and took a bite. It was the real thing, greasy overcooked meat, oily fries. What I ate when I was young but almost never as a grownup. I loved it.

Anna explained that we would wait where we were to hear from the General, rather than going to the more comfortable apartment. "At the moment it is dangerous to be outside. This place is, I think, quite safe. We have been using it as a warehouse only a short time, so it is unlikely the police or anyone else knows of it."

The time passed slowly. I sat in a chair while she lay down again on the couch. I could see that the wound, even though the bullet hadn't penetrated, had taken a good deal out of her. I got up and used the bathroom. At one point, Oleg came back and told her something. She confirmed that the message had been relayed.

"Now we wait some more," Anna said. She stretched out on the couch.

After a while, I dozed off. The sound of a telephone woke me up. The room was dark, except for a lamp on a table that threw a small pool of light around it. I looked at my watch. It was after midnight.

Anna put the phone down. "I'm sorry," she said.

"About what?"

"I have just been informed that General Pankov is dead."

Chapter 38

"The caller did not identify himself," Anna said. "He said the General died of a heart attack. Heart attack is often given as the cause of death. He also suggested that we might as well turn ourselves in, since we no longer have anyone to protect us. Of course, we do not know if this is true or not. But we shall proceed on the assumption that it is true."

"Why should we believe him?"

"I tend to believe him because he called me on my cell phone. The only way he could get the number was by intercepting the message I sent to the General."

"Well," I said, "it looks like now our only choice is to find our own way out of this."

"It seems so. Do you have any ideas?" she asked.

"As a matter of fact, I do." I remembered when we arrived seeing cartons stacked up against a wall. "You said this was a warehouse. So I assume those cartons downstairs are full of merchandise for sale. Am I right?"

"Yes. We have everything from refrigerators to computers to sacks of grain."

"Does any of it go out of the country?"

"Most of it. That's where the buyers are." She paused. "I see what you are getting at. We ship mostly by truck. The trucks go to Germany. Poland. Greece. All over."

"What about the borders? Won't they be watching?"

"In all probability, yes. But we know people at the borders. Especially Finland. It is a border we use very much. We have very good connections."

"So I get smuggled out with the contraband."

"Exactly. An excellent idea."

"You think it'll work?"

"If it doesn't, I shall be very unhappy."

"Me, too."

For the rest of the night, we were in the office going through manifests to decide which shipment would be the ideal one in which to smuggle me over the border. The office was the room we had originally entered. It consisted of a beat-up pine table that served as a desk, a few wooden chairs, and a row of file cabinets. I couldn't do anything but watch as Anna pulled notebooks out of the file cabinets and studied lists.

By three a.m. my head ached. I needed sleep, a hot bath, hot coffee, any or all of the above. "Here's one," she said, holding up a sheet of paper. "I think this might be what we're looking for. There's a truck scheduled to leave tomorrow for Helsinki. It's carrying aviation parts."

At first light, she began making phone calls. I couldn't tell what the conversations were about, but she seemed impatient with the people she was speaking to and not satisfied with what she was hearing. Finally, she turned to me and said, "Apparently something has happened at the Finland Station. My contact says we should not ship anything through there for a while. The rats are all over, asking questions, taking people away, interfering with business. It is obvious we shall have to find another route."

"You think it has anything to do with me?"

"Perhaps. Perhaps not. Who can say?" She pulled more

files and began going through them.

At last, Oleg arrived, along with the same two guys. They brought bread, cheese, and coffee. While we ate, Anna talked with them. There seemed to be a lot of arguing. It was frustrating not being able to understand what they were saying, especially because I knew they were talking about me.

My eyes were grainy. I went into the bathroom and splashed cold water on my face. I felt like I'd been doing that a lot in Russia and I was sick and tired of it.

When I went back, Anna was sitting at the table looking very much the weary executive. "We have come up with something else." She pinched the bridge of her nose. Her cheeks appeared to have sunken into her face. There were dark smudges under her eyes.

"What is it?"

"From here to St. Petersburg is a day, and from St. Petersburg to the Finnish border is a matter of hours. I think it is possible they will be waiting for you there because it is so close. Therefore, we shall fool them and go where it is far."

"And where is that?"

She forced a smile. "How would you like to go on a cruise?"

Chapter 39

"A cruise? I have a feeling you don't mean High Tea, Cherries Jubilee for dessert, the sinful Midnight Buffet. That kind of cruise."

"Definitely not. More likely, all the undrinkable Soviet wine you might want, and for dessert, if you are lucky, perhaps a babka."

"Okay. What's the story?"

"The cruise I have in mind takes place on the Black Sea."

"Didn't Stalin meet with Roosevelt and Churchill there? A place called Yalta?"

"Yes. But you shall not board in Yalta. Many government officials have summer *dacha*s there, and that means they are heavy with security. I know of another place. It is a small port by the name of Sochi. A few cruise ships depart from it. I happen to be acquainted with the captain of one of these ships."

"A business associate?"

"Exactly. And one of his regular stops is Turkey. You go on board in Sochi and leave the ship in Istanbul as just another visiting tourist. Then all you have to do is go to the airport and book a flight home."

"Sounds too easy."

"Getting off in Istanbul is easy. Getting you to Sochi and then onto the ship, that is a little more complicated."

There were more phone calls. They gave me clothes that were supposed to make me look like an assistant truck driver, along with a cap that I pulled down to cover my bandage.

"What happens if we get stopped and someone speaks to me?"

"Until you are well out of Moscow, no one will see you. After that, you will not be stopped."

"No one will see me? Does that mean you're going to put me in one of the cartons?"

"Something like that."

"Then what? What happens when we get to the port?"

"Once there, Oleg will make the final arrangements with the captain. Do you have money? American dollars?"

"Yes."

"Good. The captain already knows that you will be coming on board. He will ask for four hundred. Give him two. I do not think the rats will be there. They cannot watch every port of embarkation."

No time was wasted. In less than an hour, they had filled up a small truck with cartons. I went over to see where they were going to put me. Anna showed me a box-like space they had built under the floorboard.

"It looks pretty small," I said.

"It was as large as they could make it. I'm sorry, but it will have to do. Try it."

I climbed in and found that in order to fit I had to pull my knees up and lie on my side. "You're sure about this?"

"An agent has been shot. They don't take that lightly. It is possible they may have roadblocks."

I climbed back down to where Anna stood.

"It will not be for long," she said. "Only until you are away from Moscow."

"You've been wonderful," I said. "I want you to know how much that means to me." I put my arms around her and we held each other, then I climbed back into the box. The top went on and I was in darkness. After some banging around and movement of people and cartons, the motor started and we were on our way.

As far as I could tell, the truck had no springs. My body made a record of every hole and bump in the road. That was nothing compared to what my mind was going through in that box. It wasn't even as large as a coffin. At least in a coffin the stiff could stretch out. The longer we rode, the more I became aware of how small the space was. Thankfully, I was not in complete darkness because of air holes on the side that allowed a little light to creep in. I could also detect the very distinct smell of cabbage. I did my best to keep from thinking about coffins. What helped was running through the list of all the bad things that could happen if I weren't hidden. Still, it took all the control I had to keep from trying to bust my way out of there.

After some time had passed, the truck stopped. I heard voices. I guessed the truck was being searched. I could hear cartons being moved. The voices got louder. It meant they were coming closer. Then I heard dogs barking. Dogs! They would sniff me out for sure. I stopped breathing. Literally. I closed my eyes and held my breath. Finally, I couldn't hold it any longer. I let the air out of my lungs as gradually as possible, then breathed in slowly, thankful for any air, no matter how foul. After a while, the noises receded. I heard doors slam and the truck start up. I wondered if the cabbages had been put in to disguise the odor of a human.

I don't know how long it was before the truck stopped

once more. I heard voices, the sound of them coming closer. I was getting ready to hold my breath again when I heard my name being called. I recognized Oleg's voice. It had to mean they had come to let me out. When they took the top off the box and I was able to climb out into the blessed light and clean air, I wanted to yell my head off, but I didn't. I just said the Russian word for thank you, over and over again: *"Spasibo, spasibo, spasibo . . ."*

It took us two and a half days to get to Sochi. It was late afternoon when we rolled in. We found the ship easily enough. It didn't look like any cruise ship I'd seen advertised in slick brochures. There were no flags fluttering in the breeze. No spiffy looking people in white uniforms on deck. Instead, we found a rusty old tub that looked like it had been welded together from spare parts. A guy with a beard leaned against the rail of the gangplank, his arms crossed, a crumpled, greasy cap on his head. Oleg got out of the truck and spoke to him. Then they went up the gangplank onto the ship and disappeared from sight.

After a while, Oleg came back, pointed, and we all carried cartons aboard. One of the cartons had my suitcase hidden inside it. Once on the ship, I was taken to a cabin where I dropped my carton on the floor. He motioned again and I went with him into another cabin. There was the scruffy-looking guy who'd been standing at the foot of the gangplank. He turned out to be the captain.

"We cast off at midnight," he said in passable English. "Remain in your cabin from now until then. You will not be entered on the passenger list until after we have departed, just to be safe. All right?"

"Fine."

"That will be five hundred dollars."

"I have two hundred," I said, as Anna had suggested.

"Five hundred." I guessed he hadn't read the script. "Do you want to go to Turkey or not?"

"How about four?"

"Done."

Oleg kissed me on both cheeks and left with the others. Although we had never been able to speak each other's language, we had still been through a lot together. I felt as if I was losing a friend.

The cabin was an inside one without a porthole. There were two narrow bunk beds, a sink, and a toilet. Air was piped in through a vent in the ceiling. Unfortunately, there wasn't enough of it to overcome the aroma that came out of the toilet, even through the closed door.

I looked in the mirror and saw that my bandage was filthy. I removed it and washed my face. Only a slight redness remained. I lay on my bunk and heard the occasional sounds of footsteps outside. I listened for the noises of passengers coming aboard, but I couldn't hear much of anything. At midnight, I heard the growling rumble of the anchor being raised. There was a humming sound from the ship's engines and then my bunk began to tremble, then to shudder as if I'd put a quarter in one of those vibrating mattresses. It was happening! I was leaving Mother Russia. Even though there was still a long way to go, I knew that I was actually, finally, on my way home.

Chapter 40

Two days later, I was back in New York. The first one I called was Rosalind.

"Jake. What a relief! Where are you?"

"The airport. I just got in."

"I'm so glad to hear from you. I was worried. We all were."

"Thanks. I wanted to call from Moscow, but it wasn't possible. It's good to hear your voice again."

"Yours, too. Tell me everything. Are you all right?"

"I'm okay. How are things here?"

"All quiet on the western front."

"Cynthia? Toby? Our friend, Cormac?"

"I haven't seen or heard anything about Cynthia. Toby's been a bit anxious, but I think she's okay. As for Cormac, he's waiting to speak to you."

"I've got a lot to tell him. But I don't want to do anything on the phone."

"You've been seeing too many gangster movies."

"I've been seeing too many gangsters."

"Does that mean you had a problem over there? You sure you're all right?"

"I'm fine."

"Are you coming out right away?"

"Soon." I hesitated. "I miss you. I thought about you a lot."

"I thought about you, too," she said.

That sounded good. I didn't push it.

My next call was to Cormac. He wasn't going to like what I had to tell him. "It's me," I said. "I hear everything's all right."

"Other than expiring from the utter boredom of this place, one might agree with that assumption. Did everything proceed as planned?"

"Not quite. A few flies got into the ice cream."

"That sounds unpleasant."

"You have no idea. I'll explain when I see you. Are you still where you were?"

"Correct."

"Then I will see you as soon as I can."

After hanging up, I decided to go to my father's apartment, rest for a few hours, then take the train or the Jitney. I was beat. A couple of hours of sleep at my father's would get me going again. The downside was that there would be a lot of explaining to do. He didn't know a thing about my going to Russia.

The air that blew in through the taxi window was an unpleasant fusion of heat, humidity, and soot. The taxi driver wore a lavender turban and had no idea where he was going, but I didn't care. I was home.

My father lived in one of those old apartment houses on Central Park West with twelve-foot ceilings and rooms that had size as well as style. A big difference from the new stuff they were putting up, where three hundred square feet and a Jacuzzi in the bathroom was dubbed a Junior Four.

After a few wrong turns and a near-miss of a pedestrian, the driver found the address. The doorman buzzed my father's apartment and got no answer.

"Nobody there."

"I'm his son. Can't you let me up?"

"No."

I held out a ten-dollar bill.

"I take you up."

After he let me in and went away, I dropped my bag and walked over to the living room windows. Trees, grass, ordinary American people wandering around enjoying the outdoors. What a difference from the dour, depressing atmosphere of Russia. I soaked up the scene, along with the air conditioning. Then I lay down on the couch.

I woke up to find my father and Zeena standing over me. My father said, "I was just about to wake you."

"Dad?" For a second I had forgotten where I was; then it came back in a flash. "What's the time?"

"Almost seven."

I had to think about that before I understood he meant seven in the evening. "Good. I still have time to get out east."

"What's the hurry? Now that you're here, why not stay a while? I never get to see you anymore."

"I can't. It's important that I be out there."

"If it's so important, then how come you're here in the first place?"

He always did that to me. His logic was unassailable and exasperating.

"I was in the city, so I thought I'd stop by. I guess I fell asleep."

"Looks like you've been on a trip." He pointed to my suitcase.

"That's right. I just got back."

"Where'd you go, Moscow?"

Zeena was smiling.

"Misha," I said.

"He wanted us to know he was looking out for you over there."

"That was nice of him."

"So are we going to get the whole story?"

"How much did Misha tell you?"

"A little. But I'd like to hear the rest of it."

"I'm not sure that's a good idea."

"Why not?"

"I think maybe the less you know the better."

"Why, because there are criminals involved?"

"Exactly."

"Listen, Jakey," my father said. "The way I see it, it's very simple. Either you tell us the story—and while you're at it, you might explain how you got that nice bruise on your forehead—or you don't tell us. If you don't want to tell, that's okay. I would assume you have your reasons." He folded his arms. Folded arms was not my Dad at all. It could only mean he was angry, or annoyed, or frustrated with me. Not for the first time, I might add.

"Okay," I said. "I give up."

I told them everything, from Cynthia to Solofsky, Cormac, and Toby, and what happened in Russia.

My father smiled. "I've always been proud of you sonny, but now I'm bursting with pride. You've got great balls."

"I think you should go to the police," Zeena said.

"Nonsense," my father said. "They won't protect him. All they would want to do is get hold of the eggs and give them back."

"What's the matter with that?" Zeena said.

"There's a deal in progress. A lot is at stake."

"What about *my* father?" Zeena asked.

"Misha? What about him? He can take care of himself. We can fill him in later." He began pacing, rubbing his hands together. He spoke to me: "You're going out to see this Cormac Blather, right? And you have to figure out how you're going to get in touch with the Russians now that the KGB knows the password and all the rest of it. Is that right?"

"Right."

"We'll drive you out. Grab a bite on the way."

"Thanks, but no thanks."

"Why not? You need transportation. I have it. What's the big deal?"

"Because I don't want you and Zeena to get involved. I thought I made it clear that these guys don't fool around. People have died. I don't want you and Zeena adding to the total."

"Who's afraid? I thrive on excitement, and this is the best thing I've heard of in a long time."

"No," I said.

"What do you say, Zeena?" my father said, ignoring me. "Want to go along for the ride?"

The gold circle in Zeena's nose bobbed up and down as she nodded in agreement. "Why the hell not?"

"Okay," I said. "I'll tell you what. You can drive me out. We can talk about everything. But no way are you going to do anything else. Is that understood?"

"Of course, Jakey," my father said. "You're the boss."

Chapter 41

We left the city at eight and were in Southampton at nine-thirty, a full half hour less than it should have taken only because of light traffic and my father's inattention to speed limits. We stopped for a quick bite at the Princess Diner before heading on to East Hampton. I wanted to see Rosalind, but Blather came first. I guided my father to where I had last seen Cormac, in that old place up near Gardiner's Bay.

"Park behind the house," I said.

"What for? Nobody knows my car, so what difference does it make where we park?"

I counted to five. "Listen, Dad, let's get one thing straight. I let you drive me out here, but don't start thinking you're going to take over. This is my business, not yours, and we're going to do everything my way. Got it?"

"Of course, Jake. I said you were the boss. I wouldn't dream of upsetting your apple cart."

"Then stay in the car with Zeena until I let you know everything's okay. Okay?"

"Sure."

In a flash, that dialogue replayed itself in my mind. I realized I'd never spoken to my father that way before. Where had that assertiveness come from? I wondered if Moscow had something to do with it.

I knocked on the back door and was only momentarily surprised to see it opened by Kevin, the teenage neighbor. Cormac was sitting in the same chair I'd seen him in last. He wore his customary white suit and looked at me as if I were delivering pizza.

After greeting him, I explained that my father and his girlfriend were out in the car and would he mind if they came in.

"I certainly would mind. What we have to talk about is absolutely confidential. I don't want anyone else in the world to hear it."

"What about our friend Kevin here?"

"He will leave the room."

"They can leave the room, too, but I think you ought to consider something. My father has offered to help, and I think we can use all the help we can get."

Cormac smiled. If a smile could reek of disdain, his did. "I allowed you to assist only because I could see no alternative. Bringing more amateurs into this will only make things worse."

"I'm not letting them sit in the car. They can come inside and stay in the kitchen with Kevin." I looked at the kid. "By the way, Kevin, have you seen any suspicious characters around here recently?"

"What's a suspicious character?"

I deserved that. "I mean, anybody not local, asking questions about Mr. Blather here?"

He shook his head.

"Good." Then I went out and told my father and Zeena to come in.

The instant my father came into the room, there was a change in the atmosphere. I'd seen it before. My father was an imposing figure. Well over six feet tall, hand-tailored clothes, perpetual tan on smooth skin, chestnut hair thick and wavy. He shook Kevin's hand as if he were delighted to meet the little shit, and then Cormac's, as if in deference to his greatness. "A great pleasure," he said.

"Hummph," said Cormac.

"Listen, Dad," I said, "Cormac and I have some business to discuss. Would you mind taking Zeena and following Kevin into the kitchen? It'll only be a while."

"Not at all," my father said. He took Zeena's hand and began to follow Kevin out of the room. At the door, he stopped and came back, pulling Zeena with him. "But first, I want to say something to Mr. Blather." He gave a slight bow in Cormac's direction. "Your accomplishments and great store of knowledge have been made known to me by my son. But I must tell you, because I believe in being up front, that Jake has also told me everything about this caper, the whole story in fact . . . from the beginning."

"Has he, indeed?" said Cormac, the jowls of his face turning pink.

"Dad!" I wanted to shoot him.

"Bear with me, Jake. Before I'm finished, Mr. Blather will understand. He's a father, too, is he not?" He had not turned away from Cormac. He went on in his best super-salesman mode. "Before you get upset at what you may consider Jake's indiscretion, remember that I am his father. And who else should a son with problems talk to, if not his own father? Furthermore, I think you ought to know that I am not a novice. I have been around the block, you might say, and not once, but a few times. I have also been involved in all kinds of deals, some of which—I am not proud to say it, but it's the truth—might have been considered not quite of the kosher variety."

Cormac tried to speak, but my father wouldn't let him.

"Hear me out, Mr. Blather. I have only a few more words to say. I am here to offer you and my son my assistance. If there is anything I, or my fiancée, can do to expedite this matter, we are both ready, willing, and able to do whatever may be asked of us. You, of course, will make the ultimate decision." He took a step back and actually made a little bow. "That is all I have to say."

Although I was annoyed with my father, it was a pleasure to see Cormac disconcerted. He took out a handkerchief and wiped his forehead, then cleared his throat with a loud noise, all the while obviously struggling to find the words he needed for a reply. "Well," he finally said. "Dear me. You are nothing like your son, if I may say so."

"We are two sides of the same coin," my father said.

Where did he get this stuff?

"That may well be," Cormac said. "Nevertheless—"

"Do you understand what I'm saying?" my father interrupted. "You're in a lot of trouble here, and I think you can use all the help you can get."

I was sorry he had used my exact words.

"Please!" Cormac said. "Please, sir. Allow me the privilege of speaking before you burst in again. I was about to say—"

"After all," my father interrupted again, "with the General dead, your main squeeze is out of the picture. So I think it's going to take all of us to figure out what to do next."

"What General is dead?" Cormac asked.

"Dad! Put a zipper on it!" I said.

My father put his two hands together as if praying and bowed his head. "Forgive me. I got carried away." He looked at me. "Your turn."

"Things didn't go that smoothly in Moscow," I said to Cormac. "There were a few complications."

Eggs

"Perhaps you would explain."

"Of course. But first, I want everyone else to leave the room. That includes you, Dad."

Without another word, my father, Zeena, and Kevin went out. When the door had closed behind them, Cormac said, "Was your father referring to General Pankov when he said the General was dead?"

I told him the whole story and concluded with an apology. "I'm sorry it didn't work out."

"You said Pankov gave you specific instructions. What were they?"

I related the General's instructions, specifically how insistent he was that I remember to tell Cormac about someone named Constantine.

When I finished, I couldn't help noticing a ghost of a smile playing about his thick lips. "What's with the smile? It looks to me like we're done."

"Constantine."

"So you know this guy. Big deal. They know him too."

"There is no one with that name."

"Then it means something else, is that it? It's some kind of code?"

"Not quite. There is a person. Their people will search for Constantine, but they will not find him."

"Why not?"

"I told you that the General and I have known each other more than forty years. We did business together, much of it while he was assigned to the embassy in London. Partly because he was not always available, and partly because we needed a third party to carry out certain duties, such as transport, the picking up and delivering of various items, he recruited a low-level clerk to assist us. For reasons to which I was not privy, he said he had every reason to have trust in this

231

person. He assured me that this person would never betray us. And he was proven to be right. Constantine was our go-between all these years."

"Who is he? And what makes you think he's still here?"

"He must be, or the General would not have given the name. He is obviously at the consulate in New York. I am sure that after all these years he has risen in the hierarchy and presumably has a position of importance."

"And the KGB won't be able to figure out who he is?"

"We must hope not."

"Okay. Let's assume our contact is still viable. But what about Russian contacts? How do we get the money the General arranged?"

"I am hopeful that my friend Constantine will know what to do. There is no doubt that he and the General have been in touch, and there is every reason to assume that the General had a fallback option."

"Then our next step is to figure out how to get in touch with Constantine without getting trapped. We have to make sure they haven't got on to him before we make any contact."

"Quite right," Cormac said. "Do you have any suggestions?"

"As a matter of fact, I think I have a good one."

"Excellent," my father said. He was standing in the open doorway. "What do you have in mind?"

"How long have you been listening?" I asked.

"Not long, but long enough."

"All right. You might as well come in. Bring Zeena and Kevin with you."

When they all returned, I said to the kid, "Thanks, Kevin. You can go home now. Mr. Blather doesn't need you any more tonight."

Cormac said nothing. Kevin frowned. It was obvious he

did not want to go, but he went without complaint.

When he was gone, I looked at Zeena, who was sitting demurely—if you could call anyone with a gold ring in her nose and a diamond stud in her lip demure—in the armchair opposite Cormac.

"How good an actress are you?" I asked her.

"Fantastic," my father said. "That's what she does. She's an artist. A performer. She also speaks Russian. She can do anything you want."

"Is that right, Zeena?" I said.

"Don't be stupid. Of course."

"And you are willing to help. Right?"

"Definitely."

"Then I think there's an interesting role for you to play in a little drama I have in mind."

"Would you care to share your idea with the rest of us?" Cormac said.

"Sure." I spelled it out.

"Could this be hazardous to the health?" my father asked.

"I don't think so," I said. "But we can't rule out the possibility."

"How do you feel about that, sweetie?" my father asked Zeena.

"Piece a cake," Zeena said.

Chapter 42

Playing safe, we spent the night there. Before I went to sleep, I called Rosie and told her I was visiting a friend nearby. She knew what I meant.

Zeena's assignment the next morning was to call the Consulate General in New York and ask for Constantine by his real name, Ivan Lechenko. She was to say she was his niece visiting from Kiev, was in New York for only a short visit, and that her parents had insisted she call her favorite uncle.

"He will, of course, be suspicious, although he does have a niece in Kiev," Cormac said. "It is unlikely, however, that she would be in New York."

"We can't worry about that," I said. "When you get him on the line, say hello, how are you, blah, blah, blah. Tell him your dear father's old friend, Mr. Constantine, sends his regards. Then suggest you have lunch together at the Metropolitan Museum. It'll make it easy for him, because the Consulate is on East 91st Street. Tell him to meet you in front of the museum at noon."

"Suppose he says he can't make it?" Zeena said.

"If Cormac is right about Constantine, he'll come."

I tried to convince Zeena to redo her hair and remove her nose ring and the diamond stud.

"No way," she said. "You're talking about my individuality here. If you want, I'll cover the diamond with lipstick."

I could see there was no use arguing. "But you need a different dress, something a little plainer."

"Okay," Zeena said. "That, I'll agree to."

We'd have to go into town for the dress, which meant I'd finally have an opportunity to see Rosalind. "I'll get Rosalind to come along and help pick one out," I said. I called, and told her to meet us across from the movie theater complex in East Hampton.

Rosalind was already there when we drove up. I ran over, put my arms around her, and kissed her. When I let her go, I said, as casually as I could, "Just my way of saying hello."

"Well, hello back," she said, with a half-smile.

"Thanks for coming," Zeena said. "I wouldn't want these clowns picking out a dress for me."

The two of them walked away from us and headed for the stores. In a very short time they were back, with Zeena holding a shopping bag.

"It's perfect," Rosalind said. "We found a simple summer dress, black, with narrow straps. She looks beautiful in it."

I explained to Rosie that we would have to leave her because we were going back to the city right away. Our plan was to stay at my father's apartment before our scheduled meeting the next day. She said she understood.

Driving back, Cormac said, "It is vital that we determine that our friend is above suspicion. We must be absolutely certain that he is not followed. If we see that he is, then I very much fear we shall have to devise some other means of achieving our objective."

"How are we going to find out if he's being followed?" my father asked.

"I've got an idea," I said.

"One after the other," my father said. "Keep it up Jakey, you're doing great."

After a restless night and a tense morning, the four of us were in my father's car in a No Standing zone on Fifth Avenue, a half-block north of the museum. Zeena was wearing her simple black dress. Cormac's disguise was a plain white shirt without a tie, a pair of twill pants, and a NY Yankees baseball cap. To make sure he positively wouldn't be recognized, we had added a false beard and mustache.

At exactly twelve noon, a white-haired man walked past our car. Although it was a sunny day in August, he carried a tightly furled umbrella and wore a dark gray pinstriped suit.

"There he is," Blather said.

I said, "All he needs is a bowler on his head and he could pass for the great appeaser of World War II, Neville Chamberlain."

"Ivan was at the London Embassy for two tours of duty. He became an Anglophile. He even drinks tea with milk."

"Okay," I said. "We let him stand at the curb in front of the museum, as arranged. If anyone happened to be eavesdropping on his phone conversation, they won't see anything unusual. We'll let him wait a few minutes, then Zeena will do what she is supposed to do. Now everyone go to your places."

My father and I left the car. Cormac stayed. My Dad went to the other side of the avenue. I moved closer, where I would have an unobstructed view.

The man with the umbrella reached the sidewalk in front of the museum steps and looked at his watch. Zeena got out of the car and began walking toward him. I had to admire her. She was well aware that bad things could happen, but it did not slow her down.

She came up to the man supposed to be her uncle and threw her arms around him. He did his best to keep from being startled. I don't think he expected such a beautiful young woman to kiss him like that. He quickly recovered, gave her a smile, and kissed both her cheeks in return.

A taxi pulled up and two women got out. Zeena took the man's arm and all but pushed him into the taxi. This was my idea. Instead of going into the museum, Zeena was to get into one of the many taxis that stopped to discharge passengers. If there were watchers, they would not expect it. When they saw what happened, they would have to make a sudden move in order to follow them. If they did, my father and I would be there to observe everything.

The door slammed and the taxi took off. I watched for a sign of somebody making a run, either for a taxi or to a waiting car. I didn't see any unusual movement. I checked the street to see if a car suddenly pulled out. Again, nothing. My father and I ran back to the car where Cormac was.

"Did you see anything?" I asked.

"I saw nothing overt," said Cormac.

"Neither did I," my father said.

"Me neither," I said. "I think we're okay."

"Let us not be prematurely sanguine," Cormac said. "We must wait and see what Lechenko has to say. What he tells us may put us more in the throes of gloom than of good cheer."

"You're not much of an optimistic chap, are you?" my father said.

"I have always had a doleful nature," Cormac replied.

"While you're being doleful," I said, "we'll drive over to 2nd Avenue and 79th Street. I told them to find themselves a booth at the rear."

"I hope you chose a decent restaurant," Cormac said. "I have been deprived of quality food for too long in that wretched house in the Springs."

I didn't bother to tell him we were going to a deli.

Chapter 43

We found them in the back of a long, narrow restaurant that was as noisy as a jet take-off. Zeena and her *uncle* were sitting across from each other.

"Greetings, Ivan," Blather said. He grandly gestured for my father and me to join Zeena on one side of the booth, while he managed to get his bulk onto the bench on the other. "How good it is to see you again, especially in these circumstances when it is imperative to have friends in the right places."

"Mr. Blather," the man said. "You know it has been an honor and a privilege to serve the General, and incidentally yourself, these many years."

His voice had a hollow sound, as if it were coming from inside a cave. In fact, he himself looked as if he rarely ventured forth into daylight. His skin was a pale green tinged with gray, something like a sick tomato that will drop from the vine before it begins to ripen.

"My respect for you, sir, is equally great," said Blather. He then introduced all of us to Mr. Ivan Lechenko.

The waiter appeared and tossed menus onto the table with the special nonchalance that only a waiter in a New York deli has.

"Excellent," Blather said. "Before we get down to business, I think it best that we order our lunch. I haven't been to a good New York delicatessen in years."

Blather, my father, and I ordered corned beef sandwiches. Blather instructed, "Please be sure that the meat has plenty of fat throughout."

"What else?" the waiter said. "Lean corned beef is for them what don't know corned beef from pastrami."

Zeena and Lechenko ordered salad.

"I don't eat anything that has a head or a tail," Zeena explained.

"Those are my sentiments, as well," Lechenko said.

"Then what are you doing here?" the waiter said.

"You didn't used to be a vegetarian," Blather said, ignoring the waiter.

"I have learned to 'eat healthy,' as they say over here," Lechenko said, his skin giving off a green glow that would have made a pea envious.

The waiter shrugged and left. Blather leaned forward and lifted a pickle out of the bowl of sour and half-sour pickles on the table. He chomped and chewed with his eyes closed. After a contented swallow, he opened his eyes and said to Lechenko, "You know about the General?"

Lechenko nodded and made the sign of the cross. "He was like a father to me."

"Indeed he was," Blather said. "Now, I have a most important question to put to you. You know what is involved here. Did General Pankov have someone to carry on in case of his inability to function?"

Lechenko nodded.

"Who is it?"

"Mikhail Tomashevsky, the Minister of Culture."

"God's teeth!" Blather said. "That little pipsqueak. I don't believe it."

239

"It is so," Lechenko said. "He is a politician through and through. He is very ambitious. He wants to be President. The General knew of these ambitions and was able to recruit him by assuring him that the publicity generated by the return of the treasure and the Minister's part in achieving this would be of incalculable benefit to him."

"Do you think we can trust him?" Blather said.

"If the General trusted him, I am afraid we have no choice but to do the same. He already has my life in his hands."

"What you say is quite true. We must deal with what we have." Blather shoved the remainder of the pickle into his mouth. "All right, let us proceed with the details."

The waiter arrived, holding a plate in his left hand with the other plates stacked one on top of the other along his arm. He casually deposited them on the table, informing us the drinks would be along in a minute.

"I propose that we postpone discussion of business matters until we have properly disposed of these gustatory delights," said Blather. He slathered mustard on his bread, then placed it back on the corned beef, which was layered so high it looked like only a boa constrictor could bite into it. Somehow, he managed.

There was a lot of chatter around us but we were too busy concentrating on gnawing at our mile-high sandwiches to listen to any of it. Blather was the last to finish. He patted his lips with a napkin and swallowed the remains of his beer. He let out a satisfied belch.

"Let us continue, Ivan," he said. "As you are no doubt aware, the original arrangement with the General was for me to deliver one egg to Moscow. Upon receipt, a payment of one million was to be made to the account in the Cayman Islands. I believe we can still follow that procedure, except that I shall have to provide you with a different code because the original code has been compromised."

Lechenko nodded.

"All well and good," I said. "But more important is how are we going to deliver the one egg to Lechenko? And how is he going to get it to Moscow?"

"Getting it to Moscow is simple," Lechenko said. "By diplomatic pouch."

"You have access to that?" I was skeptical.

"Indeed. The ambassador and I have an arrangement. There are always quid pro quos. It will be in a sealed box addressed to the Minister of Culture."

"Okay. That sounds good. Now, how do we get it into your hands?"

"Bring it to my apartment. I will give you the address. Have it wrapped as if it were a gift. The doorman will call up and my wife will receive it."

"Deal," I said. "We'll give it a great gift wrap."

Lechenko slid out of the booth. "I must be leaving now. I shall be waiting for the delivery and will expedite it as quickly as possible. Wait one week from the day you deliver it, then check with your bank. Hopefully, the money will be there and we can finish the transaction." He shook hands all around, and left.

The waiter dropped the check on the table. My father picked it up. "Allow me," he said.

"That is very kind of you, Mr. Wanderman," Blather said. "But before we go, I must ask, is anyone interested in dessert?"

Chapter 44

The next day, all of us were back in the house in East Hampton. We began discussing the best means of transporting the precious object to Lechenko's apartment in New York.

"How about Federal Express?" my father said.

"Dad," I said. "The thing is worth millions."

Blather spoke up. "I suggest we use Kevin to transport it."

"I don't trust that little shit any more than I trust Federal Express," I said. "Besides, he's probably never been to the city in his life. He'll get lost."

"On the contrary," Blather said, "he grew up in Manhattan. He knows his way around."

"He has a point," my father said. "Nobody would suspect a kid like that."

"He's bringing my lunch," Blather said. "I'll tell him then."

I went into town and bought a gift box and wrapping. After dark, my father and I drove Cormac to a wooded area nearby. Using a flashlight, Cormac located the spot where he had hidden the case.

"How did you know you would ever find it again?" I asked.

"I followed a line that went directly in from the road to a

tree that I marked, then went at a right angle until I found a good hiding place. Going back, I counted the paces from the tree where I made the turn."

We spent another night in the house with Cormac. It was a bit more pleasant than the last time, because we felt we had made progress.

The next day Kevin showed up with his hair slicked back and wearing clean jeans and a sport shirt. The total effect of his almost-perfect features was so extraordinary, you couldn't help but stare at him. My father offered to drive him to the bus.

"Call here right after you make the delivery," I said. "Got it?"

Kevin nodded.

"Then take the next Jitney back. We'll pick you up."

After a while, my father returned with the news that he had seen Kevin onto the bus for New York. There was nothing to do but wait. It was tedious. I watched TV: soap operas, talk shows, infomercials, old, old movies. My father dug up a deck of cards and we played gin rummy for a while, but I couldn't stay with it. I kept getting up and pacing the room.

"Relax, my boy," Cormac said. "All will go well."

"You're pretty confident," I said.

"Fatalistic might be a better choice of words."

"Tell me something then. How did a fatalist like you come to be Toby's father, when it appears your interest is in men?"

"Dear me, that is a direct question, isn't it?"

"Isn't that a little personal, Jake?" my father said.

"Certainly Mr. Blather doesn't have to answer if he doesn't want to."

"At this stage of my life I mind everything, but I understand everything as well, so the answer to one of your questions is that no, I do not mind your asking." Blather reached into the bowl that was on the small table next to his chair. It was filled with an assortment of peaches, plums, and grapes. He bit into a peach. "Fruit. The elixir of life, is it not? But you want to know about paternity. The story is quite simple. When I was a young man, I was quite virile. I am not one to brag. I am merely stating a fact. I began my sexual career the way many boys of my generation and class did, with buggering at public school. I don't deny that I quite enjoyed it. I did, however, crave the attention of women as well. Bisexuality has much to recommend it. If I may quote Woody Allen, a connoisseur of sexuality, 'It doubles your chances for a date on Saturday night.'

"At any rate, Toby's mother was a very attractive young woman who had come to Britain to spend one of her school years at Oxford. She came into my shop and we began talking. There was an immediate connection, if I may say so, in spite of the fact that I was twenty years older than she. We began an affair. I had no idea she was pregnant when she left England. You can imagine both my shock and my delight, when Toby came to England to find me and to inform me that she was my daughter. I had difficulty believing it at first, but it did not take her long to convince me. Her mother had told her of my existence just before she died. How glad I was." He pulled a handkerchief out of his pocket and dabbed at his eyes. "Forgive me. I do get sentimental at times."

"That's beautiful," Zeena said.

"Thank you," said Cormac Blather.

I was feeling sentimental, too. Here was a guy I'd thought of as shallow, cynical, self-interested, who turned out to be someone with real feelings.

Scrambled Eggs

Some glory in their birth, some in their skill
Some in their wealth, some in their body's force . . .
And every humour has his adjunct pleasure,
Wherein it finds a joy above the rest.

We had calculated that it would take two and a half to three hours before we heard from Kevin. There wasn't much else to do but continue to wait. I went outside. I didn't have running shoes, so I walked. I kept up a fast pace in order to break a sweat. I wanted to keep my body occupied so that I could give my brain a rest. There was too much to think about: if all went well, Cormac would pay off his blackmailer and the good Russians would get back what was rightfully theirs. After that, there were a lot of questions: Was Rosalind going to continue her new life or decide to come back? Was it Solofsky who had Mackleworth killed? Who was the blackmailer, and what had Cormac done that he could be blackmailed for? What was Cynthia up to?

Finally I was sweating. Every part of my body was wet. I was concentrating so hard, I didn't hear the car next to me until the horn blew. It was my father.

I pulled the door open and got in.

"Kevin was jumped," my father said. "The egg is gone."

Chapter 45

We drove to the Omni in Southampton where Kevin was waiting.

"What happened?" I asked.

"I don't know."

"What do you mean, you don't know?"

"I don't mean I don't know. I mean, it was funny."

"I don't think I'm going to laugh."

"Like, after I got on the Jitney in East Hampton, it made a stop in Bridgehampton, you know? A bunch of people got on. There were these two guys. I was sitting alone. Even though there were plenty of empty seats, one of them sat right next to me, the other guy behind. I didn't like the look of them the minute I seen them, but I was stuck. As soon as the bus starts up, the guy next to me says, 'We're gettin' off the next stop in Southampton.' I go, 'What are you tellin' *me* for?' 'You're gettin' off, too,' he goes. 'Who says?' Then he pulls open his jacket so I can see he's carryin' a gun.

"So I got off with them. Right away, they grabbed the box from me and they began to shove me toward where all the cars are parked. I knew if I got into a car, I was smoked. But we weren't that far from the entrance. The ticket counter was right there, you know, behind the glass doors. I took a chance. I kicked one a them in the shins and ran as fast as I could. I was inside before they could do anything. I could see them through the glass doors, arguing. I thought they might come in after me, so I went to the desk. When they saw me do that, they took off."

"Good work, Kevin," my father said. "That was quick thinking on your part."

"They didn't scare me," Kevin said.

"You should've been scared," I said. "But what I want to know is, how did they know about you in the first place? How did they know you were carrying something they wanted? You must've told somebody."

"Nobody," Kevin said. "I didn't tell nobody."

"Let's get out of here," my father said.

We were almost back to the house, when Kevin suddenly said, "Romeo. Shit!"

"Who's Romeo?" I asked.

"My mother's boyfriend. I call him Romeo. He's the only one outside of my ma who knew I was goin' to the city today."

"You think he might've tipped these guys? Why? And how would he even know them?"

"Money. He don't work. He bets Lotto, OTB, Quick Pick, all a those. He's always hangin' out at the general store. Maybe those guys offered money for information."

"But what would he know?" I said. "You said you didn't tell anybody about Mr. Blather." I saw something in Kevin's eyes and guessed he had just remembered saying something he shouldn't have. "What was it?"

He shook his head in disgust. "Jeez, I'm sorry. My ma kept pesterin' me about what I was doin' over there every day, so I finally told her that Mr. Blather couldn't do anything for himself. That he needed me to do everything for him, like shopping, cleaning, general chores. That was all I ever said though, honest."

"That was enough." The kid looked like he was about to cry. "Okay, it's done. Forget about it."

When we returned to the house, we found Zeena and Blather playing gin rummy. Blather asked Kevin if he was all right. When told that he was, he said, "Good."

"You don't seem very upset," I said.

"We have been deprived of a million, but there are many millions still to be had."

"Sure, but let me clue you in on something," I said. "We were lucky Kevin got away from those guys, whoever they were, because otherwise they would have found out where we were and they'd be here right now. That doesn't mean they won't find us. So let's get the hell out of here before they do."

"Perhaps you're right," Blather said. He sent Kevin home, while slipping a bunch of green into his hand. "Don't burden yourself about what happened, my boy. You did your best and I am most appreciative."

"You mean, this is goodbye?" Kevin said.

"Exactly," Blather said. "It was a most pleasant interlude and I shall miss you terribly, but now it is time to move on. It will be better for you in the long run."

Kevin's lips pressed together. Once again he looked like he was about to cry. But give the kid credit. He didn't. He left without another word.

We were on our way out when Kevin came running back in, out of breath. "A car just pulled up. There's a bunch of guys in it, and two of them are the guys I told you about."

"What do we do now?" Zeena asked.

I ran to the phone and dialed 911. "This is an emergency. Call the police, tell them to come to . . . what's the address here, anyway?"

Blather said, "It's Gilda Lane. I don't know if there's even a number."

"Gilda Lane," I shouted. "Hurry."

But it was too late. The phone had gone dead.

We heard their footsteps on the wooden porch. The door opened and there was Solofsky in his luminous suit, followed by Crab. Behind him were two guys, one with a ponytail. There was another member of the group, someone I was as startled to see as if the Pope had just happened to drop by. The purple stain on his face seemed to be even more vivid than I had remembered it. So he had come here, after all.

Solofsky rubbed his hands together. It was a habit of his I liked less each time I saw it. "It is good to see you again, Mr. Wanderman." He looked at Cormac. "I presume you are Mr. Blather." He turned back to me. "Who are all these other people? Perhaps you will introduce me."

I told him, then said, "Why don't you let the others go? They don't have anything to do with this."

Solofsky smiled. "I think not. Not until we conclude our business."

"Kevin, then. He's just a neighborhood kid."

"The little *faigel?* Is he not the one carrying this on the bus?" He held out the box I had bought to transport the egg. "You are always the crafty one, aren't you, Mr. Wanderman? No, all we need now is for you and Mr. Blather to direct us to the rest of these beauties, and we leave you in peace. They are all I want. If you resist, however, then we shall have to do a lot more than we do at our last meeting. You remember?"

I remembered. I also remembered the prison in Moscow and the scared feelings came flooding back. "Cormac," I said, "let's not be heroes. Give them up. Tell him where they are."

Cormac pulled a large, white handkerchief out of his

pocket and dabbed at his forehead. "I suppose you're right. What happens to me after this is not important. I cannot risk anyone's life and limb."

My father piped up: "In that case, let me take them to where it is. We can get this over with, in a hurry."

"You can find it?" I asked.

My father nodded.

Solofsky looked around the room at each of us in turn. "This is too easy, I am thinking. I hope this is not a trick."

"It is not a trick," I said.

"All right. Pyotr and one of my men will go with your father. Putlezhev and the other will remain here with the rest of us. Please, do not attempt to do anything foolish."

My father left with Pyotr and ponytail. We sat and waited. Nobody spoke. I was disappointed and I was mad. All that work. All that effort. And the payoff was going to be Solofsky's, not ours. Still, I couldn't see that there was anything to be done about it. Solofsky was the fox and we were the rabbits.

Not much later, we heard a car pull up outside and doors slam. My father came in, followed by Pyotr and the other guy. Pyotr was carrying the attaché case. He handed it to Solofsky.

Solofsky said, "Get me something to clean off the *shmutz*."

One of his men went into the kitchen and got some paper towels.

He wiped the dirt off the case, then opened it. He unwrapped one of the eggs, examined it, rewrapped it, and put it back in the case. Smiling, he took out of his pocket the egg he had gotten from Kevin and put that in. With that, he snapped the case shut and stood up.

"I think we are concluding our business in a most satisfactory manner," he said. He nodded at Pyotr, who opened the door for him. They all went out. The Eggplant was last. He turned and looked at me before he left, but gave no sign and said nothing.

We heard their car drive away. We sat there without speaking for a long time. Then my father said, "I know you're disappointed, but it's not the end of the world."

"You know what?" I said. "I'm glad they're gone. I never want to see those fucking things again."

Blather snorted. "What is that delightful expression you Americans have? It's easy for you to say?"

"I'm sorry," I said. "You still have your neighborly black-mailer to contend with. What do you think he'll do when he learns he's going to get zilch?"

Blather shrugged. "I'm afraid I have no idea what will happen. It may be decided that I am no longer of any use, in which case the next time you see me may well be through a grid of iron bars. Or are they made of steel?"

Chapter 46

There was no longer any reason for Blather to remain in that house. We helped him pack.

"Where do you want to go now?" I asked.

"I think I should like to see my daughter."

The security guards were still there. We could tell Toby she no longer needed them. The party was over.

Toby threw herself into her father's arms. It was good to see that her reputation as a man-eating shark was undeserved. I did not have much time to reflect on this, because Rosalind was holding me close and kissing me, too. Her body was soft and warm against mine.

"Are you all right?" she asked.

"No. But I sure feel better than I felt a few minutes ago." I leaned forward to kiss her again and got a disappointing jolt when she turned her head just enough for the message to come through. Women were so good at that. They didn't have to say a word in order to let you know that no matter how much you may have thought you understood them, there was no way in the world you ever would. "What's the matter?" I said. "I thought we were over that hump."

"I'm sorry, Jake. I didn't mean for you to get the wrong impression. I'm glad to see you back and safe, and all that.

But I haven't made up my mind about anything yet."

Blather said to his daughter, "I must warn you that difficult days lie ahead."

"I know," Toby said.

"How do you know?"

"Pokharam told me. She predicted there would be crisis, difficulty, calumny, accident, treachery, perhaps even fatality."

"Ah yes, your revered Tarot reader. Well, she did not miss out on one component, did she? We've had them all. And the worst is yet to come. You must be prepared to ride out the storm, for storm there will surely be, once my nemesis learns the treasure is once again in the hands of the wrong Russians."

"Don't worry about me," Toby said. "I can take care of myself. And I expect you to stay here from now on. In fact, I insist you stay here. There's plenty of room."

Blather sank down onto a chair. "I'm overwhelmed. I don't know what to say."

"You don't have to say anything." Toby said.

We left. My father and Zeena dropped me off at my house. "Don't have to worry about gangsters hanging around anymore, do we?" my father said.

"Thanks for everything, Dad. You too, Zeena. You were both terrific."

Hugs, kisses, goodbyes.

I went into the house. It was empty, hot, uninviting. I sat on a chair in the kitchen and slowly came to the realization that despite all my great ideas about how to handle everything, I had fucked everything up anyway.

Chapter 47

Early next morning, before I even had a chance to think about what I could do next, I had a surprise visitor: the Eggplant.

"Have some coffee," I said.

"I have come to you because I am sure we can help each other."

"I can't think of anything you can do for me," I said.

"You would like to get back what you just lost, wouldn't you?"

"No," I said. "I'm glad they're out of my life."

"I was under the impression much money was involved in their return. Am I not correct?"

"Yes. But money isn't everything."

"We are talking about millions. That doesn't interest you?" I looked at him, trying to figure out what he was getting at. Without that blotch on his face, he would have been a good-looking guy. "You must be a rich man," he said.

"Are you kidding? I was a teacher. Besides, I know who sent you over here, so why would I want to get involved with you in any way?"

The Eggplant sipped his coffee. "When you were in the *Lubyanka*, I did my best to help you. You saw that, didn't you?"

"Yes. But that was for you, too, wasn't it?"

"I was sympathetic to you. They would have sent you to the gulag. I did not want to see your life ruined. Now I am asking you to do something for me. If I help you to get the treasure back, there will be a lot of money. I need some of that money."

"Who doesn't? But is it worth getting killed for?"

"For me it is."

"Why?"

"It is the price I may have to pay. That is why I have not yet told my controllers that Solofsky has taken possession of the Fabergé eggs. If they knew, they would kill him immediately."

"So what do you have in mind?"

"Here in America I have a chance to be free. I can have a new life. And I want something else, something that costs a lot of money."

"That's a lot of wants. And what's so important that you need money?"

"An operation."

"Operation?"

He put the palm of his hand over the stain on his face. "I want to get rid of this . . . this deformity!"

The force of his anger hit me. I felt stupid because I had assumed that having lived with that thing on his face for so long, he had gotten used to it. I should have realized it was not something you could ever get used to.

"When it is done, I will be able to go where they will never find me. I will have a new life."

"Are you sure they can get rid of that?"

"In this country they have done much with laser treatment. It is a long process. It is painful. And it is very expensive. But I have heard they have had great success."

"Okay, that part sounds good. But what about the rest of it? I don't mean to be suspicious or cynical or anything like that, but why should I believe you? How do I know this isn't some kind of scheme?"

The Eggplant did not seem surprised by the question. "You don't know. And I don't know how to prove to you that I am telling the truth."

That struck me as a pretty honest answer. "Let's hear what you have in mind," I said.

He leaned forward, his hands clenched. "Solofsky has the treasure in his apartment. Since he has it there, he acts like he is the Czar. I spent a few hours with him. He examined each object with a magnifying glass. He held each one as if it were an infant fresh from the womb. 'Magnificent,' he would say. Then he would hold one out in front of him and say, 'Thank you, comrade Fabergé, for designing this beauty for me.' I think he has gone a trifle mad."

"So he likes them. Who wouldn't? What I want to know is, how can you get them away from him?"

"First, we shall go there."

"Obviously. Then what? What about bodyguards?"

"Only Pyotr."

"How do we deal with him?"

"I have observed that he stays in the lobby until twelve thirty-five a.m., which is when Solofsky has finished watching Jay Leno. Then he goes home. Solofsky allows him to leave, because he does not think anyone would have the nerve to attack him in his own home. I have obtained a key to the lobby door. The minute Pyotr leaves, we will enter."

"Then what? We just knock on his door and he hands them over?"

"First we knock on his door. Then we knock on him."

"Just the two of us?"

"Why not? He is no match for us."

"Maybe not for you. But I would guess he's got guns and items of that nature handy that might offset the odds a little bit."

"I have a weapon. It will be enough to convince him. He knows me well. He will not resist once he is aware the situation is out of his control."

"You're sure?"

"Absolutely."

I went outside and paced back and forth on the deck. This was a crazy idea, I knew. It was too simple. Where did I come off to even consider doing something like this? And how did I know anything this Eggplant guy was telling me was true? He might just be using me for his own purposes. And who knew what they hell they were? It would have to be some kind of balls-driven, ego-seeking, macho-male, me-Tarzan bullshit that would make me agree.

We shook hands on it.

What was I, nuts?

Probably.

But after he left, I made a couple of phone calls.

Chapter 48

Solofsky lived in Brighton Beach on the ninth floor of a high-rise facing the boardwalk. We got there that same night and checked out the lobby. It was just before one a.m. There was no sign of Crab.

"Why isn't that creep bodyguard here?" I asked.

"I don't know," the Eggplant said.

"Maybe he's in the apartment."

"If he is, we will deal with him."

"How?"

"Don't worry." He tapped his pocket meaningfully, then opened the lobby door and pressed the button for the elevator. While we were going up he said, "Let's hope Solofsky has not yet gone to sleep."

"Wouldn't it be better that way?"

"No. I do not have a key to the apartment. We would have to wake him up. When his routine is disturbed, he becomes angry and suspicious. I want him to look through the little hole and be only mildly surprised to see me. I am quite sure he will open the door."

"And after he opens the door, then what?"

"I will enter and you will follow immediately. Then just listen and do as I say."

The higher we went the less I liked it.

We sneaked down the corridor toward Solofsky's apartment. When we got to the door, he motioned for me to stand to the side. He rang the bell. Nothing happened. He rang again. I could hear the buzzing noise from where I was. That grating sound was enough to wake him or anybody . . . unless that person was already dead. Maybe the KGB had gotten there first.

I heard the sound of a chain and the door swung open. "It's you," Solofsky said. "I was expecting . . . never mind. What do you want?"

"To come in." Putlezhev entered with me right behind him.

"What is *he* doing here?" Solofsky said, nodding at me. He seemed only a little surprised at my presence.

The Eggplant pulled a gun out of his pocket. Waved it back and forth as if it were a chicken leg. "I am sorry to have to do this Jascha, but I must have the case and its contents."

"Are you crazy?" Solofsky said. "Do you know what you are doing?"

"Yes," the Eggplant said. He motioned with the gun. Solofsky turned and we followed him down a hallway. He wore silk pajamas that had as much of a sheen as the suits he favored. Ahead of us was a lighted room with a sofa, chairs, and a wall unit containing a TV, stereo, and books. The Home Shopping Network was on.

"Did your gorilla go home, or is he coming back?" I asked. "Pyotr, I mean."

"He goes home at this hour," Solofsky said.

"Sit down," the Eggplant said to Solofsky. "Let's talk."

I decided to check out the apartment just to make sure, but I had nothing to defend myself with. I looked for a weapon. A fireplace poker would have been good, but

Brighton Beach apartments didn't have fireplaces. I picked up a vase.

"What are you doing with that?" Solofsky said. "That was my mother's."

"I won't hurt it," I said. Cautiously, I went through the other rooms and was glad not to find anyone. When I came back into the living room, the attaché case I knew so well was open on the coffee table in front of a gloomy Solofsky. I replaced the vase.

"You see?" the Eggplant said. "We have what we came for. My friend cooperated in a very reasonable manner." He knelt down and took one of the objects out of the case.

I moved forward to get a better look. At that moment, a voice behind me said something in Russian. I knew it was the bodyguard. He had come in without making a sound.

The Eggplant sighed. "We should have put the chain on the door."

Solofsky said, "What is taking you so long, you ox?"

I turned around to see Crab with a pistol in one hand and a brown paper bag in the other. "It took me a long time to find a store open that had it," he said.

Solofsky took the Eggplant's gun and gave it to Crab, removed the treasure from the Eggplant's hand, and placed it back in the case. He went into the kitchen and came back with a spoon, took the bag from Crab, and withdrew a container of ice cream from it. "My favorite," he said. "*Cherry Garcia.*"

I watched as he began spooning ice cream into his mouth. There was a grunt. I turned in time to see Crab whack the Eggplant upside the head with his gun barrel. The Eggplant stumbled and Crab hit him again. There was blood. The Eggplant fell down. Crab kicked him. Crab smiled. Then he kicked the Eggplant again. The Eggplant groaned as Crab's shoe struck the poor guy's body.

Crab stopped working over the Eggplant and looked at me. "You are the strong man, yes?" he said. I guessed he was referring to that day on my deck when I had out-squeezed him in a hand grip. "We will see how strong you are." He stepped toward me and moved the gun from his right hand to his left. Then with his free right hand he socked me in the stomach. I staggered backwards. He hit me again. I managed to turn my body so that the blow hit my side instead of my belly. But it hit my kidney, which was worse. He raised the hand with the gun in it. I was getting ready to duck when Solofsky said, "That is enough for now."

I dropped into the nearest chair, shooting pains radiating up my back. Solofsky put the cover back on the ice cream container, looked at me, and said, as if we were having a normal conversation, "I am able to eat the whole box without any trouble. But I must control myself. My weight is beginning to trouble me." He held it out for Crab. "Put it in the freezer."

When he came back, Solofsky said, "Watch them while I get dressed. Then I decide what to do with them."

The Eggplant was still on the floor. The unfortunate man had not moved, but I had a hunch he was still conscious.

Crab sat on a chair opposite me. He held the gun in his left hand and pointed his free hand at me as if it were a gun. "Bang," he said, and laughed. "Strong man, very strong man. What you gonna do now?"

He had me. I wished I had an idea what I was going to do, but I didn't. Once again, they had the eggs. They had the guns. In addition, the Eggplant was beaten to a pulp and I didn't feel so good myself. I tried to think, but the only thing that popped into my head was another quotation from the Stratford genius, a grim one:

261

Boris Riskin

Nothing in his life
Became him like the leaving of it . . .

Solofsky came back into the room. Even though it was summer he had put on his favorite costume, a black suit that looked as if it had been made for John Gotti. "Everything good?"

"No problem," Crab said.

Solofsky had the attaché case in his hand. He walked over to the window and looked out. "A car is pulling up. They are getting out."

"Who is it?" Crab asked. He went over to the window. "I don't see anything."

"Idiot! They are not there anymore. I think they are coming into the building. I want nothing to do with them." He pointed at me and the Eggplant. "Bring them."

Crab waved his gun at me. "Move."

"What about him?" I said. "He's unconscious."

"We'll see about that," Crab said. He went over to the Eggplant and prodded him with his foot. Crab hollered something at him in Russian and pointed his gun at him. The Eggplant opened his eyes. He turned over on his stomach and slowly got to his feet.

"Hurry," Solofsky said. "If you value your life, hurry!"

In the corridor, Solofsky said, "We will take the stairs."

We ran down nine flights of stairs like a bad imitation of Larry, Curly, and Moe, slipping, stumbling, gasping for air. My lungs were straining, but the pains were not as bad as they had been. While we were going down, I managed to ask the Eggplant who he thought Solofsky was running from.

"Those who arrested you back in Moscow. Nothing

else would scare him like this."

"I thought you weren't going to tell them."

"I didn't."

When we reached the lobby floor, Solofsky said, "Keep going. Maybe they are leaving somebody at the front entrance."

We continued down another flight to the basement. It was a typical apartment house cellar: dark, damp, dirty, a single bulb lighting the way to the outer door.

Crab opened the basement door. A narrow cement walk led to the street. There was an iron railing and alongside it a row of garbage cans and black plastic bags yielding up a smell of putrefying vegetables, animal matter, and God knows what else.

"Where is the car?" Solofsky said.

"Around the corner."

"Moy tvoyou mat!" Solofsky said. "Stupid. Why you don't park it in front of the building?"

"It was the only space I could find!" Crab protested.

"All right. Get it. Bring it here."

Crab headed up the ramp toward the street. I heard a sound I now recognized: *pop,* a gun going off. Crab staggered.

"Drop!" I yelled. I hit the ground. The Eggplant followed. Solofsky ran back into the building.

I looked up to see Crab pull out a weapon and fire back. I couldn't see who he was shooting at, but I heard somebody cry out. Crab stood motionless for a moment, then slowly sank to the cement. I waited for the other shooter to make a move. Nothing happened. A car came along and pulled to a stop, tires squealing. The doors opened and out came Misha, my father, and Zeena. Misha had a gun in his hand.

At that moment, another car started up and pulled away in a hurry.

"*Boychik,*" Misha said.

I got to my feet and ran to the sidewalk, the Eggplant right behind me. A body lay there, blood leaking from a wound in the chest. A gun lay beside the body. I bent down to look at the dead man's face but didn't recognize him. "Do you know this guy?" I asked Misha.

He shrugged.

"What about you?" I asked the Eggplant.

He too, shrugged.

My father said, "I called Misha, sonny. I did just what you told me."

"Thanks, Dad. You did good." That phone call I'd made to my father after the Eggplant showed up at my house this morning, telling him what the Eggplant and I were going to do, had turned out to be a good idea.

I ran back to check on Crab. The sour-faced dog was dead. I felt a twinge. In spite of everything, I didn't want him extinct.

"We go now," Misha said.

"Solofsky's inside with the eggs," I said. I thought I'd been glad to see the last of them, but I'd changed my mind. "I want them."

"Then we will get them," Misha said.

"What about KGB?" the Eggplant said.

Misha paused. "KGB? They are here?"

"I do not know for sure," the Eggplant said. "Solofsky saw some men from the window. And he was frightened. Maybe they were the ones who shot Pyotr."

"To hell with them," I said. I picked up the gun from the sidewalk. "This is America. Let's do it."

The three of us went back into the basement.

It was dark. The bad lighting produced a lot of shadows. Solofsky could have been hiding anywhere. "Solofsky," I said. "It's me."

"Jascha," Misha called out softly. "This is Misha. We are not out to harm you."

"I just want the case back," I said.

Not a sound.

"Listen, Solofsky," I said. "We're armed but we don't want any trouble. Give us the case and we walk. That's it."

No response.

"Do you hear me?" I said. "Pyotr is dead. Do you want to join him? Are those eggs worth getting killed for?"

We waited. It was quiet for a moment. There was a scraping noise. A shadow appeared from a dark corner. Solofsky came toward us holding the case in one hand, the lowered gun in the other.

I grabbed the gun and the case. "Attaboy," I said. "You did the right thing. Now you'll have to excuse us, but we're in a hurry."

I ran back out to the street, the others following. I had the case and two guns. I shoved each gun into a separate pocket. My father stood at the side of the car. Zeena was in the front seat, checking her makeup in the mirror. Misha got behind the wheel. My father, the Eggplant, and I squeezed into the back and we took off.

Chapter 49

Misha was taking a lot of tread off the tires.

I looked out the back window. There were no cars behind us. "Take it easy," I said. "Nobody's following us."

He kept his foot on the accelerator.

"Cool it, Daddy," Zeena said. "You're giving us a fit."

Misha eventually slowed down, made a few turns, then drove up a ramp which put us onto the Belt Parkway. I saw that we were heading east. "Where are we going?"

"Relax, *Boychik*. Let the good times roll."

"That's right, sonny," my father said. "Misha knows what he's doing. And you've had a pretty strenuous night. So why don't you just lean back and gather your forces together? You might just need them sooner than you think."

"What does that mean?"

"I've got nothing more to say," my father said.

It was obvious Misha and my father had an agenda. I supposed it couldn't be bad, or my father wouldn't be so laid back about it. I made an effort to let the tension go out of my body, but I couldn't. I had the attaché case on my lap. The thing was sending out all sorts of vibrations. There was so much history attached to what was inside, and not just the history of Fabergé and the Czar, but my own. What was going to happen to Fabergé's eggs now? Would we still be able to do what we planned? Would the connection with the General's man, Lechenko, still work?

I looked at the Eggplant. "How are you feeling?"

"I am all right, thank you. There is nothing to worry about." He touched the dried blood at the side of his head.

"What about your ribs? He gave you some heavy kicks."

"It is painful but it will pass. He hurt you, too, did he not?"

"Not too bad."

"What happened, Putlezhev, your old friend is not your old friend anymore?" Misha put his two cents in.

"You might say that," said the Eggplant.

"How come?"

"It is a long and boring story."

"Tell me anyway. I am not easily bored," Misha said.

"Listen, Misha," I said. "Get off this guy's case. He's on my side now. I know that for a fact. What I don't know at this point is whose side *you're* on."

"*Boychik!* You disappoint me. Who came to rescue you from that *pascudnyak*, Solofsky?"

"You."

"Exactly. You called your father. Your father called me. I didn't hesitate. When it comes to family, you can always count on Misha."

"I'm not sure exactly why," I said. "But something tells me there's more to it than that."

"What a suspicious mind you have, *Boychik*."

Maybe he was right. Why was I looking for trouble? He had saved my skin, and the Eggplant's too. But he was taking us somewhere and I couldn't help wondering where it was.

The adrenaline rush slowed. The road stretched out in front of me. I stared at it while the car rolled along. Without realizing it, my eyes closed and I fell asleep.

Back when I worked in the city, I was one of the subway straphangers. And sometimes, after one of those days that sucked the marrow out of bones, I would zonk out, even standing up. But the amazing thing was, no matter how wiped out I was, I always woke up in time to get off at the right stop.

The same thing happened in Misha's car. Maybe it was the change of speed, or the sound of gravel under the tires. My brain cleared in an instant because I recognized where I was. I knew the driveway as well as my own . . . the crushed red stone, the Belgian block edging, the outdoor sculpture on the lawn, visible even in the middle of the night because the moon shone on it like an overhead lamp.

"What is this?" I said. "Why are we here?"

"It will all be explained," my father said. "Be patient."

Misha stopped the car at the front door. We got out. Misha pushed the button. We could hear chimes ringing inside the house. A light went on. The door opened. It was Morty in his pajamas. He looked at Misha and then at us as if we were Darth Vader and friends. Then he focused on me.

"Jake, what . . . what are you all doing here?"

"May we come in?" Misha answered. Without waiting for a reply, he walked past Morty, and motioned for us to follow. We trailed after him into the living room.

"Where are you going?" Morty asked.

"To make ourselves comfortable," Misha said. He flopped into a chair. "Would you mind turning on the lights?"

My brain cells were in a frenzy. Odds and ends of information were jiggling around like sperm in search of a lodging. Things were beginning to connect. I'd read somewhere that the definition of intelligence was the ability to make connections between discrete pieces of information. But I didn't feel intelligent. In fact, what suddenly struck me was how *dumb* I was. How could I have not figured it out before? Morty, with a collection of art from all over the world, but especially European art. Morty, who had been to Europe as a young man and had gone back many times over the years. Morty, my best friend, who must somehow have gotten information about Cormac Blather and had blackmailed him all these years into selling stolen works of art and then using his share of the loot to buy legitimate art. He had claimed it was Sherri who had a rich uncle who had given them the art, but that was obviously a lie. He had to be the one Blather had talked about, the one tied up with Boris and Solofsky. I had no idea how he had gotten in with the Russians and their stolen eggs, but that didn't matter. When Boris was killed and Solofsky wouldn't cooperate, he must have contacted Misha to get the eggs for him.

"All right, Jake," Morty said. "Now what is this? Who are all these people?"

"You son of a bitch," I said. I wanted to hit him, but too many years of friendship were in the way. I put the case down and picked up the phone. "All this time we've known each other and I never suspected a thing."

"I don't know what you're talking about. Who are you calling?"

"I think some other people you know ought to be here."

I could hear it ring at the other end, once, twice, three times. *Come on, come on, wake up.* It rang again and again. They had to be home. The ringing continued . . . and then, finally, someone answered. A voice dragged out of sleep said, "Yes?"

"Toby?"

"Who is this?"

"It's Jake, Rosalind's husband. Listen to me. Get your father and Rosalind, and come right over to Dr. Morton Adler's house."

"Why? What's happened?"

"A lot. Too much to explain on the phone. But it's important. Will you come?"

"Yes."

"Get here as fast as you can." I gave her directions and hung up.

"Who did you just call?" Morty said. "Toby Welch? Why should she come over here with Rosalind? And her father. Who's her father?"

"Keep it up, Morty," I said. "I'm just beginning to realize what a great actor you are."

Morty shook his head, then pointed at the attaché case. "Is this what this is all about? Are the famous eggs in here?"

"O Jesu, he does it as like one of these harlotry players as ever I see."

"I'm not putting on an act," Morty said. "I swear I don't know anything except what you told me."

"Listen to him, *Boychik*," Misha said. "He's telling you the truth."

I looked at Misha, who was leaning back in the armchair, cigarette smoldering in his hand, a shit-eating grin on his face.

This was too much. If Misha wasn't lying and Morty wasn't lying, then I was damned if I had the slightest idea what was going on. "All right," I said to Misha. "Since you seem to know so much, I think now is a good time for you to tell us why you brought us here."

A voice came from the doorway. "I believe I have the information you want," Sherri Adler said.

Chapter 50

Sherri Adler's middle-of-the-night attire was pink meringue. It was full length and covered her completely but somehow managed to make you think you could see all there was anyhow. She leaned against the doorframe, arms crossed, like the lead in an amateur production of *Streetcar*. "What's the idea, Misha? You went back on our deal?"

"I am sorry, believe me," Misha said. "But these people are my family now. I had to choose."

"I expected Misha alone," she explained. "Not with an audience."

So it wasn't Morty, which meant I wasn't such a dope after all. That made me feel better. I was also relieved that my best friend hadn't stabbed me in the back.

"Who is this guy?" Morty asked. "What do you have to do with him?"

Sherri sighed. "I don't think you want to know."

"We all want to know," I said.

Sherri walked over to the attaché case and touched it lightly. "Are they in here?"

"Yes," I said.

"I'd love to see them . . . but it's probably better if I don't."

"Get on with it," Morty said.

Sherri hesitated. She'd always been able to get him to roll over anytime she wanted, but this time I think she knew it wouldn't happen. She shrugged. "It looks like my choices are limited."

"Cut to the chase," I said.

Sherri found a seat. "I met Misha a long time ago. Through Boris. It was also through Boris that I first heard about the Fabergé eggs. When Boris died, I tried to work with Solofsky, but it became plain he was not to be trusted. I was pretty sure he had killed Boris. That's when I called Misha. I told him everything and offered him a percentage if he would help me get possession of the eggs."

"And so I did," Misha said.

"You didn't get them," I said. "We did." I pointed to the Eggplant.

"Wait a minute," Morty said to Sherri. "What do you have to do with any of this in the first place?"

She sighed. "You know how I love art, how I always loved paintings and sculpture . . ."

"And jewelry, and tchochkes. Yeah, I know all that."

"It's always been my great passion. In order to indulge that passion, I needed money. Real money. That's what the Fabergé stuff was for. It was to be sold to get money. Just as many other things were sold. That's what enabled me to acquire the paintings and the sculpture that we have. Where do you think it all came from?"

"You mean your Uncle Osgood didn't give it to you?"

"Morty . . . Morty . . ." she said. "You can't be that naïve."

"I don't understand," he said. "I met your uncle. He seemed like a nice guy."

"He *is* a nice guy. That's why he agreed to say he was giving me these things, because I was his favorite niece and he had no one else to leave them to. He thought it was a great joke."

"I still don't understand," he said to his wife. "You're saying you bought all this stuff yourself? You sold other stuff to get the money? What stuff?"

"Now we are getting to the heart of the matter," Misha said.

"Sherri discovered a sure-fire formula for minting money," I said. "She found a cash-cow and squeezed its tits."

Sherri patted her hands together in mock applause.

"What is he talking about?" Morty said.

"I had someone who would sell things for me and allow me to keep the lion's share," Sherri said.

"The real version of an uncle," I said. "The man who coughed up the money so she could buy the art. What I don't understand is how you could be such a schmuck and never have any idea about what was happening right under your nose."

"I don't understand what's happening under my nose right now," Morty said.

"I'll explain it in one word," I said. "Blackmail."

"Blackmail!" He stared at his wife. "You were black-mailing somebody?"

Sherri did not answer. On the table next to her was an ivory carving of an elephant being mauled by a tiger. Sherri picked it up and caressed it. "You remember when we got this?"

"London," Morty said. "A long time ago. You bought it from an antique dealer. I remember you said it was a steal. You paid very little for it."

"Actually, I didn't pay anything for it," she said.

"What do you mean, you got it for nothing?"

"Well, not nothing nothing. You might say I paid, only not in English pounds."

"Come on, Sherri," Morty said. "Stop jerking me around. Tell me what you're talking about."

"All right. We used to go to Europe a lot. Especially London. You always had medical conventions to go to. That way you could write it off as a business trip. Right?"

"Get on with it."

"I loved London. It had wonderful antique shops."

"I remember you dragging me to them all the time, that's for sure."

"But when you were at your conventions, I went alone. And one day I found this lovely place . . . with the most beautiful things. The man who owned the shop was charming. His name was Cormac Blather. We got friendly, you might say. Then I realized that he was interested in being more than friendly. I didn't mind. In fact, it was kind of fun. I thought it was a remarkably apt way to pay you back for all the women you fooled around with."

She held the ivory out in front of her, smiling at it. "When I saw this, I just had to have it."

"So you fucked this guy for it," he said.

She smiled. "It was the beginning of a beautiful friendship."

"When did it turn into blackmail?" I asked.

She was about to answer, when the doorbell rang.

"I'll get it," my father said.

We waited for the new arrivals. It was going to be interesting to see how Morty and Cormac and Sherri would react to each other. There was the sound of the door opening. Then I heard my father say, "Hey, what are you doing?"

Footsteps. Lots of them. Coming down the hall toward us. My father was the first one into the room. Behind him were

Rosalind, Toby, and Cormac. And directly behind them was a guy I thought I'd seen the last of, Solofsky. And directly behind *him*, holding a gun, his complexion even more the color of asparagus than it was the last time I'd seen him, was Constantine, real name, Ivan Lechenko.

Chapter 51

"I imagine you are surprised." Lechenko said to me.

Before I had a chance to reply, Rosalind ran over and threw her arms around me. She was shaking.

"Are you okay?" I asked, ready to kill if she told me anything had been done to her.

"I'm okay. They were waiting for us when we came out. We never expected it."

"Of course not," I said. "How could you?" I felt like an idiot.

Lechenko said, "Everyone please sit down. After you have done so, place your hands on top of your heads where I may see them. You, as well, Mr. Solofsky."

"Great go-between, Cormac," I said.

"If you will recall, I had no say in the matter. He was chosen by General Pankov."

"You're right. I'm sorry. I'll bet if the General were alive, he'd be very disappointed."

"No more disappointed than I have been," Lechenko said.

"What is that supposed to mean?" I said. I was aware of the weight of guns in each of my pockets. I'd taken one from Solofsky, the other from his dead bodyguard. I tried to think of a way I could get my hands on one without getting shot.

Talking was a way of distracting him. Besides, there was a lot I wanted to know. "Before you answer that question, tell me, how long have you been double-crossing us?"

"Double-cross? A quaint American colloquialism. Completely unwarranted, I might add. If anyone has been double-crossed, it is I. And for many years, I might add."

"How is that?" I asked, still stalling.

"*You* must know, Mr. Blather. All those years I performed for the General and you. All those years you both made untold amounts of money while I drew a measly functionary's pay. And was I given any share of that money? Not a farthing. Not a sou. A pat on the head was thought to suffice. 'Good work, Ivan.' 'Well done, Lechenko.' And when the Cold War ended, and the General knew changes were coming, was any thought given to me? Once again, no."

"The General had nothing to do with your transfer to New York?" Blather said.

Lechenko's lips pressed together. "He may have put in a word, I am not sure. But does that justify years of neglect? I hardly think so. So, when he contacted me in regard to the Fabergé treasure, I saw that an opportunity had been granted to me. At last, I could have what I deserved. No longer would I be just the go-between, the detail man, the lowest of the low. I would have the treasure for myself."

"How did you think you could get away with it?" I said.

"Difficulties occurred to me, but in fact, it turned out to be quite simple. I sent out inquiries. Very discreetly, you may be sure. There were several excellent responses. I saw no shortage of opportunities waiting for the goods to be disposed of. I had only to get the treasure in my hands. And you, Mr. Blather, were going to give it to me."

"My arms are hurting," Rosalind said.

"Mine, too," Zeena said.

"What do you say, Lechenko?" I said. "How about letting us put our hands down? You're the guy with the gun. There's nothing we can do."

"Just the women," he said.

The ladies lowered their hands.

"Now, bring me the attaché case," Lechenko said to me. "I know you have it."

I got it from the table and brought it over to him. I hoped he wouldn't notice the bulges in my pockets. He didn't. He was too thrilled to see the case.

"Open it," he said.

I unlocked it. "See? They're all here. You've got your treasure. Now why don't you just take it and leave?"

"Do you take me for a fool?" He looked at me. "The moment I left, you would call the police and have me picked up before I'd gone five miles. No, I'm afraid it isn't that easy."

"Then what are you going to do?"

"That is a problem I am trying to deal with. I had a man with me at Solofsky's place, but he was unfortunately put out of commission."

"So that was *your* man shooting at Crab?"

"Who is Crab?"

"I mean, Pyotr, Solofsky's bodyguard."

"Yes, he was with me. Was he hurt badly?"

"He's dead."

"I told him to be careful, the fool."

"What were *you* doing there?" I asked.

"I have many contacts in the KGB. I have had Mr. Solofsky watched ever since Boris Organ was killed. He led me to Mrs. Organ. She, in turn, led me to Ms. Welch."

"So, it was your men who broke into Cynthia's house."

"Yes."

"They also raided Toby's house and killed Mackleworth."

278

"I did not order them to kill anyone. They were to search for the treasure, that was all."

"Very noble of you. How did you manage to find us to-night? You couldn't have known we were coming here. I didn't know it myself."

"Correct. I had learned the case was in Mr. Solofsky's hands. I had come to attempt to make a deal with him. He was expecting me. I was about to enter the elevator when I heard noises on the staircase. At that hour, I concluded it could only be Solofsky making a run for it. My companion and I raced outside and hid across the street. When he saw Pyotr, he shot at him before I could do anything about it. He was so sure Pyotr had been rendered harmless that he ran across the street and was then shot himself."

"That's when a car drove away," I said. "That was you, I suppose?"

"Yes. I circled the block and came back in time to see you leave. Mr. Solofsky was not with you. I went inside and found him, rather upset, it seemed. I persuaded him to tell me what happened. I then made a calculated guess that you might be coming out here. I further persuaded Mr. Solofsky to drive me. We went first to your residence. You were not there. Then I thought of trying Ms. Welch's place. While I mulled over the possibility of breaking in, out they came, and who should be with them but Mr. Blather."

"Blather?" Morty said. "The guy from London?"

"Please don't interrupt," Lechenko said. "Who are you?" he asked Morty.

"The guy whose house you're in."

"I shall have need of you in a moment." He continued: "It was not difficult to intercept them and learn they were coming here. But let us get on to other matters of more pressing urgency."

"Yeah," I said. "Such as how you're going to make a getaway without getting caught."

"Mr. Solofsky will assist me."

"You're going to trust him?"

"For a share of the treasure, he will cooperate." He spoke to Solofsky. "Isn't that so?"

Solofsky smiled, and lowered his hands. "Of course. What do you want me to do? Kill them?"

"It would solve a lot of problems, but I am afraid it might create new ones. I think, perhaps something to tie them up with. Rope, tape, something strong." Solofsky started to leave the room. "A moment," Lechenko said. He spoke to Morty. "Now it is your turn. Where do you keep what I am looking for?"

"The basement."

"And where might that access be?"

"From the back of the kitchen." He pointed. To the right was a dining room and beyond that, the kitchen.

"Is there egress from the basement to outside?"

"No," Morty said.

"Good. What about from the kitchen?"

"There's a door leading to a deck."

Lechenko looked at Solofsky. "Take off your clothes."

"What?"

"I am quite aware that once out of sight you might wish to leave, so I am attempting to make it more difficult for you. Naked, you might want to think about it. I also urge you to consider the consequences if you do try. If this gentleman is telling the truth, and I see no reason why he should not, your only means of egress is from the kitchen. This gentleman will stand at the entrance to the kitchen and observe that you do indeed go down to the basement. If you attempt to leave through the kitchen door, he will inform me and I will shoot you. Is that understood?"

"I assure you . . ." Solofsky began.

"It is useless to argue. Remove your clothes. All of them."

We watched while Solofsky did a strip tease. He took everything off but his shoes. A coil of hair like razor wire spread across his back. It was not a pretty sight.

"Shoes, as well," Lechenko said.

Solofsky removed his shoes and socks. "I go now?" he said.

Lechenko nodded.

Morty followed him to the kitchen and watched. Then he said, "He went down the stairs."

"Please remain there until he returns," Lechenko said.

While this was going on, I kept thinking of a way to get at a gun, but Lechenko didn't take his eyes off me long enough. One of the phone calls had brought Misha as a savior. I looked at him now as a possible source of help. But he seemed to have lost his fire. He looked back and shrugged as if to say, *whatever will be will be.* That wasn't much in the way of support. I needed a Russian like Ivan the Terrible, and instead, I got Chekhov.

My gaze then went to Cormac. He was studying Sherri, his blackmailer. Strangely, he had a trace of a smile on his lips. Sherri became aware of his stare. "So it has come to this," Cormac said. "You see where your greed has taken you."

Sherri did not respond.

The rest of them—my father, Toby, Zeena, the Eggplant—were all frozen in place, watching Lechenko as if he were a cobra waving sinuously back and forth in front of them.

Solofsky arrived with clothesline. "I am finding this in the cellar." Morty came back into the room with him.

"Tie them up," Lechenko said.

"I can put clothes on first?"

"You may as well."

While Solofsky dressed, I looked at Rosalind, trying to send a telepathic message that I was trying my best to get us out of this. She answered my look blankly, indicating my message hadn't gotten through.

Solofsky began with Misha. He trussed him like a loin of pork, pulling the cord as tight as he could. If he thought he was going to get any satisfaction from hurting Misha, he was mistaken. When Solofsky finished with him, Misha said, "Is that the best you can do?"

That was not a clever thing to say, because Solofsky answered by smacking him across the face with the back of his hand, leaving a clearly visible red welt.

Solofsky tied the Eggplant next, then my father and Blather. As he was tying Blather, Morty said to Sherri, "This is the guy you had the affair with? This fat guy?"

"He looked different in those days."

"Shut up," Solofsky said.

I knew I had to make a move. Solofsky had apparently forgotten that I had taken his gun. But the minute he saw me and the bulges in my pocket, he was sure to remember. Who knew what could happen next? Once he had the gun, he might shoot Lechenko. That wouldn't be so terrible, but then he might do the rest of us.

"I wish you would hurry," Lechenko said.

Solofsky approached. I turned to the side so he would only see one pocket. Sure enough, he spotted the one gun, but not the other. He bent over me and whispered, "Say nothing and you will be spared." He reached into my pocket, pulled out the weapon, and quickly slipped it into his waistband. Then he began to tie me.

The moment had come. I had to make a move. I punched

him directly on his nose. I could feel it flatten under my fist. Blood spurted out. He tottered back, hollering in pain. Out of the corner of my eye, I saw Lechenko's arm come up. I yanked the gun out of my pocket and attempted to whack Solofsky on the head. But he moved. Or I missed. My blow caught his cheekbone and opened a gash. There was more blood. Lechenko couldn't shoot because Solofsky was in the way.

"I kill you," Solofsky roared, and began pulling at the gun in his waistband.

I didn't wait for him to get it out. I swung the gun barrel again and this time he crumpled, fell, and didn't move.

I pointed the gun at Lechenko. He pointed his gun at me. I was breathing hard, sucking air. "What do we do now?" I said.

"Perhaps we can make a deal," he said.

"You're good at that, aren't you?" I said.

We stared at each other. It was a draw. Then I thought I heard the sound of a door opening. I listened carefully. I was right. Someone was coming down the hallway. I looked past Lechenko to see Detective Catalano and another man come into the room. They both held guns. My other call had paid off, too.

Chapter 52

"Drop your weapon," Catalano said.

Lechenko hesitated, but only for a moment, then let it fall. I picked it up and handed it to the detective, along with mine.

"Who's that on the floor?" Catalano asked.

"Solofsky," I said. "He's got a gun, too."

"Get the weapon and cuff 'em," he told the other detective. He spoke to Lechenko. "And who might you be?"

Lechenko told him.

"So you're in on this thing, too?"

"Not at all. I was trying to rescue a treasure that belongs to my government, that is all. When they learn of my activities, they will give me a medal."

"Is that so? In the meantime, I'm taking you in."

"You don't have the right. I have diplomatic immunity. You will find my card in my wallet."

"Maybe I'll look for it later. Right now, you're heading for the pokey." He snapped handcuffs on Lechenko. "Take 'em out," he said to the other cop.

There was some difficulty getting Solofsky to stand up. Solofsky mumbled but didn't stir. The detective went into the kitchen and came back with a glass of water. He let it spill out onto Solofsky's face. That brought a response. He got

Solofsky to his feet, cuffed him to Lechenko, then marched the two of them out.

When they had gone, I asked Catalano, "What about the diplomatic immunity stuff? Is he going to get away with that?"

"Probably. It wouldn't be the first time these jokers have gotten away with murder."

"It would be a shame if he does," I said. "But I'm glad you showed up, anyway."

"And I'm glad you decided to cooperate instead of obstruct."

Making a few phone calls had turned out to be one of the best things I ever did. "How did you find us?"

"I had the apartment house staked out. I watched the whole thing."

"You *watched?* Are you kidding me? Why didn't you jump in?"

"You were doing okay. I figured I'd take it through to the end and see what I could catch. Followed you out here and waited."

"Glad I could help," I said. To the others, "This is Detective Bill Catalano from the New York City police. He's been after Solofsky for years."

"I am delighted," Misha said. "But perhaps you would be good enough to release us from these ropes."

Catalano produced a knife and cut everyone free. Misha pulled a handkerchief out of his pocket and patted his forehead. Catalano pointed at him. "I've had an eye on this guy, too."

"He saved us tonight before you did," I said. "Besides, from now on he won't be giving you any trouble. He's practically a relative. Once he gets to be part of my family, he's going to be a straight arrow. Right Misha?"

Misha smiled. "As straight as an arrow can be."

Catalano said, "We'll see if he keeps his nose clean. Just because he's a relative doesn't let him off the hook." He picked up the attaché case. "I'll be taking this with me."

"Good," I said. "The only time I ever want to see those things again is in a museum."

I felt as if I'd come up for air after a long dive. The Fabergé eggs were out of my life. Sure, the money would have been good to have, but I knew it wasn't important. I looked around the room. "Everybody's here except Cynthia," I said. "Too bad she missed the end of the story."

"Don't worry about Cynthia," Sherri said. "She met a megabucks real estate developer from Palm Beach. She's with him right now, cruising on his hundred-twenty-foot yacht with a captain and a crew of six."

"That solves her problems," I said. "But what's going to happen now with you and Cormac?"

"I should like to know the answer to that question as well," Cormac said.

"So that woman is the blackmailer," Toby said. She looked like a tiger about to attack.

"Correct," I said. "You weren't here when it was all discussed. It seems that Mrs. Adler and your father have known each other a long time."

"I know what I did was wrong," Sherri said.

"You made my life quite miserable for thirty years," Cormac said.

"I apologize."

"Not good enough," I said. "You've got to do more than that. Whatever you have that gave you a hold on Cormac, you should give it up. Right now." I turned to Cormac. "What does she have, anyway?"

"Certain documents from my early days of working with

286

the General. They contain some incriminating information."

"What do you say, Sherri? This is your chance to redeem yourself. Give that stuff to Cormac. He deserves to live the rest of his life in peace."

"It's the least you can do," Morty said.

"That's right," my father said. "It's time to be a good person."

"Isn't it too late for that?" Toby said.

"No, my dear," Cormac said. "I have no interest in revenge. I should be delighted to know that it is all over."

Sherri said nothing. She looked at each of us in turn, then went out. A few minutes later, she returned with a manila envelope. "There are no copies."

"How can we be sure of that?" I said.

"I swear it," she said.

Cormac took two sheets of paper from the envelope and read through them. He sighed. "Does anyone have a match?"

Misha handed him a book of matches.

"What may I burn these in?"

"Use this," Morty said. He gave Cormac a silver bowl.

Sherri was about to protest, then stopped.

Cormac struck the match and, with a shaking hand, put the flame to the papers. When the flame caught, he dropped the papers into the bowl. We watched them turn to ash.

"That's that," Toby said.

"That's almost that," I said.

Chapter 53

Misha took my father and Zeena and the Eggplant to Brooklyn. I gave my father the keys to my car, which I'd parked near Solofsky's apartment house. We agreed to make arrangements for me to get it back.

Morty said he would drive the rest of us home. When we got to Toby's, I asked Rosalind if she wanted to get out, or come back with me.

"I'll go with you," she said.

At first, being alone together was awkward. I found it difficult to speak. I offered to make some tea.

"Don't bother," Rosalind said. "It's very late."

"What do you think's going to happen with Morty and Sherri? He got a pretty nasty surprise."

"I think they'll work it out."

"I hope you're right."

I made some tea anyway. Gradually, we began to relax. We talked until the sky began to lighten. She told me a lot about myself. It seemed there were a few flaws in my character that she felt ought to be improved. I couldn't say it was enjoyable hearing that I was impatient, intolerant, cynical, and quick to anger, but I was so glad to have her back home that a catalogue of my faults was more than bearable. In fact,

I would have let her flay me with a butter knife if she had the urge.

There was something else going on. My body was quivering with the desire to get my hands on her and it seemed that, despite my failings, she had the same feelings in regard to me.

"But first," I said, "I want to read you something." I reached for my book of Shakespeare's sonnets.

"Please don't. Take off your clothes instead."

"In a minute. Listen:

> *Whoever hath her wish, thou hast thy Will,*
> *And Will to boot, and Will in overplus;*
> *More than enough am I that vex thee still,*
> *To thy sweet will making addition thus,*
> *Wilt thou, whose will is large and spacious,*
> *Not once vouchsafe to hide my will in thine?*

I grinned at her. "Didn't that get you hot?"

"Either you're getting senile, or you must be joking."

"I'll explain. *Will* means this." I put one hand between my legs. "And *will* also means this." I put my other hand between Rosalind's legs.

"Oh," she said.

"So I repeat, *Wilt thou, whose will is large and spacious, Not once vouchsafe to hide my will in thine?*"

"Oh," she said again. "That's a different story."

It went well. No, better than well. There was music in the air. Fireworks in the sky. Rosalind made sounds that indicated she was having some really good moments. And I was eighteen again.

Okay, not quite eighteen . . . maybe a few decades beyond, maybe more like thirty-eight.

In between making love, I told her about the Eggplant and his obsession to have a normal face. Her answer to that was the brilliant suggestion that Sherri should be the one to pay for his operation, since she was the one who had profited all those years.

"I'm sure she'll agree," I said. "Considering she's got no choice."

As for Cormac and Toby, I knew they would have a good life together now that Cormac was free of threat. Toby could continue to plan every aspect of Middle America's life, and Cormac could sit in the back of his shop and drink gourmet coffee.

All that remained was for me to figure out what I was going to do with my time. Obviously I had to find something challenging to do.

"I have an idea," Rosalind said. "Why don't you become a private investigator? After all, you did a great job on this case."

"Some great job. I was supposed to arrange for the transfer of the eggs and collect millions of dollars. All that happened was that some people got beaten up and others got killed."

"But the eggs are ending up where they belong. The Russian government must be very grateful. In addition, the plot by the KGB to take over the Secret Service is not going to work. You did that. You're the one who should get the credit."

"Well . . . I guess I had something to do with it," I admitted.

It was intriguing. Certainly the excitement level was high in that kind of a job. The recent past was solid proof. What clinched it was that Rosalind was for it.

So we agreed I'd give it a try. I'd do what it took to get a license, and set up shop in the house. I could advertise in newspapers, in magazines, and on the Internet.

The next thing was to come up with a name for this new company. And a slogan, of course.

It wasn't hard to do. In no time at all, we had it.

In fact, it sort of wrote itself:

W. SHAKESPEARE CO.

Private and discreet investigations.

Suit the action to the word, the word to the action.

About the Author

Boris Riskin went to the University of Michigan, where he studied playwriting with Kenneth Rowe, but switched to fiction shortly thereafter. He worked at a variety of jobs from dishwasher to busboy to factory worker to salesman of discounted clothes to high fashion women. He has published short stories in *The New Yorker* and a variety of literary magazines.

A Brooklyn native, he has traveled the world. This included living in France for a few years. One of those years was spent studying at the Sorbonne. The other was on a honeymoon. But New York is where his heart is, as well as family and friends.

He and his wife, Kiki, a sculptor, have a daughter and son. They eventually discovered Sag Harbor at the eastern end of Long Island where the bay and ocean are nearby and the air is filled with creativity.

e kept
ly
ewed

BAKER & TAYLOR